Dedicated to
my sister Maggi Deere (née Masterson),
my brother-in-law Eddie Deere,
and my nephews Kevin and Bobby.
With love.

FRANKIE'S MANOR

FRANKIE'S MANOR

Anna King

LITTLE, BROWN AND COMPANY

A *Little, Brown* Book

First published in Great Britain in 1998
by Little, Brown and Company

A CIP catalogue record for this book
is available from the British Library.

ISBN 0 316 88155 4

Typeset in Palatino by
Palimpsest Book Production Limited,
Polmont, Stirlingshire
Printed and bound in Great Britain by
Creative Print and Design Wales, Ebbw Vale

Little, Brown and Company (UK)
Brettenham House
Lancaster Place
London WC2E 7EN

CHAPTER ONE

''Ere, get a move on, Rosie, love, I'm near dying of thirst.' The beer-soaked bar counter was packed to capacity. Flat-capped men in grimy shirts and baggy trousers, held up by braces, stood alongside more smartly dressed customers, all leaning over the bar clamouring for service, eager for their first pint after a hard day's work.

Despite the raucous shouts for attention, the atmosphere in the Red Lion in Mare Street, Hackney, on this Saturday evening in June, was good-natured; though whether it would be the same by closing time was a different matter.

It was barely five months since the death of their immensely popular and much-loved sovereign, but the new king was fast becoming as well liked as his late mother, and the people of London were looking forward to a new era under Edward VII.

Nineteen-year-old Rose Kennedy, one of three barmaids in the busy public house, looked down the long counter. 'Hold your horses, Bert, I've only got one pair of hands. I'll be with you in a minute.'

Sliding two brimming tankards towards two of her regular customers she took the proffered half-crown and was about to go to the till for change when the older of the men said, 'Keep the change, Rose, 'ave a drink on me.'

'Aw, thanks, Fred, that's nice of you.' Rose smiled gratefully before moving on to serve Bert Cox. 'Here I am, then, Bert. The usual, is it?'

Taking a tankard from beneath the counter Rose expertly drew a pint of bitter. As she did so, Sally Higgins, a well-endowed, attractive blonde woman in her late twenties, stopped by Rose's side and said sharply, 'Here, I hope you ain't thinking of pocketing that tip. You know the rules. All tips go into the kitty.'

Rose flicked a disdainful look at her. 'I haven't forgotten, Sally. I always share my tips . . . unlike some I could mention.'

The woman bridled, her hard eyes glittering dangerously. Placing a coarse hand on her ample hip, she hissed, 'And what's that supposed to mean, Miss High an' bleeding Mighty?'

Sensing trouble, the men at the bar stopped talking, their expressions tense as the grim-faced blonde moved nearer to their favourite barmaid. Then, as if out of thin air, a heavily built man of dapper appearance materialised between the two women, effectively defusing the situation before it had the chance to gather momentum. 'Now then, girls, what's all this, then? I don't pay you to stand gossiping. Get on with your work, the pair of you.'

Henry Dixon, landlord and owner of the Red Lion, raised a long-suffering eyebrow at the men gathered at the bar. 'Women!' He sighed heavily, evoking murmurs and nods of sympathetic agreement from his male customers. Henry Dixon was forty-eight, a tough East-Ender, who could handle himself against any of his equally rough clientele. He might have been good-looking, but for a badly broken nose, the remnant of a vicious fight in his youth. A widower for the last five years, he had no intention of remarrying. His late wife of twenty years had made his life hell, and he wasn't about to put himself through that living nightmare again. Women were easy enough to get when the mood was on him, and being the owner of a thriving business certainly helped matters along in that department.

A faint whiff of lemon drifted beneath his nose, causing him to glance at the girl by his side. Most of the women with whom he came into contact nearly drowned themselves in cheap perfume, usually to hide that they hadn't washed recently. But not Rose Kennedy. Oh, no, Rosie was different, and that was what caused most of the trouble between her and Sally Higgins.

Before Rose had put in an appearance just over a year ago, Sally had been the main attraction behind the bar, but the pretty, younger arrival had ousted Sally from the limelight. Not that Rose had set out to steal Sally's thunder, far from it, for Henry Dixon had never seen her flirt or put herself about with any of the men. She was friendly and sociable, but squashed any unwanted attention from the customers – which only whetted their appetites, as they vied to be the first to succeed in taking her out.

When Rose had first started working at the pub, a customer had taken one look at the sweet face surrounded by a cascade of curly, burnished copper hair and remarked tactlessly, 'Bleedin' hell, a Rose between two thorns,' which hadn't pleased either Sally or the other resident barmaid, Rita Watkins.

But while Rita had gradually warmed to her workmate, Sally never had, and took every opportunity to put the younger woman down.

Still, he wasn't in the business of playing nursemaid, and despite Rose's inexperienced looks, she knew how to take care of herself, and she drew the punters in. Mind you, she might become an even bigger asset if she stopped wearing those dowdy clothes. She looked like a bloody housemaid in those high-necked blouses and straight black skirts. In fact, he had been meaning to have a word with her about that. Even though she was popular, men liked a bit of female flesh to ogle over their beer: it made a change from looking at their harassed, worn-out wives.

Sally and Rita now . . . Well, they knew what men liked to see, and weren't shy of showing off their ample curves; even if the curves in question were a little overripe for Henry Dixon's tastes. Fingering his neat black moustache, he pulled Rose to one side. 'I want a word with you later, before you finish your shift'll do. Meanwhile, leave the serving to Sally and go and help Bill collect the empties, else they'll be drinking straight from the pumps.'

Rose looked apprehensively at her governor. 'I was going

to put the money in the kitty, Mr Dixon, I always do, you
know that.'

The landlord clicked his tongue impatiently, 'I ain't
bothered about your bleeding kitty, love, you can fight
that out amongst yerselves. Now collect them empties, and
get them washed, or do I have to get them meself? And tell
Bill to get a move on, there's a barrel needs changing on the
end pump.'

Biting back a sharp retort, Rose lifted up the bar flap and
walked into the noisy, smoky throng of people jammed
tightly together on the sawdust floor, bracing herself for
the sly gropes and *accidental* brushes against her person.
Sally and Rita took all such encounters in their stride – Sally
actively encouraged them. The friendlier the barmaid, the
better the tips, was Sally's motto, besides which, it was all
part and parcel of their work. But Rose found she did well
enough without letting herself be groped by any man who
took a fancy to her.

Weaving expertly through the crowd, she stopped by a
table where a small, wiry man with a shock of white hair
was enjoying a brief rest and a gossip with several market
traders. 'The governor's on the war-path, Bill,' she said
warningly. 'He wants a barrel changed, and we're running
short of glasses, so you'd best get a move on'.

Bill Austin, the cellarman, potman and general dogsbody,
gave a loud, impatient sigh. 'Have a heart, Rosie, love, I
ain't hardly stopped for a breather all day.'

Rose smiled in sympathy at the elderly man. 'I know, Bill,
I know, I'm only passing on the message . . . Oh, and I'll
need some help making more sandwiches soon – the last
lot have nearly all gone.'

Moving on, Rose heard Bill declare loudly, 'Bleeding hell.
Put a broom up me arse, an' I'll sweep the floor as I go along,
an' all.' The joke was an old one, but it still brought forth
a gale of laughter from all who heard it.

One wag called out cheerfully, 'Don't let Dixon hear you,
Bill. I heard tell he was on the look-out for a cleaner,'
whereupon more laughter erupted throughout the pub.

Rose made several trips back and forth, balancing empty
glasses and tankards on a large pewter tray, stopping

occasionally to have a few words with some of her regulars and their wives before returning to serve behind the bar.

Over an hour later, as she came from the kitchen carrying yet another load of hot pies and thick-cut sandwiches, the pub door opened and a woman of about thirty, in a bright blue dress, cut low at the neck, and an array of assorted gaudy feathers perched on top of a mass of dark hair, walked in jauntily. The face beneath the garish display was heavily painted. Shoving her way forcefully through the drinkers, she yelled, 'Lock up your sons, and keep an eye on your husbands, girls, Rita's here.'

A wide smile spread over Rose's lips, her amusement tinged with relief, for if Rita was here it meant that her own shift was nearly over.

Ten minutes later Rose was standing in the office at the back of the pub, waiting for the landlord to hand over her wages. Seated behind his desk, Henry Dixon cast a critical eye over her. She was an eyeful, there was no denying that. With that mane of coppery hair tumbling around her shoulders, and a pair of deep blue eyes looking out of an oval face over a snub nose sprinkled with freckles, it was little wonder she was so popular with the locals. But it was the passing trade he wanted to attract, and as pretty as she undoubtedly was, she could do with livening her ideas up about the way she dressed. Not that he wanted her to look too much of a tart – he already had two of those working for him – but . . .

'Is anything the matter, Mr Dixon? Only you said earlier you wanted to have a word with me.' Rose waited patiently for him to speak, a pink flush spreading over her face and neck as she found herself under close scrutiny. Embarrassed, she pulled on a pair of white gloves, then fiddled nervously with the clasp of her black handbag. The sound of a chair being pushed back on the wooden floor brought her eyes up quickly, her expression turning wary.

Before she could say any more, Henry Dixon pushed a small pile of coins across the desk saying tersely, 'Here you are, Rosie, girl, your wages, though it's not much for a week's work . . . Not that I'm saying I underpay you, don't you go thinking that,' he amended hastily. 'The wages I pay are the same as you'd get anywhere else – in fact, a sight more than in some pubs I could mention.'

'Yes, I know that, Mr Dixon,' Rose replied hurriedly, confused by the way the conversation was going and already beginning to inch nearer the door.

'Hold your horses, girl, I ain't gonna jump on you. I just wanted a word, quiet, like.'

Feeling a little silly, Rose relaxed, then stiffened, her slight blush burgeoning into a dark red stain of anger as the import of the landlord's words slowly dawned on her.

'. . . I don't expect you to dress like the other two, but if you could just liven yourself up a bit, you know, show the customers a bit of—'

'I'm not in the habit of showing my body off to all and sundry,' her voice was low and angry. 'My job here is to serve behind the bar, collect the empties and help prepare the food, all of which I do very well. Now, I don't mind helping out with other jobs around the pub when we're busy. Like last week, when that delivery from the brewery turned up an hour early and you were down at the bank. I had to help Bill unload the barrels into the cellar, he couldn't manage on his own, not at his age, and it was blooming hard work, I can tell you. But I didn't complain. It had to be done, and I was on hand and, like I said, I don't mind helping out.' She paused for a moment, regretting mentioning the incident in case it reminded Dixon that Bill was getting too old for his job, then she jutted out her chin. The elderly cellarman would be the first to tell her to stick up for herself. 'What I won't do is dress myself up like – like a prostitute, just so you can get all the local riff-raff in off the streets to gawp at me. If I wanted to go on the game, I'd do it properly and above board, not like Sal—'

With a roar, Henry Dixon pushed back his chair and rose to his feet. Stretching his bulky frame over the table he glowered at his rebellious employee. 'Like Sally, you was about to say, wasn't you, you stuck-up little madam? Well, let me tell you something! There's nothing wrong with what Sally and Rita do in their own time. It's what all women do, one way and another. Even respectable little wives soon fall on their backs when they want the housekeeping, so you tell me where's the difference! Anyways . . .' Suddenly uncomfortable he dropped his gaze. He hadn't meant to go on like that, but she'd got him riled, looking at him as if he'd asked her to drop her drawers when all he wanted was to keep his business thriving. There was nothing wrong with that, was there? But he didn't want to lose Rose. She was a good worker, and honest, and they were qualities that weren't that easy to come by. He ran a hand through his oiled black hair. Gawd! He wished he hadn't started this now, but he had, and he wasn't about to back down. Dropping his voice to a reasonable pitch he said, 'Look, I ain't expecting you to do anything you don't want to, but I ain't running a charity here, I've got to make me money as best I can. You know what it's like round the East End – there's pubs every couple a hundred yards and a landlord in each one trying his best to get his share of the custom. And you'd benefit an' all, 'cos if my takings go up, then you'll get a rise. Now, I can't say fairer than that, can I? So, what d'yer say, Rose, eh? Chuck those old clothes and get yourself something decent, something that—'

'Something that shows a bit of *tit*.' Rose glared at her employer. 'Well, I'm sorry to disappoint you, Mr Dixon, but my *tits* are staying right where they are. Covered up and out of sight. And if you don't like it, you can get yourself another barmaid. As you're always saying, there's plenty of women who'd jump at the chance of a job.'

A heavy fist banged down on the desk, making Rose jump. She composed herself quickly, though she couldn't stop a feeling of dread creeping through her. She didn't want to lose this job. Despite a few drawbacks she liked it here, she was comfortable and at ease, well, most of the time and, above all else, she was settled. If Mr Dixon sacked her, she'd have to start looking around for another job, the prospect of which didn't appeal to her one little bit.

'Don't push your luck, girl.' Dixon's knuckles were white as he gripped the edge of the desk, his lips tight with anger. 'Now, I'm giving you fair warning. Don't you ever speak to me like that again, d'yer understand? I won't put up with it, not from you or anyone else.'

Rose stood mute, her courage dwindling by the minute. She hated confrontations, but there was a limit to anyone's endurance. What he had asked of her went against every grain of her nature, and there was no way she was going to give in; unfortunately, it looked as if her employer was of like mind.

'Here, take your wages and get out before I really lose me temper.' The coins were shoved roughly across the polished desk and Rose had to jump forward to catch them before they rolled on to the floor. Without looking at the irate man, she took out her purse, dropped in the coins then turned to leave. Her face was still flushed, and she was annoyed to note that her hands were trembling. At the door she hesitated. Then, sounding calm and steady, she asked, 'Do I still have a job to come back to on Monday?'

Henry Dixon couldn't trust himself to answer. Instead he nodded curtly, then sat down heavily, pulled a thick ledger towards him and opened the pages, silently dismissing her.

When the door closed after her, he leaned back in the chair, a wry smile tugging at his thin lips. Well! Who would have thought she had it in her to talk back to him like that? She'd always been so obliging up till now – to a point, that is. She never let anyone in the bar take liberties with her, and he'd heard her answer back to Sally on numerous occasions, but he'd never guessed she had such a temper. Well, now he knew, and it was obvious she wasn't going to fall in with his plans as easily as he'd imagined. So what was he going to do about it?

He should have been feeling furious, but instead he experienced a sneaking admiration for the way Rose had stood up to him. A soft laugh escaped his lips. 'She's got the better of you this time, me old son, and it ain't often that happens.'

From out of nowhere, a disturbing thought crossed his mind, causing him to shuffle uneasily in the chair. Then he sat up straighter, his face set determinedly. 'Bugger him. It's my pub, and I'll do what I bleeding well like. And he ain't around to stick his nose in anyway, thank Gawd!' he declared to the empty room.

Feeling somewhat better, he squared his shoulders and bent over the ledger, but the nagging uneasiness persisted.

Still upset from the heated conversation with the landlord, Rose took her share of the week's tips from a scowling Sally and headed thankfully for the door. Not wanting to stop and chat with anyone she kept her head down and walked purposefully towards the front of the pub. She was nearing the exit when she sensed a sudden change in the atmosphere.

Miraculously a space appeared in the crowd letting through a tall, dark-haired man in his early thirties, his expensive navy suit and brocade waistcoat setting him instantly apart from all other men present. The fingers holding a gold-tipped walking cane were adorned with gold set diamond rings, while an equally impressive heavy gold bracelet rested against the cuff of a pure white linen shirt. Flanked on all sides by burly minders who glanced menacingly at the onlookers, he stood for a moment, his dark eyes sweeping the pub as if searching for somebody before moving on. Frankie Buchannon, a well-known and often feared man, swept on through and, with each step he took, a path was cleared to make his progress easy.

A few men, arrogant in their familiarity, slapped the broad back, saying cheerfully, 'Welcome back, Mr Buchannon.'

'Hello, Frankie, me old mate, when did you get out?'

'How are yer, Frank? Good ter see yer back.'

'Would yer like a drink, Mr Buchannon, sir?'

Frankie Buchannon strode on, acknowledging a man or woman here and there with a curt nod, like a king bestowing a greeting on his subjects. Then his features broke into a wide smile, which transformed his moody countenance to reveal a strikingly handsome man. He stopped in front of a dumbfounded Rose and gazed down fondly at her. 'Hello, Princess, pleased to see me, are you?'

Rose could only stand and stare, open-mouthed, at the tall man leaning over her, then, a wide grin splitting her face she cried, 'Frankie! I thought you weren't coming out until next August. What happened? Why didn't you let me know? Ooh, Frankie . . . Oh, it is good to see you.' Gabbling excitedly, she grabbed hold of the outstretched hands, her blue eyes fixed on his face. 'And why didn't you answer any of my letters? I thought you'd forgotten about me.'

Frankie gripped the slender hands, his eyes tender. 'You know I ain't one for writing, Princess – but forget you? Never! Never in a million years,' he said softly. Then, aware of prying eyes and cocked ears, he added, 'Look, let's find a table where we can talk,' and his hands pulled at hers as he tried to guide her further back into the pub where they could have some privacy. Reluctantly she shook her head. 'I'd love to, Frankie, honestly, you know I would, but Aunt Mary will be waiting for me to get home, and I don't want her worrying.' The disappointment on her face mirrored that on his own, but with a regretful sigh he let her go. 'Well at least have a drink with me . . . Just a quick one, I promise,' he pleaded, the beseeching look in his dark brown eyes rapidly melting her resolve.

'All right, Frankie, but I'm not sitting down. I don't want to get too comfortable,' she said, knowing from past experience how persuasive he could be. At any other time she would have been more than happy to spend some time with this man, but her aunt would be waiting for her at home and, as fond as Rose was of Frankie, her aunt Mary came first. 'I'll have a quick drink at the bar with you, then I'll be off. You do understand, don't you?' The last words were uttered in the form of a command, rather than an apology, and Frankie, looking down into the wide blue eyes, smiled ruefully.

'Yeah, I understand, Princess.' His broad arm came to rest familiarly around her shoulders as he led her towards the bar. 'I don't like the idea of Mary being on her own any more than you do – though she wouldn't thank me for saying it, the stubborn old cow.' The last words were spoken with affection, and that in itself was rare for there weren't many people whom Frankie Buchannon held in high esteem.

Still holding Rose close to his side, Frank leaned one elbow on the bar, his foot resting on the brass rail, his baleful companions keeping the other patrons at arm's length. Rose fell silent, her body resting against Frank's in complete harmony, her contentment marred only by the presence of the strong-arm contingent that always seemed to accompany him. A slight tremor of misgiving ran through her, which she instantly dismissed. There was a lot she didn't like about the way Frankie ran his life, but the essence of her feelings for him remained the same, and always would.

She had known Frankie Buchannon most of her life and looked upon him as a member of her small family. And as such, any disquieting thoughts that threatened to impair her feelings for him had always been swiftly crushed, as they were now. Glancing up sideways into the merry brown eyes, she was struck by how kind they were, and wondered, not for the first time, how anyone could be frightened of this man. Oh, she wasn't a complete fool: she knew he had his hand in a number of shady enterprises, and was well aware that his money didn't come from honest graft. She smiled wryly. Considering he had just come out of prison for the umpteenth time, only a complete imbecile would remain blind to the nature of his work, and she was neither stupid, nor blind, but it would be true to say that her vision was blinkered where Frankie Buchannon was concerned.

Thoughts of protection rackets and sweatshops crept into Rose's mind and, just as quickly, were gone. There was only one Frankie Buchannon she knew, and that man was kind and protective. The other Frankie was pushed back into the dark recesses of her mind, the part that protected her from knowledge that would surely erode her love and loyalty for the man who had looked out for her from the moment when, as a small child, he had held her in his arms for the first time.

Taking a large gulp of the gin and orange he had bought for her she nudged him sharply in the ribs. 'Well, come on, then. Aren't you going to tell me how you got released so early? I thought I was seeing things when you walked through the door.'

With one arm still snaked around her waist, Frankie inclined his dark head and answered, with a smile and a broad wink, 'I was innocent, wasn't I? I told you that all along . . . 'Ere!' He pulled back from her, his eyes expressing mock horror. 'Don't say you didn't believe me, Princess?'

Rose shook her head, laughing. According to Frank, he was as innocent as a newborn babe. Then, suddenly conscious of time slipping away, she finished her drink and said, 'Look, Frank, I'll have to go. Aunt Mary will be—'

'Yeah, yeah, I know. Hang on a minute and I'll walk you out.' Draining his glass, he threw a couple of florins across the bar. 'Cheers, Rita, have one for yourself, darling.' He gave Rita a broad wink and was about to turn away when he spotted the landlord coming out from one of the rooms at the back.

Henry Dixon saw Frankie at the same time, and couldn't hide the look of alarm that crossed his swarthy face.

Relishing the other man's obvious discomfort, Frankie cried, 'Well, well, if it ain't me old mate Henry. How you doing, me old son? Still watering the beer, are you? Gawd help us, you look like you've seen a ghost. Ain't you pleased to see me, mate?'

Dixon stood stock still, the shock at seeing Frankie Buchannon standing in his pub momentarily rendering him speechless. Then his eyes flickered to the young woman Buchannon held so possessively, and his stomach lurched in fear. The harsh words he had so recently spoken to Rose now came back to haunt him.

Dixon was no coward, and in his life there had been few people who could frighten him, but Frankie Buchannon was different. The man was dangerous, ruthless to those who had the misfortune to upset or annoy him, and he, Henry Dixon, a man who should have known better, had committed the unforgivable. He had unintentionally upset someone dear to Buchannon's heart. You stupid, bleeding bastard, he cursed himself mentally. What the bloody hell did you think you was playing at, talking to Rosie like that, when you knew how Buchannon felt about her? But he had imagined Buchannon to be safely locked up behind bars, and in his eagerness to attract more custom he had put himself in grave danger.

Swallowing hard, he put out his hand in a gesture of welcome. 'Hello, Frankie. I didn't expect to see you for some time yet. How d'yer manage to get out so early?'

His hand was left hovering in mid-air for a few embarrass-
ing moments, the ambiguous gesture drawing unwelcome
attention from the eagle-eyed punters at the bar. A few,
less audacious than their companions, began to shuffle
away from the bar, not wanting to stay around in case
there was trouble. Then Frankie's hand shot out, clasped
Henry's warmly, and an audible sigh of relief escaped the
lips of all present. Repeating what he had told Rose, Frankie
said, 'I was innocent, wasn't I?' His eyebrows rose in mock
indignation. 'Me lawyer says I can sue the coppers for false
imprisonment, but I don't think I'll bother. It was worth it
just to see their faces when they had to let me out.'

'Frankie! I'll have to go,' Rose extricated herself from the
tight hold.

Frank looked at her benevolently. 'Sorry, Princess.' Taking her arm he paused once more and, turning back to
Henry, said laughingly, 'I hope you've been taking care of
me girl while I was away, Henry.' Before the startled man
could answer, Frankie pulled Rose close, adding to her, 'He
has, ain't he, Princess? He ain't been taking liberties with
you, has he?' Then he threw back his head and laughed
uproariously at what he deemed a preposterous notion.

'Don't be silly, Frank,' Rose said, glancing over at her
employer and smiling. 'Mr Dixon has always been the
perfect gentleman. Now, please, if you're going to walk
me out, get a move on, or you'll have Aunt Mary after you
for making me late.'

Rose had barely gone two steps from the bar when she
was rudely shoved to one side and there was Sally, painted
face wreathed in smiles, provocative body planted firmly
in front of the celebrated customer. 'Frankie! Gawd help
us, I thought they'd locked you up and thrown away the
key. You ain't gone and tunnelled your way out of the nick,
have you?' Ignoring Rose, she grabbed Frank's arm and laid
her face against his shoulder. 'Here, let me show you to a
table. They was all taken, but I'm sure one'll be free any
minute now.' She tilted her chin up to the handsome face
and winked. 'If you know what I mean.'

Frankie stared down into the attractive face, a face that
had often lain on a pillow next to his but which had long

since lost its appeal for him. He felt a strong urge to fling
her violently away from him, but he restrained the impulse.
Not out of any chivalrous sentiment, but because Rose was
present. It was absurd, he told himself. Here he was, Frankie
Buchannon, a name that could send shivers of fear through
many a man, yet this woman, Rose Kennedy, could see no
wrong in him. And it was terribly important to Frankie that
Rose's good opinion of him remained unchanged. Bearing
this in mind, he smiled tightly and said to the hovering
Sally, 'Thanks, Sal, but I think I can manage to get a table
for meself.'

Unperturbed, Sally clung even tighter to the man she still
regarded as her property, even though it had been over a
year since he had last shown any interest in her. Stroking
the front of his chest, she whispered huskily, 'D'yer fancy
stopping by me place later, Frankie? You know, for old
times' sake.'

Impatient with the cloying attention, Frank tugged his
arm free, saying drily, 'No, thanks, Sal. I don't like queuing.'

This remark was greeted with loud guffaws from all
within earshot, and Rose, embarrassed for Sally, looked
away from a face that had turned pale beneath the mask
of powder and rouge. The smile on the older woman's
painted lips faltered for a few seconds, then, she said
nonchalantly, 'Suit yerself, Frankie, your loss, not mine,'
before she turned and engaged a young docker in banter,
her shrill laugh echoing falsely in the air.

Rose felt a wave of pity as she hastily left the pub. She
didn't like Sally, and she knew that the feeling was mutual,
but even so she didn't like seeing her hurt.

Seeing Rose leave the pub, Frankie detached himself from
his henchmen and hurried after her. Out on the street he
caught her arm. 'Hang on, Princess, I thought you was
gonna wait for me. What's the matter?'

Rose stared up at him, her eyes accusing. 'That was cruel,
Frankie. I know you're not interested in Sally any more, but
there was no need to talk to her like that, especially in front
of a crowd.'

Frankie looked away, his teeth worrying his bottom lip
as he sought for the right words to appease Rose. He

didn't want to fall out with her, especially not over a slag like Sally. Adopting a contrite manner, he said sheepishly, 'Yeah, you're right, love. Tell you what, when I go back in I'll apologise and buy her a drink. How about that?'

He had no intention of doing any such thing, but Rose brightened immediately. 'Well, make sure you do.'

Eager to change the subject, Frankie asked, 'How's Mary these days? Her legs any better, or are they still playing her up?'

At the mention of her aunt, Rose felt a growing surge of anxiety to get home and began to back away. 'About the same. Look, Frank, I've got to go. And, Frank . . . instead of just asking after her, you should go round and visit. You know how much she thinks of you, and how she's been worrying ever since you went inside. The least you can do is go and see her, and set her mind at rest.' She had been about to add, 'You owe her that much,' but her aunt wouldn't thank her for pointing out Frankie's obligations. Nor would she want him coming to see her merely out of a sense of duty – or, worse still, guilt.

His head drooping, Frankie shrugged. Then, he said, 'Yeah, you're right, Princess. I'll get round as soon as I can, I promise.'

Satisfied that she had stirred his conscience, Rose smiled. 'Thanks, Frank. I'll be seeing you soon, then. 'Bye . . . And, Frank . . .' Her face seemed to melt with emotion as she added, almost shyly, 'I'm glad you're back home. I missed you.' With a cheery wave she walked off into the balmy twilight.

Frankie watched the slim figure hurrying down the narrow street, his eyes thoughtful. He went back inside the pub and called one of his men to his side. 'See she gets home safely,' he said.

There was no need to explain further. With a deferential nod, the man answered, 'Righto, Mr Buchannon.'

Seated comfortably at a table at the back of the pub, Frankie pondered over the last five months. It had cost him plenty to get himself released. Coppers, lawyers and other minor servants of the law had had their palms greased, and that money would have to be replaced. He glanced at the bar, to where Henry Dixon was busy serving drinks. Dixon was about the only landlord round these parts who didn't pay him protection money, and that was only because Rose worked for him. Still, she wouldn't always be working here, and when that day came, Henry Dixon would receive a visit. A very expensive visit.

CHAPTER TWO

Coming out of the chip shop, Rose hugged the steaming paper parcel to her chest, breathing in the appetising aroma. Lord, she was hungry. She'd been working in the pub since ten o'clock that morning and was now dead on her feet. Thinking of the pub brought to mind what had occurred earlier with Dixon. She began to laugh quietly – the blooming cheek of the man! But what if she'd gone along with his wishes? Good God! She could just imagine her aunt's reaction to seeing her niece sloping out of the house wearing a blouse or dress with half the top missing. Bad legs or no, Mary Miller would beat the living daylights out of her charge, and when she had finished, she'd go after the man responsible for putting such an idea into her head, even if she had to crawl all the way. The image created such an extraordinary picture in Rose's mind that she had to smother her laughter, otherwise passers-by would think she was mad. Humming softly she quickened her step, anxious to get home. She couldn't wait to see her aunt's face when she told her Frankie was out of prison and asking after her. She'd be over the moon at the news.

Turning the corner into a narrow side-street of small terraced houses, she was three doors from home when a cloaked figure seemed to rise from the shadows out of nowhere. Her cry of fear was quickly replaced by one of anger when she saw who it was. Her chest heaving from fright, she said angrily, 'Bloody hell, Jack, you nearly scared the living daylights out of me, jumping out on me like that.'

Before her visitor could answer, pounding footsteps crashed on the cobblestones behind them, then a short, stocky man, his fists bunched ready for action, stopped in his tracks when he saw who was with the woman he had been ordered to protect.

Constable Jack Adams, his hands clasped behind his back, looked with disdain at Buchannon's man and said disparagingly, 'It's all right, Perkins. You can report back to *Mr* Buchannon that Miss Kennedy has reached home safely.'

Perkins, a known thief and bully boy, glared at the tall, uniformed figure, his upper lip curling back in a sneer. 'Yeah, I'll do just that, *Constable*,' he said cockily. 'Mr Buchannon'll be very interested to hear how you was waiting for her – *very* interested indeed.' Then, tipping his flat cap in Rose's direction he added, 'Good night to you, Miss,' before he swaggered back the way he had come.

'Do you have to be so nasty, Jack?' Rose was pulling her latch-key through the letter-box. 'The poor man was just looking out for me. There was no need for you to be so rude to him.'

Jack Adams stood back, perplexed and annoyed by Rose's attitude. 'If you'd let me meet you and walk you home after you finished work there wouldn't be any need for anyone else to look out for you. Anybody would think you were ashamed of me, the way you carry on. You don't even like me coming in for a drink when I'm off duty, and when I do, you act as if you barely know me. Look, Rose . . .' He took her arm, then let go as he saw her expression. Lord! She was infuriating at times. In a more conciliatory tone he said, 'I'm sorry, love. It's just that, well, I want people to know we're walking out together. For a start it would stop other lads from giving you any aggravation and—'

'I can look after myself, Jack. And I've told you before. I don't want everyone at the pub knowing my business.'

Jack's eyebrows nearly disappeared into the rim of his black helmet. 'Well, I don't care who knows, but we'll forget about that for a minute. Let's talk about him.' He jerked his head back down the street, towards where the stocky man had disappeared. 'And the person who sent him. I've told you before how I feel about you mixing with the likes of Buchannon and his sort. He—'

'Oh, oh, that's a good one, Jack. And just what *sort* of people do you think I serve in the Red Lion? Dukes and duchesses? Anyway,' she faced him, suddenly suspicious, 'how did you know Frankie was out of prison? He only came out today.'

Immediately on his guard, the uniformed man looked down at his heavy black regulation boots and said hesitantly, 'Well . . . Actually, Rose, he came out nearly two weeks ago. He's been back on this patch since his release.'

Rose stared up at him in disbelief. 'Two weeks ago! Rubbish! He couldn't have, he . . .' She trailed off. So, Frank had been out all that time and hadn't bothered to get in touch until now. Well, he must have had his reasons, she thought loyally. Even so, she couldn't help but be hurt that he hadn't tried to see her or her aunt sooner.

Swallowing hard she turned away from the sympathetic grey eyes staring down at her. 'Yes, well . . . Frank's a very busy man,' she said, carelessly. 'Now, if you'll excuse me, my aunt's waiting for her supper.'

'Rose, please,' Jack begged, 'Don't be like that. I know I should have told you he was out, but . . . well, I sort of hoped he'd stay away from you. And if you weren't working in that place, you might not have seen him for months.'

Studying the silent figure, Jack moved nearer, his hands going out to embrace her. They dropped to his sides as she pushed open the door and stepped into a dim hallway. He put one foot over the doorstep and asked hopefully, 'About the pub, Rose. Have you thought any more about leaving. I mean, with your education, you could . . .'

Rose tossed her head, her eyes darting down the hall to the open door of the parlour where she knew her aunt would be waiting for her. 'Could what, Jack? Get a better job? Well, maybe I could, but the pub suits me for now. It's near home, and I can earn good money with tips, and you know how I'm placed. Aunt Mary hasn't got anyone else and I have to be nearby in case she needs me. So, unless you can find me a well-paid, respectable job that's within walking distance of home, keep your nose out of my business.'

Alarmed by Rose's unusually sharp manner, Jack nevertheless blundered on recklessly. 'But what about Buchannon? Please, Rose, stay away from him. He's not the lovable villain you think he is. God, if you knew only half what I know about him, then—'

Rose whirled on him angrily, the mass of copper curls bouncing around her face and shoulders. 'Now, you listen to me, Jack Adams. Frank Buchannon has been good to me and Aunt Mary. She's known him all his life. His mother was her best friend, and when she died Aunt Mary took Frankie in until he was old enough to look after himself. He's never forgotten it. Oh! What am I doing telling you all this? You know damn well how my aunt feels about Frank – and that goes for me too. So don't come round with your tales because I don't want to know. Just because you and me have gone out together a few times it doesn't mean you can tell me what to do or who to see. Now, if you don't mind, I'll say good night.'

Jack, bemused, found himself staring at a closed door. He swore softly. He waited a few minutes longer, hoping Rose would regret her harsh words and come back, but the door remained shut.

He cast one more hopeful glance at the green-painted door, then with purposeful strides resumed his beat.

CHAPTER THREE

Mary Miller, seated in a well-worn brown armchair by the hearth, laid her knitting in her ample lap, her pale blue eyes lighting up with relief at the sound of Rose's voice in the hallway.

Mary was a stout woman of fifty-three, with a plump, smooth, kindly face that belied her formidable character. Her hair, which at the moment was wound tightly in steel grips and covered by an old pair of knickers to keep them in place, was a warm brown colour without a trace of grey, which was more than could be said of many a woman her age. In essence she would give her last sixpence to someone in need, yet her razor-edged tongue could slice you to shreds if you had the misfortune to cross swords with her.

Although it had only just gone nine o'clock, she was already dressed for bed in a flowery cotton nightgown that fell in folds around her swollen ankles. Now, as the voices in the hallway became more audible she leaned forward in her chair, straining to identify the male voice talking to her niece. She was about to call out when she recognised Jack Adams's familiar tone and sank back, letting her large body relax.

Mary never felt easy until Rose was safely back from the pub, but it was more than that. Without Rose's presence, the small terraced house that she had lived in since her early childhood seemed devoid of life, empty and cold, and sometimes frightening. For the past few years, since her legs had started playing her up, Mary had been forced to slow down her busy lifestyle. Her once numerous cleaning jobs had been taken over by able-bodied women, who could still clamber on to chairs and tables to take down heavy curtains and wash ceilings, spend hours on their knees scrubbing floors, and still have enough energy to tackle a week's washing, as she once had.

Not that she could be termed a cripple – far from it. But tasks that had once been effortless now took three times as long, with a good rest afterwards. And people who could afford help weren't going to employ someone like Mary, not when they could take their pick of strong, willing women eager to earn a few extra shillings.

And slowly, as time passed and she found herself with nothing much to do but look after her own home, Mary's fierce independence had begun to deteriorate. Where once her days had been full, they now stretched emptily from one week to the next. Day by day she had clung to Rose a little more until now her life seemed to revolve around her niece. And the older Mary got, the more she fretted. She had every reason to worry: Rose was a striking young woman, and it wasn't unknown for some to fall prey to the riff-raff that prowled the back-streets of the East End.

Suddenly her nose picked up the tantalising aroma of fish and chips and her stomach rumbled in anticipation of the treat to come. Blast that Jack Adams, keeping Rosie talking while Mary's supper was getting cold. With an impatient tut, she wondered if she should go out into the hall and get it for herself, because if it wasn't put into the oven to keep warm it wouldn't be worth eating.

She started to heave herself from the chair, then stopped mid-way as the voices in the hallway were raised.

Maybe they were having a fight, and if that was so Rose wouldn't thank her for poking her nose in. And if they *were* . . . Well, good! Mary had never been over-fond of the police, with good cause. And out of all the men in London, of whom Rose could have had her pick, she had to go and get tangled up with a bleeding copper.

Mary's chest rose in hopeful expectation at the now

whispered but still evidently angry words that infiltrated the parlour. With luck, Rose was telling him to get lost, and if she was, it would be worth the fish supper getting cold. Mary leaned her head back against the white, lace-edged antimacassar and thought back to the day she had first brought Rose home with her, and the events leading up to her taking charge of her niece's life. Her mind drifted back to her own youth, as it often did, these days. Her parents had died when she was seventeen, leaving Mary and her sister Ruth, who was a year younger, alone in the world. The two girls, torn apart by grief and ravaged with fear at finding themselves alone, had formed a bond, hitherto unknown to them.

They had both been working in a machine factory in Bethnal Green at the time of their parents' death, and although the wages were poor, they survived by sharing every penny they earned. Mary had always been frugal unlike Ruth, who could never hang on to a penny and preferred instead to roam the markets, with one eye on the clothes stalls and the other on any presentable man who walked by. But, to give her her due, in those first early days Ruth had tried, yet as time passed and grief diminished, she returned to her old ways. It wasn't her fault. She had always been feckless and irresponsible, with a tendency to plod along in a good-natured fashion, smiling impishly whenever her parents, and later Mary, had remonstrated with her for her slipshod ways. Knowing that her sister would never change, and fearful of the future, Mary had put in all the hours she could at the factory, hoarding away the extra money she made, and refusing to listen to Ruth's pleas for a loan when she found herself broke, which was a regular occurrence.

When Ruth was nineteen, she met and married a young labourer within the space of three months, without informing her elder sister until after the wedding. Mary was at first hurt, then furious. There was a heated argument, in which both women said things they didn't mean. Ruth had stormed off with her new husband, vowing never to return.

Left alone, Mary threw herself into her work, leaving

herself no time to feel sorry for her lonely state. She would arrive home feeling so tired that she couldn't even think straight, let alone dwell on her abject misery over Ruth's hasty marriage and departure.

Ten years passed, during which she received a dozen letters from Ruth, each apologising for her behaviour and promising she would come and visit soon; but she never did. And as time went on, Mary hardened her heart. It was the only way she knew how to cope with the shattering sense of betrayal her sister had left in her wake.

On Mary's thirtieth birthday, her next-door neighbour and only friend, Mabel Buchannon, died suddenly, creating yet another void in Mary's lonely life. It was to Mabel that Mary had turned when Ruth had run off, and over the years she had been glad of the cheerful Irishwoman's friendship.

Mabel had been a widow for seven years, so when ten-year-old Frankie Buchannon found himself an orphan, Mary stepped in, took the boy into her home and looked after him until he could fend for himself, an accomplishment he had achieved by the time he was eleven.

Two days after his twelfth birthday he announced that he wasn't going back to school, and nothing Mary could do or say would change his mind. She tried coaxing and bribing before resorting to threats but, throughout it all, Frankie remained steadfast, until Mary finally admitted defeat. Frankie had always been old for his years, due mainly to his mother having constantly referred to him as 'the man of the house'; poor Mabel had used the term affectionately, but Frankie had taken the words at face value and had developed a wisdom and maturity that went far beyond the normal scope of a boy his age. And from the day he declared his intention of leaving school to the day he turned fourteen, he became adept at avoiding the truancy officer, leaving a belligerent Mary to protest her innocence as to the whereabouts of her charge until Frankie no longer had to worry about school.

During those years he contributed to his keep, tipping a small pile of silver on to the kitchen table every Friday night, from odd jobs he did around the local shops and markets. His first official job was as an errand boy for a large clothing firm, but taking orders and being treated like a dogsbody hadn't suited Frankie's independent temperament, and after only two weeks he left to find regular work down at Ridley Road market.

Mary couldn't remember exactly when it had dawned on her that things weren't quite right, nor when the first uneasy niggles began to plague her mind. Frankie's plausible explanations as to the varying amounts of housekeeping he gave her and the odd hours he worked had satisfied her at first; after all, she'd had no reason to suspect him of lying. Even when she had visited the Ridley Road market and found no sign of him she had told herself that he must have slipped off to get something to eat.

Only once did she mention to Frankie that she had been at the market and hadn't been able to find him. She had made light of it, insinuating that he had been skiving off to meet some girl, but he hadn't laughed at the joke. Instead he had carried on eating his supper, the noise of the knife and fork scraping along the china plate the only sound in the room. His meal finished, he had sat silently at the table before raising his head in Mary's direction. Then, in a voice so quiet she had to strain to hear his words, he'd said, 'It's been good of you to look after me, Mary, and I'll always be grateful to you for taking me in when Mum died, but I think it's time I started to look after meself. After all, I'm not a kid any more – am I?' He had been smiling as he spoke, and when he saw the tears of alarm spring to Mary's eyes he had gone to her, had taken her trembling hands in his and gently chastised her: 'I'm only thinking of you, Mary. What I mean is, well . . . I don't want to cause you any worry. D'yer understand?'

And she'd understood. The matter was dropped and never mentioned again.

After that, Frankie began staying out later and later. Some nights he didn't come home at all, and as he got older his absences became more frequent, but still Mary raised no objection. She was afraid to, in case he left her for good. She had never been one for the men, unlike her younger sister, and the prospect of being an old maid had never frightened her – but being left alone did, so she bit her tongue and stayed silent. Yet for all the worry he caused her, Mary had never regretted taking the boy into her home. Even when the police became regular visitors, Frankie had only to look at her, with those cheeky dark eyes and that affectionate grin, and her anger would melt away. He could have charmed the knickers off a nun if he'd wanted to – still could, for that matter.

The letter from Ruth came out of the blue. When Mary had read the scrawled message begging for help, all past differences were instantly forgotten. With Frankie, now a strapping seventeen-year-old, at her side, Mary had made the short journey to a dilapidated tenement block in Whitechapel where she had found her sister huddled, dirty and unkempt, in a squalid room at the top of the building. Lying beside her, in a broken, wooden box was her three-year-old daughter, so weak with hunger and neglect, she could only look up at the visitors with wide, glazed eyes.

Frankie had immediately taken control. Within an hour he had found, and brought back with him, an elderly doctor, who was protesting loudly at being dragged from his surgery to the godforsaken hole he found himself in. To give him his due, he had tried to help Ruth, but she had been beyond the aid of mere mortals. The only thing Mary could do for her was provide her with a decent burial and take care of her orphaned child. The first task was performed with sorrow, the second with joy, for from the moment Mary brought Rose home, she looked upon her as the daughter she would never have.

She never found out what had happened to Ruth's husband, or what circumstances had led to her sister ending her days in such dire straits, but she thanked God she had arrived in time to save Rose before she, too, had suffered the same fate as her mother.

Frankie, too, had instantly taken to the child, and even when he moved out, some months later, not a week went by when he didn't turn up with a small present for Rose, and after he left Mary would always find money on the kitchen table. The amount varied, but even if it was only a few shillings, there was always something. She used the money she'd saved over the years to send Rose to a decent school, determined that her niece would have a good start in life, which she did; she found a job in an office in the City, which she kept until her aunt became ill.

For years Mary had been battling with crippling pains in her feet and legs, and when Rose came home one day to find her nearly in tears with the pain – and frustrated because she hadn't been able to get to one of her cleaning jobs – she promptly found employment in the Red Lion so that she could be nearer to home.

Mary had wept at seeing her beloved niece having to work in a pub, but Rose had been adamant. As soon as Frankie heard of Mary's plight, he had immediately offered to pay someone to come in during the day to see to her and the housework. His generous offer hadn't been well received: Mary, furious at the idea of some busybody – as she put it – poking and prying into her drawers and cupboards, hadn't minced her words. The dropsy might have slowed her down and she might not be able to do as much as she had in the past, but while she could still manage to wipe her arse, she shouted, she wasn't going to have anyone running round after her and sticking their nose into her business.

Mary gave a long sigh, eased herself out of the sagging armchair and into the small kitchen to butter some bread and make a pot of tea for when Rose finally got rid of Jack Adams. While she waited for the kettle to boil, she wondered what Frankie would have to say about their Rose going out with a copper. Although Mary hadn't seen as much of him over the past few years, she knew he was always there if she needed him – when he wasn't in prison.

Her eyes dimmed as she thought of her Frankie banged up behind the grim walls of the Scrubs. She should be used to it by now, she mused silently, she'd visited him there often enough. But this time had been different.

Up until now, Frankie had never been jailed for longer than a few weeks, but on his last appearance at court, the judge had sentenced him to eighteen months for beating up the owner of a nearby factory when the man had refused to pay protection money.

A spark of anger flared in Mary's pale blue eyes. Frankie was no angel, and Lord knows he was no stranger to the law – he had been ducking and diving since he was eleven – but he wasn't violent. No! No. He wasn't violent, never had been. Her head bobbed up and down furiously on her thick neck, the affirmative, defensive action adding strength to her conviction. She'd admit that, in the past, Frankie had stolen to provide for her and he had paid for his early crimes. But he was straight now. Over the years he had built up a small empire, and he had worked hard to achieve his success. He owned several businesses, the nature of which she wasn't quite sure – Frank had always been vague about his ventures – but it was all legal and above board. Just because he had been a tearway in his youth, the local police had never given up hounding him, turning up on his doorstep every time a crime occurred in the neighbourhood. And the latest incident just proved how vindictive the coppers were. They hadn't been able to pin anything on him legally, so out of sheer spite they'd set him up on a false charge. Bastards!

The sound of the front door banging jerked Mary from her reverie. Picking up the plate of buttered bread, she moved slowly into the parlour saying, 'About bleeding time. Those fish an' chips'll be stone cold by now.' As she put the plate on the table, she glanced up at her niece. Her eyes narrowed at the look of anger on Rose's face. 'What's up, love? You fallen out with Jack, have you?'

The hopeful note in her voice wasn't lost on Rose, who immediately began to bustle around the small room. 'No, not really. We just had a disagreement about something. Nothing important . . . Look, let's leave it for now, eh, Auntie?' She was overcome by tiredness and all she wanted now was to eat her supper in peace. She knew better than to mention Jack's scathing comments about Frankie to her aunt. Seeing the worried frown creasing Mary's face, Rose smiled. 'Honest, Auntie. Everything's all right. I'm just tired, that's all. It's been a long day.'

Mary would have probed further, but hunger got the

better of her, and instead she said, 'Well, let's get started on supper, then. Gawd! I knew it! I knew they'd be ruined.' Mary had opened the greasy parcel and, as she settled herself at the table, she grumbled on for the next five minutes about her meal being cold, remarking between mouthfuls, 'You should've brought them in and put 'em in the oven to keep warm if you was gonna stand chattering on the doorstep.' Rose listened half-heartedly to her aunt's diatribe without comment. If there was one thing her aunt loved more than food, it was a good moan. Rose carried on eating and let Mary's voice wash over her without much notice.

When there were only three chips left in the paper bag, Mary pushed them away, saying pettishly, 'You know how cold grease lays on me chest, Rosie. I'll probably be up half the night with wind now.'

She felt a sudden urge to shout, 'Well, nobody forced you to eat them,' but she kept quiet. Her aunt could be maddening at times, and on occasions like this, Rose found it best to ignore her. Gathering up the remnants of the meal, she carried them into the scullery, calling over her shoulder, 'I'll make the cocoa now, Auntie. I don't know about you, but I'm ready for my bed.'

Mary, her niece home, her stomach filled, and feeling better for a good grumble, answered amiably, 'Yeah, all right, love. D'yer want any help?'

'No, it's all right. You let your supper get down.'

Rose waited for another comment on Mary's irregular digestion. When none was forthcoming she started to pre-pare their nightcap. While she waited for the milk to heat, Rose pondered on whether or not to tell Mary about Frankie being out. Of course she'd have to tell her, there was no question of that; the problem was when rather than if. And if she told Mary about his early release now, the delighted woman would keep her up all night talking about it. She really didn't feel like hearing again about how the police had it in for Frankie, not tonight. She just wasn't in the mood. Especially after the row she'd just had with Jack on the same subject.

Carrying two steaming cups of cocoa into the parlour, she

decided to leave it until tomorrow. Mary would probably give her hell for not imparting the good news straight away, but by then Rose would have had a good night's sleep and be able to deal with the truculent, maddening and often irritable woman – whom she loved more than words could ever say.

Flopping down in the armchair opposite her aunt, Rose slipped off her shoes, propped her feet on the fender and laced her hands around her cup. She peered over the rim at Mary.

'Hot enough for you, Auntie?'

Mary glanced up, surprised. 'What? Oh, yeah, thanks, love.'

Rose smiled to herself. The veiled jibe had gone unnoticed.

Later, when Mary had retired to the brass bed in the corner of the room, Rose sat on by the empty grate, her thoughts centred on Jack Adams. She had only known him a year, but it sometimes felt as if she'd known him all her life. They had met one night when she was on her way home from the pub, and a group of young lads had barred her way in the street. They hadn't meant any harm, but Jack, who had been watching from the other side of the road, had thought differently. He had sent them running off, then walked with her the rest of the way.

At first, they had been just friends, meeting occasionally by chance in the street. Then he had begun to turn up on a Sunday afternoon in Victoria Park where she sometimes went when it was fine. It was nearly five months before he asked her out, and had escorted her to a show at the Hackney Empire. She had not wanted him to take their friendship too seriously, so she had limited the times she agreed to go out with him, not because she didn't like him but because of her aunt's animosity towards the police. Yet, despite her reservations, she'd found herself growing more fond of him than she'd anticipated. He was good company, when out of uniform – and when she could keep him off the subject of Frankie Buchannon.

She also had a sneaking suspicion he was working up the courage to ask her to marry him. Giving vent to a long drawn-out sigh, she cupped her face in her hands and stared gloomily into the fireplace. She was fond of Jack, more than fond, in fact, but not enough to marry him – at least, not at the moment. Maybe in time her feelings for him would grow stronger, but for now she was happy as she was.

She wasn't ready to settle down and start a family. Jack would insist she gave up her job – and what about Aunt Mary? She couldn't leave her on her own, and her aunt and Jack, although civil enough to each other, would never get on living together, not while Frankie remained in their lives – which he was and always would be. Jack's main ambition in life was to lock him up and throw away the key, but her aunt thought the sun shone out of him . . . 'And so do you,' a voice in her head came back at her. No! It would never work between her and Jack. Then again, she might be mistaken about him wanting to marry her. If that was so then she had nothing to worry about. After all, there was no law that said a man and woman couldn't be just friends, was there? And if Jack did start to get too serious, well, then, she'd just have to put him straight, wouldn't she? A wide yawn split Rose's face and she shivered as she got up.

As long as she lived, her aunt would always come first in Rose's affections. She owed everything to the elderly woman asleep in the corner of the room. And if that meant she had to remain single, then so be it. Rose snuffed out the lamp and went up to her bedroom, which she had shared with her aunt until Mary's legs had become too swollen and painful to manage the stairs.

The tiny landing held only two rooms: one was the small boxroom that had once been Frank's and was now used to store bits and pieces of old furniture; the other, a larger room, was now Rose's domain. It was furnished sparsely, Rose had never liked clutter, and held a brass double bed, similar to the one downstairs, a dressing-table with side mirrors, a chest of drawers and a tallboy. On the floor beside the bed lay a bright, multi-coloured mat, which Mary had taken a year to weave and which cushioned Rose's feet from the cold impact of the bare floorboards first thing in the morning.

Before she fell asleep, Rose remembered that she had promised to spend tomorrow morning down Petticoat Lane with Jack. She wondered idly if he would remember – or, indeed, if he would bother to come round for her after their argument this evening.

CHAPTER FOUR

Petticoat Lane on a Sunday morning was a thriving, bustling, noisy mass of humanity. People from all walks of life flocked together every weekend to the East End market, widely renowned for its numerous stalls and rich atmosphere. Holding Jack's arm, Rose sniffed the hot June air in delight, savouring the glorious summer's day, and the mixed aromas of coffee, fresh-baked bread and fried food that wafted under her nose.

'Hungry?' Jack looked down at her affectionately.

From beneath a wide straw bonnet Rose nodded, smiling. 'Oh, yes, yes, I am, actually.'

Delving into the pocket of his navy pin-stripe trousers, Jack took out a shilling and offered it to a stall-holder, who handed over a greasy paper with four apple fritters inside.

'Hmmm, oh, Lord, it's boiling!' Rose spluttered, fanning her mouth as the piping hot filling scalded her mouth.

Jack watched in amusement as she blew furiously on it before popping it into her mouth again. He took one for himself and remarked, 'You're in a good mood today.'

Rose glanced up at him guiltily. It was the first time this morning that Jack had alluded to last evening's heated exchange. She answered lightly, 'I'm not making any apologies for speaking up for a friend, Jack, and in Frankie's case he's more like family. If you want my good humour to continue, you'd better drop that particular topic of conversation'.

Throwing up his hands in mock surrender, Jack said, 'Okay, Rose. I won't say another word about him! At least, not today.'

Rose laughed at the look of false penitence displayed on Jack's face.

Walking on in companionable silence, Rose took stock surreptitiously of the man at her side. Jack Adams was twenty-five, of medium height for a man and slim built, with grey eyes and a mop of dark brown hair he wore combed back from his face. He wasn't what could be termed handsome, yet the strength in his features showed character, an attribute far more attractive than mere good looks. 'When you've finished admiring me, maybe we could go for a drink. I'm gasping for a beer.'

Rose's eyes widened at the words, then she punched his arm and cried, 'You should be so lucky, Jack Adams. If you must know, I was looking at that piece of pastry you've got stuck on your cheek.'

Swiftly Jack put his hand to his face, and his lips twitched wryly when he found no evidence of his snack.

'It's no good you denying it, Rose. I'm trained in observing people, and you were definitely giving me the once-over. Not that I'm complaining, mind. I have that effect on most women.'

As if to give credence to his jocular opinion, three young women, all dressed in their Sunday-best clothes and matching bonnets, jostled against Rose in the crush, their eyes fixed in open admiration on her companion. Giggling coquettishly they made a great play of brushing past Jack, while the man himself, delighted at the attention, flirted shamelessly with his admirers for a few seconds before he took Rose's arm and led her on through the crowd. 'There! What did I tell you, Rose? Women just can't leave me alone!' he crowed triumphantly. 'It's a curse, but I suppose I'll just have to live with it as best I can.'

Rose refused to rise to the bait, and said impishly, 'I wouldn't get too carried away, Jack. I know those three girls, and they'd go after a broom if it was wearing trousers.'

Jack's grin broadened, and he chuckled. 'Why, Rose, I do believe you're jealous, but you've no need to worry,

I—' He broke off, his attention distracted by the sight of a well-known pickpocket. 'Hang on a minute, will you, love? I won't be long,' he said, before pushing his way to where a shabbily dressed man was loitering by two middle-aged women examining a display of crockery.

'Morning, Nobby. Nice day for it.'

The man spun round, his mouth dropping open at the sight of Jack Adams hovering over him. 'Nice day for what, Officer? I ain't doing nuffink wrong,' he blustered. His shifty eyes narrowed as he muttered, 'Anyways, yer off duty so it ain't none of yer business.'

'Oh, no, Nobby, never off duty, me,' Jack replied, good-naturedly. 'So make sure your fingers stay firmly in your pockets!'

The man muttered a soft oath and shuffled off, out of the sight of prying eyes. Jack smiled grimly. He didn't know why he'd bothered. The market was swarming with characters like Nobby. Venues like Petticoat Lane acted like a magnet to the low-life that flourished in crowded places, and unless he could catch them in the act he was powerless to stop them.

'Who was that?' Rose asked, when Jack rejoined her. 'He looked like a desperate villain to me. Do you think you should have gone after him on your own?'

Jack made to reply, then, realised she was teasing him and guffawed.

For the next two hours he had to wait patiently for his longed-for beer while Rose browsed among the stalls, picking up a few purchases on her way. He wondered why women took so long to shop: his mother, dead now for the past three years, had been the same, going down the markets for hours on end and coming back with just the week's groceries. Whenever he wanted to buy something, he went out, bought it and came home. Finally, at the end of the market, they stopped at a pub noted for its good food and sat outside, between a wooden bench and table, with platefuls of steak and kidney pudding, boiled potatoes and peas.

Throughout lunch, the two chatted, at ease in each other's company. When her plate was empty, Rose pushed it away and picked up her lemonade. 'That was lovely,' she said, 'though you can't beat a proper Sunday dinner of roast beef, potatoes and Yorkshire pud – well, not in my opinion, anyway.'

'I'll drink to that.' Jack raised his tankard. 'That reminds me. What's Mary doing for her Sunday dinner? She's not sitting at home nibbling a bit of cold toast, is she?'

Instantly on the defensive, Rose snapped, 'Don't be silly, Jack! As if I'd scoff down a dinner knowing Aunt Mary was going hungry. How do you think she manages when I'm at work all day? She's perfectly able to cook herself a meal. If she wasn't, I wouldn't be sitting here with you now.' Then, seeing the sheepish expression on Jack's face, she relented. 'Sorry, Jack. I know you didn't mean any harm, it's just my guilty conscience talking. You see, my aunt used to love coming down here on a Sunday morning. She knew a lot of the stall-holders so it was like an outing for her every week. Now she can't even get round the shops near home for very long and – oh, go away!' She flapped her hand at a wasp hovering near her drink and continued, 'It's just that I always feel bad about leaving her at home. That's what I meant by having a guilty conscience. It's silly, I know, but I can't help it. Anyway, cheers.' Raising her glass, she touched Jack's tankard with it and added, 'Lord, it's hot today.' Languidly lifting her face to the sun, she closed her eyes against the glare of its rays.

Jack let his gaze linger on the figure opposite him, his eyes softening with tenderness. Rose looked so lovely. She had taken off her bonnet, and the sun picked out golden highlights in the dark copper hair that fell in twisted curls around her face and down over her shoulders. The dark red cotton dress she was wearing suited her but, then, as far as he was concerned, Rose would look beautiful in a canvas sack. The temptation to propose to her was overwhelming, but he contained it. Not here, he told himself. This wasn't the time or place, but soon, he vowed, soon.

Deep down, though, he knew the reason behind his reluctance to ask Rose to marry him. While the words were left unsaid, he could go on hoping she would say yes, but when he got round to asking her, there would be no going back. And if she refused him, what then? Even if they carried on walking out together, there would almost certainly be an awkwardness between them that hadn't been present before. And Jack didn't want to risk spoiling the easy, affectionate friendship they enjoyed. So he would hold his tongue, though for how long he didn't know.

'Now who's being given the once-over?'

Taken by surprise, Jack started. 'Guilty, Your Worship.' He drained his tankard and pointed to Rose's half-empty glass. 'D'yer want another one, love?'

'Hmm, yes, all right, then I must be getting back. Like I said before, I don't like leaving Aunt Mary too long on her own on Sundays. It's the only day we have together – though the way things are going at the pub, I might soon have to work on Sundays as well.'

'Why? I thought you'd made it clear to Dixon that you wouldn't do that.'

'I know, but things change. The other two barmaids have to take their turn working on Sunday, and I don't want them thinking I'm getting any special favours. Rita doesn't mind too much, but Sally's been having a moan. Then again, Sally's always moaning where I'm concerned. Though I must admit, she's right in this case. It isn't fair that they have to work at the weekend when I don't.'

'I don't see why,' Jack said, indignantly. 'You don't get paid as much as they do, and you cover for them when they have their day off during the week. Besides, it's different for them. They've probably always worked in some pub or other – neither of them would know how to do anything else – but you're only filling in time until you can find something more suitable or until your circumstances change.'

Rose's head jerked back. 'What do you mean, until my circumstances change?' she demanded. 'My aunt's got a good few more years yet. She's as healthy as you or I. Just because she can't get around like she used to doesn't mean she's ready for the knacker's yard just yet.'

Jack stared at her in dismay. 'Good Lord, Rosie, that thought never entered my head, I swear it didn't.'

The distress in his voice humbled Rose. 'I know you didn't, Jack, and I'm sorry. It's just that I'm a bit sensitive

where Aunt Mary's concerned, as you might have noticed.'
A smile of apology touched her lips. 'As for the other business, well . . .' She shrugged. 'Seeing as my *circumstances*
aren't likely to change for the foreseeable future, it looks
as though I'll be at the pub for a while yet and, that being
the case, I'll have to knuckle down and do my share of the
work, Sundays included.'

Jack rose from the bench, shaking his head. 'You stick
to your guns, Rose. Dixon won't let you go, you're too
popular with the locals, and if you give in on working
Sundays, he'll start to take advantage of your good nature.'
Leaning across the wooden table, he winked slyly. 'He
might even ask you to start dressing like the other two,
and I can't see you in plunging necklines with your face
painted. Mind you, that would get the men flocking into
the Red Lion, wouldn't it? I'd pay a few bob to see that
myself.'

Chortling loudly he strode off into the pub, which was
fortunate because the look on Rose's face would surely have
aroused his suspicion.

A smile tugged at the corners of her mouth as she watched
him disappear into the pub. Dear Jack. What would she do
without him? The very idea gave her a jolt and sent her
stomach into a wave of nervous fluttering, while a voice in
her head admonished her, 'You carry on being so blooming
touchy every time he mentions Aunt Mary and you'll soon
find out. Then you won't have to worry about turning down
a wedding proposal – which you don't know for sure he's
thinking of anyway. He'll get fed up with having his head
bitten off for no good reason, and that's the last you'll see
of him. So be warned!'

The sun had become hotter and Rose reached for her
bonnet. She was about to tie the ribbons under her chin
when a shabbily dressed man brushed past her. 'Oops,
sorry, darlin', 'ad one too many. Me apologies to yer.'
Rose glared up at him. The man stank of beer. But as he
staggered away, something nagged at her. She had seen the
man recently, he had been . . . Oh, my Lord!

It was the man in the market, the pickpocket Jack had
gone after. Bending down she grabbed her basket and

pulled aside the length of material she had purchased earlier. She searched frantically for her purse. It was nowhere
to be seen. She looked around wildly and saw the culprit
running back into the market. Her heart sank: it would be
virtually impossible to catch him in that crowd – but she
was going to have a bloody good try.

'Rose! Rose! Where're you going?' Jack had reappeared
and his police training had come instantly to the fore.
'What's happened, love?' He slammed the drinks down
on the table, spilling a mixture of lemonade and beer. Rose
spun round, her face etched with worry. 'That man, the one
you stopped earlier! He's taken my purse, Jack! It's all the
money I have to get me through the week! I'm going after
him, he can't have—'

'Oh, no, you don't,' Jack said, grabbing her and depositing
her back on the bench. 'I'll take care of it. You stay here
until I come back. Promise me, Rose.' He shook her urgently
before he set off at a run. Stunned by what had happened,
Rose slumped miserably against the hard edge of the table,
unaware of the inquisitive glances of the other customers,
and waited anxiously for his return.

CHAPTER FIVE

Nobby Summers strolled through the crowd at his ease. He was a dab hand at this game: he'd already lifted three wallets and two purses this morning. It would take more than a bleeding copper to put him off his trade. Grinning gleefully he ducked down a side alley, took a furtive look around to make sure he wasn't being watched then pulled the wallets from his inside pocket and began to check the contents. His grin broadened at the sight of the folded banknotes. Stuffing the wad into his pocket, he was about to look in the purses when a shadow fell over him. Straight away he was on his guard, ready to defend his pickings, his aggressive stance faltering as four men loomed into view.

'Well, well, well. You've had a busy day, by the looks of it, Nobby. I'll have to be careful you don't run me out of business.' Frankie Buchannon looked down at the grubby pickpocket with good-natured amusement. He'd had a profitable morning and was feeling amiable. Three new shops had opened on his patch, which meant more money for him. Two of the owners had agreed to pay him immediately; the third, however, a burly Irishman, had refused – until he had been shown the error of his ways. It was so easy it was boring. All Frankie had to do was express concern over the likelihood of their premises being robbed or smashed up in such a crime-ridden area, or if that tack failed, he reminded them of the shops that had mysteriously burned down overnight, destroying the owners' livelihood and often their homes. They paid up quickly enough. He had collected nearly fifty pounds already this morning: he preferred to make his rounds at the weekend, to give his clients time to accumulate their takings – and his cut of the profits. In the past a few men had been foolish enough to go to the police, which they had lived to regret.

It was true that Frankie had been brought to book on many occasions, but the police had never been able to make a serious charge stick. Witnesses suddenly disappeared or became reluctant to give evidence, which left the frustrated officers having to charge the elusive racketeer with lesser crimes that carried only short sentences. And while Frankie was incarcerated, his men made sure that those law-abiding citizens who had helped put their governor behind bars were made to suffer the consequences. But Frankie's last sojourn in the Scrubs had been different. The man he had attacked had been of sterner mettle, had refused to be intimidated by threats, determined to see his assailant behind bars.

When the judge had passed sentence, Frank had remained impassive, but beneath his calm façade he had been thoroughly shaken. The most he had been expecting was a couple of months – after all, he hadn't seriously injured the man, just given him a few slaps to show he meant business. But the judge had taken the opportunity to get the well-known racketeer off the streets for as long as he could.

Two months later, the plaintiff had unexpectedly confessed that he had lied about Frankie's involvement in the beating he had suffered. His retraction was prompted by the sudden disappearance of his only daughter while playing in the park. The six-year-old child had been found some hours later, distraught but unharmed, clasping a snippet from the local newspaper regarding Frankie Buchannon's arrest and subsequent imprisonment. The message hadn't been lost on the frantic father.

But the powers-that-be weren't going to let their quarry get off that easily: the new evidence was kept from the newspapers, and months of legal wrangling followed, during which Frankie had been forced to dig deep into his pocket to effect his release. And that after paying a fortune to a supposedly first-class defence lawyer who had been less than useless.

Well, he was out now, and he had no intention of ever going back inside. The days of ducking and diving one step ahead of the law were finished. From now on, things were going to be different. He, Frankie Buchannon, was about to become a legitimate businessman – at least, on the outside. To this end he had acquired a factory sweatshop in Stoke Newington, its previous owner having lost his lucrative business to Frankie in a rigged game of cards, just a week after his release, Now he had his eye on a similar venture in Dalston. Oh, yes, he was coming up in the world. Soon, in the eyes of the law he would be above board . . . with the help of an enterprising book-keeper he had just hired, and he would keep his other activities flourishing. He owed it to his men, who knew no other way to earn a living; without their loyalty and endeavours to keep his nefarious dealings thriving in his absence, he would have had nothing to come out to.

So Frankie beamed benevolently on the wretched creature before him. He, too, had started out in much the same way but Frankie Buchannon hadn't been content to remain a petty thief. He had always dreamed of becoming Someone, a man to whom others looked up, a man of importance away from the criminal element. Men like Nobby Summers had no such ambitions, and even if he had this man, like many others of his ilk, lacked the intelligence and guile to achieve his goals.

Frankie gave the other man a condescending slap on the back. 'Be lucky, Nobby,' he said.

Slumping back with relief, the shabby man brightened. Anxious to stay on good terms with the legendary Frankie Buchannon, he fumbled in his pocket, took out the leather purse he had recently stolen and held it up to his idol. ''Ere yer are, Mr Buchannon, a little present fer one of yer ladyfriends.'

Frankie raised a conspiratorial eyebrow at his men. 'Thanks, Nobby, but I think I can afford to buy me own presents, thanks all the . . .' Frankie stiffened and the hairs on the back of his neck stood on end as he looked down at the expensive leather purse. He recognised it at once. He'd had it made especially for Rose's eighteenth birthday. Now he ripped it from the man's hand and stepped closer to him. Nobby cringed in terror at the change in the man standing menacingly over him. 'Where did you get this from? Answer me, you miserable little bastard! C'mon, speak up! Where d'yer get it?'

'It was just some young tart, Mr Buchannon. Outside the pub down the end of the market, I didn't mean—'

Frankie gripped him by the throat and hissed, 'The young *tart* is a good friend of mine, a very good friend of mine, you stinking little thief, an' you know what happens to people who hurt me friends, don't yer?'

'Please, Mr Buchannon, sir, I didn't know. 'Ere, I'll take it back to 'er. Just let me . . .'

Frankie threw the man against the wall and stepped back, his eyes cold. Snapping his fingers, he said quietly, to the men waiting behind him, 'Break his hands.'

Nobby's eyes bulged in fear. 'No, no, Mr Buchannon, please. Give me another chance. Oh, p-please, Mr Buchannon – No, no – *noooo!*'

The three men moved in silently on their prey. One held him down, forcing his own filthy scarf into his gaping mouth to stifle his screams. Then there was a sickening sound of breaking bones, followed by the man's muffled, agonised sobs.

Frankie stood back in the shadows, his face impassive. He gained no pleasure from such tasks, but men like Nobby Summers had to be taught a lesson. He would tell others of his ordeal, and the reason behind it. It would serve as a warning to others, and in time the entire East End would know that Rose Kennedy was under his protection. It would also remind people that this was Frankie Buchannon's manor, and anyone caught stepping out of line would be dealt with severely.

Frankie turned on his heel and walked quickly away. Like trained dogs, the three men hurried after him.

'I'm sorry, Rose, I couldn't find him. But don't worry, I

know where he hangs about and I'll get your purse back for you. You have my word.' Jack, crestfallen at having failed to catch the thief, looked apologetically at Rose. 'Look, let me get you a drink, it'll help calm you down.'

'I don't need calming down, thank you. What I need is to get my purse back.' Rose struggled to hold back the tears. The rent man was due tomorrow and the larder at home was practically empty. She normally did the shopping on a Monday before going to work. It didn't matter so much as far as she was concerned; although meals weren't included in her wages Mr Dixon didn't mind his staff having the odd sandwich now and then. And there were often sausage rolls and meat pasties left over at the end of the day. Rose had no fear of going hungry until her next pay day. But there was still the rent to find and food for her aunt – and her aunt Mary did like her food.

Oh, dear Lord, what was she going to do?

Jack was furious with himself for having failed to catch Nobby. Oh, he'd find the miserable wretch, but whether he would be able to recover Rose's property was another matter.

'It's all right, Jack, it isn't your fault. It's just one of those things. I'll manage somehow.' Rose, her face pale, smiled up at him weakly. Her plight tugged at Jack's heartstrings. Should he offer to loan her some money? He knew how fiercely proud she was, yet surely in these circumstances she wouldn't refuse.

He was about to make the offer when he saw the four men strolling towards them. 'Hello, Princess.' Frankie moved towards Rose, his hands enveloping hers, a genuine warm smile on his lips.

Rose's heart lightened at the sight of him. She beamed up into his handsome face, and as his strong arm went protectively around her shoulders, she felt her anxiety lift. Since she was a child, she had always felt this way whenever Frank was around; warm, safe and comforted. It was as if there was nothing and nobody in the world who could harm her. There was nothing so terrible that he couldn't make it better; she trusted him implicitly and it showed in her eyes and the way her body relaxed against his. He was the father she had never known, the brother she had been denied.

As Jack watched them together, he felt a terrible desolation steal over him. With it came a rush of anger. His face set in mulish lines, he stepped forward, only to find his way barred by the powerful trio accompanying Frank. With an oath he shouldered the men aside. 'Don't you ever go anywhere without your bodyguards, Buchannon? Are you too scared to go out by yourself?'

Frankie grinned and hugged Rose closer to his side. He and Jack Adams had crossed paths frequently in the past, and Frankie had been mildly amused when Rose had first started seeing the young constable, before he had gone inside. He had hoped the friendship would have fizzled out by now. Maybe if he'd been around more at the beginning he might have been able to nip it in the bud, before it had had the chance to develop any further.

He knew he had neglected both Mary and Rose over the past few years: he had gone round regularly to make sure they were all right until Rose had started work in the City, but then his visits had become infrequent; and for that he felt guilty. Mary Miller had been like a mother to him and he would never forget her kindness. But even the closest of families drift apart, and he knew Mary harboured no ill-feeling against him for his continued absences. Still, he should have been around more often. If he had kept a closer eye on the two women, Rose would never have landed up in the pub or with Adams. But things were going to be different from now on. Oh, yes, very different. He glanced at the glowering policeman. There was no way his Rose was going to end her days tied to a copper – not if he had anything to do with it.

'Oh, I'm not scared, Constable. I just like a bit of company. Though, come to think of it, you might be better off with one of me boys following you about, 'cos you don't seem to manage too well on your own, now, do you, Constable?'

A deep flush suffused Jack's face, but before he could reply, Frankie turned to Rose, took the soft leather purse from his pocket and said softly, 'You ought ter be more careful, Princess. In future, don't leave your purse lying around. There's a lot of thieves about.'

'And you'd know all about that, wouldn't you, Buchannon?' Jack interrupted.

Heedless of the tension between the two men, Rose stared at the purse she thought she'd never see again and cried in delight, 'Oh, Frankie! Where did you find it?' She snatched the precious object from him, and hurriedly checked to see if the contents were still intact. Then she frowned. 'I didn't have this much, Frank. Why there's . . .' she was sorting deftly through the coins, her forehead creasing in bewilderment '. . . goodness, there's nearly ten pounds here. I only had a few sovereigns and some small change, there must be . . .'

Frankie's hand closed over her fingers. 'Don't worry about it, Princess. The bloke I got it from won't be needing it. Look on it as . . . *compensation* for the shock he gave you.'

Rose's eyes widened in alarm. 'Frank . . . you didn't . . .'

Jack caught Frankie's arm and growled, 'What have you done to Nobby, you vicious bastard? If any harm's come to him I'll—'

Indolently arching one eyebrow, Frankie looked first at the hand grasping his arm and then at the angry face. 'Know him by name, d'yer, Adams? He must be a friend of yours, then – but you needn't worry, I didn't lay a finger on him. You know, you should be more careful with the company you keep, Constable. It's lucky for Rose I was in the neighbourhood, otherwise she wouldn't have seen her purse again. Mind you, though, I'd've thought she'd be safe with a copper by her side. Still . . . just goes to show, don't it?'

Goaded beyond endurance Jack clenched his fists, sorely tempted to punch the self-satisfied grin off the hated face. It was with great restraint that he stifled the urge. That was exactly what Buchannon wanted him to do, and he wasn't stupid enough to risk losing his job through his own personal vendetta.

Rose had become uneasy at the chilly atmosphere between the two men and stepped between them. 'That's enough, the pair of you.' Linking her arm through Jack's, she said,

'Thanks for finding my purse, Frank. I'll sort out what I had, and give the rest in to the police station. I'm sure I wasn't the only victim of that man this morning, and I wouldn't like anyone else to go through what I have.'

The surprised look that passed across Frankie's face drew a loud chuckle from Jack, but before he could say anything else Rose dragged him out of the path of his antagonist. She wasn't going to have them squabbling in the street like a pair of five-year-olds. Shooting Jack a warning glance to behave himself, she said to Frankie, 'Try to pop round to see Aunt Mary, Frank. She doesn't know you're out yet, I thought I'd surprise her later. It'd be grand if you suddenly appeared at the door.' If he did just that she might avoid Mary's anger at not being told earlier. Rose had meant to break the news to her aunt that morning, but what with the rush to get ready when Jack turned up on the doorstep at the crack of dawn . . . she hated herself for wanting an easy way out of her problem, but nevertheless she asked hopefully, 'Could you come round in the morning, Frank? If you make it before ten, I'll be at home. I don't start work until eleven tomorrow.'

'I'll see what I can do, but I ain't promising, all right?'

Rose breathed a sigh of relief. 'Thanks, Frank . . . Oh, and thanks for the purse. I'll see you tomorrow . . . maybe.'

Still clutching the furious Jack's arm, Rose strolled away happily. Frank wouldn't let her down, she was sure. And once he turned up, her aunt would be so pleased to see him she'd forget her niece's errant forgetfulness – with a bit of luck.

Frankie watched them go, his face closed.

CHAPTER SIX

'I told you it was a mistake, didn't I, Rose? All along I said it was a mistake. Just those bleeding coppers out to make a name for themselves, and not worrying about sending an innocent man to prison.' Mary was in her element, bustling around the large room that served as parlour and kitchen as fast as her swollen legs would allow, heedless of the pain she would endure later for this disregard of her infirmity. It would be a small price to pay for such a wonderful evening.

Frankie was out of the nick, and his first port of call had been her house. Well, maybe not his first, but what difference did that make? He'd come round, hadn't he? And him a busy man like he was. No wonder Rose had been a bit off last night: the poor girl must have been bursting to tell her about Frankie's release but had decided to surprise her with a visit from the man himself.

And what a surprise it had been when Frank had poked his head around the parlour door, his mischievous grin lighting up the room. And not just the room either. Seeing him standing in the doorway, as large as life, his handsome face beaming down at her in that familiar, loving way, she had been filled with such a surge of emotion that she had felt fit to burst. Thank goodness she'd had a good tidy-up this morning while Rose was out down Petticoat Lane. The mantelpiece, dotted with ornaments on either side of the old bronze clock, was shining, as was the glass-fronted cabinet by the wall. The double bed in the corner by the window was covered with a new patchwork quilt she'd made, adding a splash of gaiety to the room. The table was covered in her best white embroidered cloth, and the woven rugs that lay atop the scrubbed, faded oilcloth had been given a good beating that morning. She had even ironed her best antimacassars to cover the backs of the battered armchairs. It was as if she'd had a sixth sense about the impending visit. And it wasn't just a five-minute visit either. Oh, no!

Her Frankie was here for the entire evening. He had brought a case of her favourite stout, and a bottle of port, saying that they would drink a toast to his freedom later. So that must mean he intended to stay. Normally he would just pop his head round the door saying, 'Can't stop, Mary. Just dropped in to see how you are,' before disappearing as quickly as he'd come. Even on those other occasions when he'd just got out of the nick, he normally only had time for a flying visit. But not tonight. He had taken off his jacket, loosened the top button of his white shirt, and was sprawled easily in one of the comfortable armchairs by the open grate. Oh, it was so good to have him here like this. It was just like old times. Her and Frankie and Rose, all together in the parlour, shutting out the rest of the world from their cosy little family . . . Well! Not exactly like old times, she amended grimly, her euphoria temporarily dampened by the presence of Jack Adams, sitting upright on a straight-backed chair at the table, his face set in tight lines of silent disapproval. Well! Bugger him. This was her house, and if he didn't like the company, he could bleeding well piss off.

She couldn't understand why Rose had asked him to stay after Frankie had turned up unexpectedly. She must have known Jack's presence would put a dampener on the evening. No! Sod it! Jack Adams wasn't going to spoil her night. Mary was suddenly anxious to prove to Frankie that the policeman's presence hadn't been her idea. She cast an aggrieved look in Jack's direction. 'Don't let us keep you, Jack. We know you've gotta get up early for work.'

Jack shifted on the chair, then pulled it tighter under the

table, resting his arms on the surface in the attitude of one settled in for the duration. 'Oh, don't worry about me, Mary,' he said easily. 'My shift doesn't start until eleven tomorrow so I'm in no rush to get home, but thanks for being so considerate.' He smiled broadly at her, determined not to let her rile him. Though it wasn't easy. Specially that crack about 'bleeding coppers sending an innocent man to prison'. Good God! Was she really so blind to Buchannon's faults? And the answer came back swiftly. No. Mary Miller wasn't a stupid woman. She was only doing what countless others had done before her: closing her eyes to the dark side of a loved one – as did her niece.

For a brief moment, Jack almost envied Frankie. To be able to engender such devotion and loyalty in two strong, forthright women like Mary and Rose surely said something about the man. Then his mind shifted to the countless beaten men and distraught women Buchannon had left in his wake, and his heart hardened once more.

Rose, coming in from the scullery with a tray of tea, stopped in the doorway, her teeth nipping at her bottom lip in dismay at the scene before her – and the undeniably heavy atmosphere. Oh dear! She would have to get Jack away from here before things got any worse.

Like her aunt, she had been delighted to see Frankie turn up at the door, though for slightly different reasons. She had been on the verge of telling Mary that he was out of prison when he had arrived, saving her a tongue-lashing from her aunt.

It was unfortunate that Jack had been there when Frank arrived. Another five minutes and he would have left. But the moment Frank had stepped into the house, Jack had dug himself in, refusing to acknowledge that his presence was unwelcome, in a bloody-minded effort to antagonise his adversary.

Jack glanced up at Rose, saw her annoyance and lowered his eyes. That he was upsetting Rose and Mary was painfully evident, and for that he was genuinely sorry, but he had no intention of leaving. If he had to stay here all night, then so be it. He wasn't going to leave until Buchannon did. The policeman in him upbraided him for his childish behaviour, while another part of him, the part that was achingly vulnerable where his pride and Rose were concerned, resolved not to be browbeaten.

Seeing the stubborn set of Jack's chin, Rose blew out her cheeks in exasperation. He was acting like a spoilt child, and Frank was no better, deliberately shutting Jack out of any conversation or making comments about the police, calculated to provoke him into heated retaliation, which he had resisted – so far!

Setting the tray down on the table with a loud thump, Rose looked at Jack crossly. He remained steadfast, merely smiling gently and saying, 'Thanks, love. I could do with a nice cuppa. I've never been over-fond of beer – it muddles the mind and I can't afford that, not in my line of work.'

Rose bit back a retort that this was the first she'd heard of Jack not liking beer, and poured out a cup for herself. She sat down on the arm of Mary's chair, leaving Jack to pour his own. The slight wasn't lost on either man, and Frankie raised his glass in Jack's direction. 'Quite right, Constable. We can't have members of the police force running round drunk. Gawd knows, they make enough mistakes when they're sober. Cheers!'

'Frank!' Rose said warningly. Then, at Frankie's infectious grin and his broad wink, she found herself laughing, which only served to fuel Jack's smouldering anger.

Rose's defection, as he saw it, was the last straw. He pushed back his chair, clenched his fists, and ground out slowly, 'We've managed to put you away enough times, Buchannon, and you'll go down again . . .'

Mary had just taken a large gulp of stout so was temporarily silenced, but then, spluttering and coughing, she shouted, ''Ere, don't you start slinging round insults in my house, Jack Adams. Frankie here is family, you ain't. So if you don't like the company, then piss off out of it.'

'Aunt Mary!' Rose cried, aghast, but Mary was unrepentant.

'Don't you Aunt Mary me, love. I ain't one for mincing

me words, never have been. If your friend wants to come here, then he'll treat me visitors with respect. If he don't, then he ain't welcome.'

Jack had risen to his feet, his face burning with rage and humiliation. As much as he'd told himself not to get riled, there was only so much flesh and blood could stand. Yet, curiously, he didn't hold any animosity towards Mary. He understood the reason for her hostility, and that reason was sitting just a few feet away. Studiously ignoring the amused glance of the man opposite the irate woman, Jack said quietly, 'I'm sorry if I've offended you, Mary. I'd never hurt you on purpose, but I ain't one for mincing words either. I only give respect where it's deserved, and that doesn't include thugs and bully boys.'

Outraged, Mary struggled to get out of the chair, her face alight with rage. 'Clear off! Go on! Get outta my house, you ungrateful sod you!'

Frankie leaned forward, motioning Mary back into her chair. ''Ere, come on, old girl, don't get yourself all upset on my account, it ain't worth it.'

Jack stood, pale-faced, watching the scene, his hands clasped tightly behind his back for fear that he would lash out at the mocking figure of Frank Buchannon. The other man was obviously enjoying the situation.

Then Frankie turned his dark, brooding eyes on Jack, who saw the malice in that glance, and knew that his adversary was willing him to start a fight. Jack drew himself upright. Well, Buchannon was out of luck this time. If there was any more upset in this house, it wasn't going to be laid at Jack Adams's door.

Turning on his heel, he nodded to Mary, then said to the white-faced Rose, 'Are you going to see me out, love? Or am I in disgrace with you too?'

Rose shook her head wordlessly and walked slowly from the room. After a moment's hesitation Jack followed her.

'Mind how you go, Officer.' Frankie's voice floated after him. 'If you run into any trouble on your way home, just mention me name and you'll be all right.'

Rose was waiting by the open door, her face downcast by the events of the evening. Apart from having her purse stolen it had been such a lovely day – and it could have been a wonderful evening. She hadn't seen her aunt so happy in a long while, and now it had all been spoilt. She didn't know whether to laugh, cry or shout. When the hand came to rest on her shoulder she pushed it away angrily. 'Don't say a word, Jack, just don't say a word. You've said quite enough already.'

'Now, just a minute, Rose,' Jack interjected, his anger matching her own. 'In case you hadn't noticed, I wasn't the only one chucking insults around.'

'No, I know that. But if you'd gone home when you intended to, there wouldn't have been any call for any unpleasantness.'

'Oh, so I should have scuttled off like a cornered rat the moment Mr God Almighty came in, should I? Well, thank you, Rose. I was under the impression you liked my company. I even thought we had an understanding between us, but it looks like I was wrong, don't it?' Jack, his face growing redder by the second, pushed past her and out of the open door.

'Jack! Don't be so childish! All I meant was that . . . Well, you must have known there'd be trouble if you stayed. I don't mind so much for myself, but Aunt Mary was so pleased to see Frank. She was really looking forward to a good night and . . .'

'And I spoilt it.' Jack finished her sentence, staring over her shoulder down the dimly lit hall. Loud laughter could be heard now coming from the parlour. His face tightened and he stepped into the street, his eyes darting down the narrow road to where two shadowy figures were leaning up against the wall of the end house. Buchannon's flunkeys. He might have known they'd be hanging about somewhere, eager to protect their master.

Rose made to close the door, then stopped. 'All right,' she flung at him. 'Yes! If you want the truth, you did. I don't know what you hoped to gain by stopping on where you clearly weren't wanted, but all you did was upset my aunt. And, like I've told you before, Jack, my aunt Mary comes first with me, and always will.'

'And not just your aunt, eh, Rose? We mustn't upset

dear Frankie either, must we? Oh, dear me, no. Not Mr Wonderful who—'

'Ooh, go to hell, Jack!' Rose gave the door a mighty shove and it slammed shut with a bang.

She hadn't gone more than a few feet when a furious hammering started on the door. She went back and yanked it open, glaring at the figure on the doorstep, then gasped in shock as he stormed past her and into the parlour. Hurrying after him, she stopped in the doorway, her mouth hanging open as she listened to his calm voice, directed at the two figures sitting by the open fireplace.

'You've got your way this time, Buchannon. I'm going. But not because you've driven me away – it would take a bigger man than you to do that – but because I don't want to cause any more upset for Mary or Rose. But I'll tell you this, Buchannon, and I'm only going to say it once, so you'd better listen hard.' Jack paused, his heart thumping wildly in his chest at the import of what he was about to say. Then, keeping his eyes firmly on the other man, he said, slowly and deliberately, 'I love Rose, and if she'll have me, I'd marry her tomorrow – and even if she doesn't feel the same way I'm still gonna be around, until Rose tells me differently. So you'd better get used to the idea. Both of you.' His eyes flashed to Mary. ''Cos I ain't going nowhere.'

This time Rose didn't follow him out, and when the door banged noisily, she dropped shakily on to one of the two hard-backed chairs by the table, clasping her trembling hands in her lap.

Mary was the first to break the silence. She craned her neck towards her niece and demanded fiercely, 'What's all this malarkey about getting married? You ain't mentioned it before, or don't you confide in your auntie any more? If there was any wedding plans in the offing, I'd've thought I'd be the first to know, instead of hearing it from that snotty-nosed little bleeder.'

'Auntie!' Rose roused herself from the initial shock of hearing Jack's proposal. She'd been expecting it, yes, but not like this, not in front of others – and definitely not in anger. Raising her head she looked hard at Mary, and when

she spoke, there was a steeliness in her voice that neither
Mary or Frank had heard before. 'Don't speak about Jack
like that, Auntie. I thought you liked him. You've never
said anything before. But you were horrible tonight, nasty,
and there was no need, no need at all. Jack didn't deserve to
be treated like that. No one does.' That she should jump to
Jack's defence so readily was evidence of her feelings, and
as Frank watched the lovely face set in defiance against her
aunt, he experienced first an alarming sensation in the pit
of his stomach, then surprise at the intensity of his reaction
to her outburst. Afraid that his feelings were written on his
face, he glanced up warily at the women, but they seemed
to have forgotten his presence as they faced each other in
their first serious altercation.

Twisting her large body further round in the chair, Mary
frowned at her niece. 'No need! No need? Well, let me tell
you, girl, there was a bleeding need. If he hadn't shouted his
big mouth off, then *I* wouldn't have had the *need* to tell him
what I thought of him. Anyways . . .' Mary took a swig of
the port Frank had poured for her and swallowed it noisily.
'I didn't say anything before 'cos I didn't think there was
anything serious going on. But Gawd blimey, girl, I didn't
spend all of me savings to educate you just so's you could
marry a bleeding copper, especially one that insults me in
me own home. Oh, no, me girl. You can do a lot better
than the likes of Jack Adams, so the sooner you tell him
he's wasting his time the better. And if *you* ain't got the
guts to tell him, then I will.'

For the first time in her life, Rose disliked her aunt. Then
her gaze shifted to the watching Frank. She realised that it
wasn't Aunt Mary's fault she was acting like this: the whole
charade was being acted out for Frank's benefit. It seemed
that the two of them were living in a private little world
of their own where outsiders weren't welcomed. Suddenly
she had no desire to join them in it.

An image of Jack's hurt face swam before her eyes, and
a lump came into her throat. Poor Jack. She shifted on the
chair, conscious of the four eyes staring at her, willing her
to join them and close ranks against the outside world . . .
a world where Jack lived. Suddenly she couldn't do it. As

much as she loved these two people, she still had a life of
her own to live, and if she wanted to prove it, she must
make a stand now. Before she had a chance to change her
mind, she rose to her feet and announced, 'I'm sorry, Aunt
Mary, but if Jack isn't welcome in this house any more, then
I'll have to go to his.'

Mary looked balefully at her determined niece, and in
that brief, tense moment, she saw not Rose but her sister
Ruth, and knew that if she wasn't careful, history might
repeat itself. But the stubbornness that had been a trait
since childhood reared its head once more. Mary drew her
chin into her neck and waved her arms shouting, wildly,
'If that's what you want, then I ain't stopping you, girl. You
do what you want, you always do. But if you're thinking
of getting married, then you'll have a bloody long wait
'cos you're under age. You need my permission before
you marry anyone, so don't hold your breath.' Mary's
large breasts were heaving in agitation while the stubby
fingers holding the glass of port shook violently, spilling
the blood-red wine on to the front of her blouse. 'But I'll
tell you this for nothing. If you do marry that copper, don't
expect me to be sitting in church giving me blessing 'cos I
won't be there. I never thought you could be so sneaky, me
own flesh and blood. Planning to get wed, with not so much
as a by-your-leave to the very person what brought you up
. . . Still, you're just like your mother, only I never noticed
it till now.'

'That's not fair, Aunt Mary,' Rose said hotly. 'I didn't
make any plans behind your back. It was as much a surprise
to me as it was to you when Jack started talking about
getting married and—'

'So, you're not gonna marry him, then! Well, that's all
right.' Mary, mollified, beamed magnanimously. She hauled
herself round in the chair, nodded towards the silent figure
in the armchair opposite, and crowed, 'Well, this has been
a night and a half, eh, Frankie? Gawd blimey, I thought
for a while we was gonna have a copper in the family.'
With that she threw back her head and let out a roar of
laughter. 'That'd be a turn-up for the books, wouldn't it,
lad?' Then she leaned forward and tapped Frankie's knee

soundly. 'Mind you, if there had been a wedding, you'd most likely have known all of his friends. That would've been a knees-up to remember, eh, Frankie?'

Frankie smiled. A smile that didn't reach his eyes. And those same forbidding eyes looked at Rose, who was holding on to the edge of the table, her face pale. He said quietly, 'Yeah, it certainly would, Mary. But that's not gonna happen – is it, Princess?'

Rose met his gaze, the ominously silent command, and lifted her head defiantly. 'I don't know, Frankie, I'll have to give it some thought. Like I said, Jack's proposal took me by surprise. But you never know, there just might be that knees-up in the future.' Rose walked swiftly across the room to Mary, bent down, pecked the elderly woman's cheek and said, over-brightly, 'I'm going out, Aunt Mary. I won't be long but don't wait up if I'm a bit late. I'll be back as soon as I can.'

'What? It's gone ten. Where're you going at this time of night?' Mary started to rise from her chair, only to be pushed gently down by a restraining hand.

When the front door closed softly behind her niece, Mary was astonished to discover that her eyes were filled with hot tears.

'Leave her, Mary. Let her go, she'll be back,' Frankie said, reassuringly. 'You know she doesn't like being told what to do. Now, who d'yer *really* suppose she takes after?' He grinned into the stricken face.

'But, Frankie,' Mary wailed, 'what if she's gone after him? I said some rotten things about the lad but he's decent enough. He's just not good enough for my Rose. Ooh, Frankie—' She grabbed frenziedly at his hands. 'What if she goes and marries him just to spite us? Oh, it'd break me heart, Frankie, it would, it'd break me heart.'

'Don't worry, old girl. Our Rosie wouldn't do anything to hurt you. She thinks the world of you. I tell you, she's just showing us she can't be ordered about. She'll be back soon. And I promise you she ain't gonna marry that copper. You have me word on that.'

Mary gazed tearfully into the compelling brown eyes. What she saw there sent a chill up her spine. 'Frankie!

You ain't gonna hurt the lad, are you? I mean, just 'cos I don't want him to carry on seeing Rose, it don't mean I'd want any harm to come to him.'

Frankie chuckled. 'Who me? Hurt someone! Now, Mary, you know me better than that. I wouldn't hurt a fly, me. And anyhow she can't do anything without your say-so. You're still her legal guardian, and until she comes of age she's gonna have to do what you tell her. Besides, there's more than one way of skinning a cat. Now, then, you sit there, drink your port, an' stop worrying. I've said I'll fix things, and I always keep me word, don't I, Mary?'

Mary didn't hear him. A sudden worrying thought had entered her mind. She had never formally applied to be named as Rose's legal guardian. She had just brought her home and brought her up. Rose had been registered at school under her father's surname, and when anyone had queried Mary's relationship to the child, Mary had simply told the truth: that Rose was her dead sister's child and that she was looking after her niece as the father couldn't be found and she had no other living relative.

A chill closed around Mary's heart. She had no legal hold over Rose. But, then, she had never imagined she would need one.

CHAPTER SEVEN

Hurrying through the dimly lit streets, Rose could just see the outline of Jack's shadowy figure up ahead.

Behind her she heard stealthy footsteps, but her own didn't falter. She knew whose they were: one of Frankie's men was trailing her, and the thought gave her comfort. The streets around this area weren't the safest place to be at night, and even though Jack was in earshot, if anybody was lurking in a nearby alley, a would-be assailant could easily jump out and overpower her before she could cry out for help.

If Rose was concerned about being accosted, Jack on the other hand was praying for such an occurrence. He couldn't remember ever being as furious as he was at this moment, and nothing would have pleased him more than if some thieving bastard tried to tackle him. The savagery of his thoughts shook Jack to the core. Blast Buchannon! The man brought out the very worst in him! Then, *Get a hold of yourself, man,* he admonished himself. *Don't let Buchannon drag you down to his level.*

Yet still Jack's anger raged. And it was fortunate, indeed, that any opportunist didn't cross his path that night.

He had barely let himself into the two-roomed flat he rented in a large house opposite the Berger's paint factory in Morning Lane, when a soft knock sounded on the front door. 'Who the bloody hell's that at this time of night?' he cursed, beneath his breath. The two other occupants of the

house, an elderly couple on the second floor, often came
to him with their problems and usually he was only too
pleased to help, but tonight he wanted to be left alone
with his thoughts. Even so, he composed his features into
a pleasant smile, which turned to genuine delight when he
saw who his late-night visitor was.

'Rose!'

Now that she was here, Rose was undecided what to do
or say next. It hadn't been easy for her to walk out on Aunt
Mary and Frank, but even if Jack had been just a casual
friend she would have done the same. The couple she had
left behind her couldn't be allowed to think they had the
right to dictate whom she saw and when.

And Jack wasn't merely a casual friend. The outrage and
fierce protectiveness that had gripped her when Mary and
Frank humiliated and jeered at Jack were a final indication
of Rose's true feelings.

'Are you coming in, love? Or have you just come to tell
me it's over between us?' The deep voice was laden with
uncertainty.

When Rose looked up into those sombre grey eyes, filled
with love and a silent plea for reassurance, she knew where
her future lay. It wasn't fair to keep Jack hanging on any
longer – but what was she going to do about her aunt?
Then his hand came out tentatively and touched her arm.
All the love and tenderness she had repressed for so long
finally spilled out and, with a muffled cry, she buried her
head against his broad chest.

Tenderly Jack led Rose towards a brown and yellow-
patterned settee, gently lowered her on to the sagging
cushions and dropped to his knees in front of her.

'Oh, Jack, I'm so sorry. I mean about how Aunt Mary
spoke to you. It was only because Frankie was there. She
would never have been so rude otherwise.'

'I know, I know, love, and I do understand. She was only
speaking out of loyalty to Frank, and if I hadn't been so bull-
headed about staying, none of this would've happened.'

'I was just as bad. I should have stood up for you straight
away, but I was so worried about upsetting Aunt Mary, I
forgot about your feelings.'

Gripping her hands, Jack smiled up into her despondent face. 'It doesn't matter. All that counts is that you came after me, and I can't tell you how much that means to me, darling.'

They gazed at each other lovingly for a long moment, neither wanting to break the magic. Although Rose had been to Jack's home before, it had always been in the daytime, and only ever for a short time. But this was different – oh, so very different. In the cosy room bathed in soft light from the wall lamp, it seemed as if they were the only two people in the world. It was a heady new experience for Rose, and when a delicious tingle of delight raced up her spine she shivered in glorious anticipation of the new, powerful emotions sweeping through her body. Giving vent to a nervous laugh she cast her eyes down and stuttered, 'Goodness, Jack. This settee's blooming awful. It could give you a bilious attack just by looking at it. I thought you were going to get a new one . . . I . . .' She felt herself sinking into the old, cushioned seat as Jack sat down beside her. He gently lifted her chin to study her in awe, as if unable to believe his luck at having her here beside him. The intensity of his naked adoration humbled Rose, while at the same time it gave her new confidence.

Lifting a hand to his curly, brown hair, she whispered shyly, 'Did you mean what you said about marrying me, Jack? Or was that just a ploy to antagonise Frank?'

Jack's head flew back, sudden hope springing to his eyes. 'Of course I meant it. I wouldn't have said it otherwise, but I didn't think you . . .'

Rose laid her fingers across his lips. 'I didn't think so either, Jack, not until tonight. I've been holding back because of Aunt Mary – Because I can't see us all living together happily, especially not after tonight, and I can't leave her on her own, she needs me. But . . . but I need *you*, Jack. I love you and I want to be with you, only . . . Oh, Jack . . . Jack, what are we going to do?'

Impassioned with hope, Jack gripped the small hands and lifted them to his lips. 'Rosie, darling, I never thought I'd hear you say those words, and I know it's not going to be easy. But I'll win Mary over, you see if I don't. By the time

I'm finished, she'll think – Hell! I don't know what she'll think, but somehow I'll make sure she comes round.'

Rose laughed softly. 'You're a fool, Jack Adams, but that side of you only makes me love you more.'

With a loud cry, Jack pulled her to her feet, and danced her round the small room. Unable to resist his impulsive, giddy mood, Rose giggled weakly as they waltzed past the two straight-backed chairs, round the small, oval table and past the crammed bookcase. Then Jack slipped on the mat by the fireplace, stumbled, tried to catch his balance and with a comical twitch of arms and legs crashed noisily to the floor, taking Rose down with him. They landed with a thump, both laughing uproariously. A furious banging started up from the ceiling below: Jack's elderly neighbours' good opinion of him didn't extend to having their sleep disturbed.

Smothering their laughter, Rose and Jack tried to get up, only to collapse again in a huddle. They lay still on their backs, trying to catch their breath, then Rose propped herself up on one elbow and gazed at Jack as if hypnotised by his steady grey eyes. Bending her head she lowered her lips on to his, and when his arms came around her, she joyfully gave herself up to his embrace. There was no more holding back, no more hesitation, only a fierce, passionate desire to belong to him. All other thoughts were blocked from her mind as she gave herself to the man she loved.

At the height of their passion, Jack, exerting every ounce of will-power, pulled away, fighting to stay in control. Rose wasn't the type of woman to give herself lightly, but he must make sure she knew exactly what she was doing. If he took advantage of her now . . . oh, God, how he wanted to . . . and she regretted it later, she might never forgive him. His breath coming in ragged gasps, he said huskily, 'Are you sure, Rose? You have to be absolutely certain this is what you want. I don't want you to have any regrets. If you . . .' Soft, willing arms enfolded his neck pulling him down on to the pliant body beneath him, and he hesitated no longer.

It was done. There was no going back now.

*   *   *

'So, you've come home, have you? I don't know why you bothered. It's nearly morning.'

Rose had left Jack at the door, refusing his offer to come in with her and slipped quietly into the house, hoping to go unnoticed, but Mary was waiting for her. She sat up in the brass bed, a majestic sight with her arms folded beneath heavy breasts, her plump face and neck quivering with anger. Her pale blue eyes, normally so benevolent when directed at her beloved niece, now glared at the young woman standing nervously in the doorway.

Rose gripped the door jamb, in trepidation. She knew that when her aunt had been drinking, she became a different woman: belligerent and nasty. Yet never had Rose imagined that side of her aunt's character would be turned against her. Her eyes flickered to the empty port bottle on the floor by the bed and she felt the muscles in her stomach contract painfully.

'On your own, are you? Or is your fancy man waiting outside? If he is, he'd better stay there, if he knows what's good for him.' Mary's voice was strident and harsh. She sneered drunkenly, 'Frankie's man came back to let us know where you'd gone, as if we needed telling. Huh! Then Frankie went soon after, leaving me all on me own – as bleeding usual. Oh, I'm not blaming the lad, he had things to see to. But you . . . you an' your fancy man had to go and spoil me big night, didn't you? You couldn't have put me first for once. Oh, no, not old Mary. Leave her, she'll be all right. Give her a bottle an' she'll be fine.' She paused for breath, her chins wobbling in a paroxysm of drink-fuelled outrage. And even though in Mary's mind a voice shouted, 'Go easy, woman, go easy. Leave it till the morning,' she yelled, 'Cat got your tongue, has it? Still, I don't wonder at it. I'd be bleeding ashamed an' all if I'd stayed out all night with a man. I thought you was better than that, me girl, but it seems I was wrong. Like I said, you're just like your mother. She could never keep her hands off the men either.'

Rose's feet felt like lead. She stood inside the open doorway, biting her tongue, determined not to answer back while Mary was in this mood. 'Please, Aunt Mary, don't start. It's only just gone twelve!'

'Don't start? *Don't bleeding start?*' Mary was screeching now, her heavy body thrown forward in the bed, her hands clutching at the gaily-patterned quilt as if for support. 'How you've got the gall to stand there and act all innocent after what you've done this night, I don't know. An' don't tell me you've been playing bleeding dominoes or just talking all this time. There's only one thing a man and woman get up to all night, and that should only be after they're married. Well! If you're hoping this'll make me change me mind, then you can bleeding well think again. I've said it once an' I'll say it again. That bastard copper ain't setting foot in this house again, not as long as I'm in it. Oh, oh, that's it! You turn your back on me! Why don't you? Go on, then, go, get outta me sight. Go on, get on up to bed. It was hardly worth your while getting out of the other one, was it?'

Heartsick at the sheer venom in Mary's slurred voice, Rose turned away, in muted denial of what was happening. Bewildered by the turn of events she wasn't even aware that she had begun to climb the narrow stairs until Mary threw a last scornful retort, spittle spraying from her mouth, at her retreating back. 'An', don't you come crying to me if you suddenly find yourself up the spout, 'cos I won't lift a finger to help you. And neither will Frankie. Not after you turned your back on him tonight. It'll be either your fancy man or the workhouse. An' *he* might not hang around now he's got what he wanted.'

Mary swung her swollen legs over the side of the bed and hobbled after her niece. Hanging on to the doorknob she shouted up to the slim figure, 'I mean it, girl. I ain't having any trouble brought to this house. I couldn't bear the shame. Not after all these years of harping on about me wonderful clever niece. Gawd help us! The Virgin Mary couldn't hold a candle to my Rose. Oh, no. Not my Rosie. And wouldn't the neighbours have a field day to see me pure, innocent Rose come waddling down the street with a bastard bulging in her stomach. Well, I won't have it, Rose! D'yer hear me?'

Gripping the banister until her knuckles turned white, Rose bent her head against the ferocious attack. What could she say in her own defence? Nothing! And her silence only emphasised her guilt. Burning tears stung her eyes. Then, on legs that had turned to jelly, she stumbled up the stairs to the sanctuary of her room.

CHAPTER EIGHT

When Rose came down the following morning, she wasn't sure what to expect. She had lain awake most of the night listening to her aunt's drunken ramblings and accusations and was in no mood to tolerate a squalid repetition of the previous night. She needn't have worried. Mary, her plump face peaceful in sleep, lay sprawled on the bed, dead to the world.

Looking down on the smooth features, Rose found it hard to imagine that her aunt could have uttered such vitriolic words but she had, and they had created in Rose a new hardness.

Not bothering to keep quiet, Rose set about her early-morning ablutions with relish. When she was dressed and sitting at the table with her morning cup of tea, she stared unblinkingly at the supine figure, wondering if she should wake her. Just as quickly she dismissed the notion. Last night she had taken her aunt's abuse without retaliation, telling herself that it was the port talking. Nevertheless, the harsh words had cut deep, and even though Rose knew that her aunt would never willingly hurt her, the fact remained that she had, and badly. Maybe Mary wouldn't even remember all that had transpired, but Rose would. Although time would eventually deaden the hurt, it would never erase the painful memory.

Suddenly Rose felt a great desire to get away from the house – away from her aunt – for if Mary should wake now, Rose wasn't sure that she would be able to stop herself from giving vent to the torrent of pent-up emotions battling for expression within her. And just to be on the safe side, she would stay away from her aunt for as long as possible. Instead of coming home for her lunch, she would get something to eat at the pub, and maybe by this evening Mary would have calmed down. Having decided on this course of action Rose felt marginally better, though not much. She picked up her bag, then stopped, her eyes filled with pain, to look down on the sleeping woman. She murmured, 'Oh, Aunt Mary, how could you?'

The sound of the front door banging penetrated Mary's deep slumber and, with a startled jerk, she opened her eyes, only to close them again as a knife-like pain seared though her temples. She lay quietly for several minutes, trying to get her bearings, then gingerly opened one eye and groaned. Gawd Almighty, she felt bloody awful. There was a dull thumping in her head, and her mouth felt as dry as a bone behind lips that seemed glued together. Running a thick, furred tongue over her teeth she grimaced at the foul taste in her parched mouth and croaked hopefully, 'Rose . . . Rosie, love. You there, darlin'?' When no answer was forthcoming, Mary turned her head carefully towards the mantel clock and realised, heart sinking, that her niece had already left for work. 'Bleeding hell, girl! You could've woke me with a cuppa before you left,' she grumbled irritably, as she endeavoured to lift her heavy legs over the side of the bed. When her feet encountered the cold floor she shivered and reached for her black woollen shawl. Still muttering to herself, she waddled into the scullery, each step bringing with it fresh agony.

It wasn't until she was seated in the armchair with a large cup of almost black tea, that memories of last night began to filter into her fogged mind. And with the remembrance came the first stirrings of guilt. She found herself shifting uncomfortably in the chair as further recollections pushed their way down the hazy tunnel of her mind. 'Oh, my Gawd! What've I done?' Her hands trembling violently, she lifted the cup to her trembling lips. The events of last night were fuzzy, but she could remember enough for hot beads of sweat to form on her agitated face. Again she whispered piteously, 'Gawd help me, what've I done?' The knowledge that her bitter attack on Rose had sprung from panic at her niece's open defiance in defence of Jack Adams did nothing to assuage the mounting shame that was consuming her. As an image of Rose, her lovely face stricken in pain, floated in front of Mary's blurred vision her body seemed to grow heavier, the guilt weighing her down. With an oath she threw herself forward in the chair, as if to thrust away the memories that taunted her. Then her gaze alighted on the empty bottle, half hidden under the bed.

The port. That was the cause of all the trouble. She never got nasty on beer, or even on just a few glasses of the sweet red wine. But she had consumed a whole bottle of it. Gawd help her, whatever had she been thinking of? And Frankie – he should've known better than to leave her alone with a full bottle. Now, now, none of that, she reprimanded herself sternly. Don't go blaming Frankie. He didn't force it down your throat. But she had been so bloody mad when that Jack Adams had spoilt her evening, and then Rose not coming back home till the early hours. Well, not exactly the early hours. Oh, sod it! She could think about the whys and wherefores till the cows came home, for all the good it'd do. The best thing would be to carry on as normal until she had the chance to talk to Rose. Yes, that was the thing to do, keep busy. Rose would be back in a few hours for her lunch so she'd get the place tidied up and open the back door and windows to let some air into the house. Her nose wrinkled in disgust: the place reeked of booze and Frankie's cigars. The smell was worse than a docker's armpit.

She'd cook Rosie a nice lunch, and while they were eating quietly she would apologise. And she *was* sorry – Lord, she'd never been so sorry about anything in all her life as she was about last night. So what if Rosie had stayed at that fellow's place most of the evening. It didn't mean anything, did it? Course it didn't. She shook her head emphatically, then winced as another blinding shaft of pain seared her temples. Gawd! Never as long as she lived would she ever touch another drop of port! Never. Fumbling down the side of the chair she lifted up a small tin, in which she kept her store of medicines, and swallowed three aspirins, then rested her head against the back of the armchair to give the white tablets time to take hold.

It was an hour later before she felt able to rise, and when she finally lurched to her feet, a grim smile of determination settled on her lips. She'd make things right with Rosie the minute she walked through the door. She'd get down on her knees if she had to: where Rose was concerned she had no pride.

But Rose didn't come home for lunch. The steak and kidney pie Mary had lovingly prepared grew cold as she waited for her niece to appear. And as each hour passed so Mary's repentant mood melted away, leaving in its place an angry resentment that seemed to grow and gather force with each passing minute.

So it was that by the time Rose arrived home, Mary had worked herself into a state of indignant fury. Even then, things might have been smoothed over, if Rose hadn't gone immediately to her room pleading a headache, and stayed there until the following morning. Once again she left the house while her aunt slept, giving Mary no opportunity to speak.

And human nature being what it is, by the time Rose had calmed down enough to talk to her aunt, that formidable woman, incensed by her niece's aloof attitude, had taken umbrage and had even convinced herself that maybe her behaviour that night hadn't been as bad as she'd first thought. So the words of apology were left unsaid, and both women, equally stubborn, refused to be the first to capitulate.

A long week followed, bringing with it a tension between aunt and niece that had never been present in all the years they had lived together. Now they were near to buckling under the strain.

Rose went to work each day as normal, arrived home later to a frosty reception, then departed silently to meet Jack at his flat. The little time the women spent together they passed in stilted small-talk, until Rose mumbled a quiet goodnight before escaping up the stairs to her room.

Downstairs, Mary would sit up in her bed, her eyes

bright with unshed tears as she urged herself to make peace with Rose. Her last thought every night was to try to make amends in the morning, but when morning came, and Rose brought her her tea, a hopeful, cautious look on her lovely face, something inside Mary refused to yield. She would take the tea with a bluff 'Ta', then ignore the young woman standing by her bed.

Of the cause of the conflict, there was no sign. Neither Frankie nor Jack had set foot in or near the house since the set-to, both men thinking privately that it would be better to let the women sort out the dilemma by themselves.

A week to the day of the start of the trouble, Rose, her Sunday dinner eaten without the usual appreciation of the joint of beef and Yorkshire pudding, pushed away her plate and stood up. She said coolly, 'I'm seeing Jack this afternoon. We're going to hear the band play in Vicky Park.'

Without looking up from her plate, Mary said gruffly, 'I hope it keeps fine for you.'

Rose picked up her plate, and said brusquely, 'Have it your own way, Auntie. I was only trying to be friendly.'

Left alone, Mary stared after the slim form disappearing into the scullery. This was killing her. She so wanted things to be back as they used to be. Well! You'd better buck your ideas up, woman, else the next time Rosie speaks to you, it'll be to tell you she's leaving. And it's no good you going on about her not being old enough to get married without your consent, 'cos if it comes right down to it, you ain't got any legal hold over her. Mary's head dropped. She had never imagined once during the past sixteen years that she would need the power of the law to keep her niece by her side: she had always thought that love and family loyalty would keep them together. Of course, she had known that Rose would marry one day – it was only natural – but in Mary's daydreams, Rose had first enjoyed a long courtship with a man of means, giving Mary the chance to get used to the idea of Rose leaving her. And, of course, the man would be someone of whom Mary approved and whom she liked. In Mary's vision, Frankie was at Rose's side, standing in for the father Rose had never known, as he smilingly gave her away.

Somehow over the past couple of years this last picture had become awkward. She knew now that Frankie would never be smiling the day he gave Rose away at the altar, if he ever did. Like Mary, he didn't think any man was good enough for Rose, but never in their wildest nightmare had either of them imagined their precious little girl would tie the knot with a copper.

A loud yell came from the other room. Mary's head jerked back and, without stopping to think, she called out, 'You all right in there, Rosie?'

Rose appeared in the doorway holding a cloth around her hand. 'I think so. I caught my hand on one of the knives. Serves me right for chucking them about. Still, no harm done.' She hesitated, as if she had been going to say more, then turned back to the sink.

Mary had started to rise, ready to inspect the wound, when Rose turned away. Disappointment almost gagged her and she clutched at the table for support. This had gone on long enough. It was obvious that Rose wasn't going to make the first move, so it was down to her. Mary was ready to make amends now, more than ready. She couldn't change what had happened, any more than she could change Rose's mind about Jack Adams, but she could make life easier for them all.

Sounds of pots and pans and crockery being stacked noisily in the sink resounded from the scullery, bringing a ghost of a smile to Mary's lips. Rose sounded like she was in a right old temper out there. Mary shuffled to the scullery doorway, her hand rubbing at a place beneath her pendulous breasts as if to ease the sudden tightness around her heart.

'I'm sorry, Rose.'

There! She'd said it. Just two little words, yet those two words transformed Rose. Spinning round from the stone sink, her soapy hands still clutching the heavy roasting dish, she stared in undisguised joy at the awkward figure.

'Oh, Aunt Mary,' she breathed, 'oh, it's all right. It was as much my fault. I should have said something sooner, only I—'

'Yeah, I know, love,' Mary muttered clumsily. 'I ain't

the easiest person to talk to. Anyway . . . We still friends, Rosie love?'

For answer, Rose almost flung herself against the huge body, her words tumbling over each other in her relief. 'Oh, of course we are, Auntie. How could we ever be anything else?' Standing back a pace, Rose saw that Mary's pale blue eyes had become suspiciously bright, and found her own suddenly blurred. Then, in a voice that was both happy and tearful, she babbled, 'I don't think I could have gone on much longer living like this, it's been awful, really awful.' It didn't matter any more about whose fault it had been, or why, and in this moment, Rose would have accepted blame for the Crucifixion, if by doing so it would smooth things over. 'I'm so sorry about what happened, Auntie. It was all my fault, and you were quite right to be angry, but I promise you things will be different from now on. Just . . . just don't let us ever fall out again.' She hiccuped. 'I don't think my nerves could stand it. I love you so much, Auntie, and – and I can't bear it when you're angry with me.' Overcome with emotion, Rose fell against the stout figure and buried her head in the soft folds of Mary's neck.

Mary patted the slim back, blustering, 'Yeah, all right, we were both in the wrong. There's no need to tear the arse out of it,' yet the relief in her voice was unmistakable. Mary prised herself free from Rose's embrace; her eyes darted uncomfortably over her niece's head. 'I should've known better than to drink all that port – not that that's an excuse. Like I've been telling meself all week, nobody poured the stuff down me throat. Anyways . . .' She fought for the words to express her feelings. She wasn't used to emotional outbursts, and this was evident in her restless movements and the uncomfortable flickering of her eyes.

'Auntie, it's all right, there's no need for you to explain,' Rose cut in, not wishing to rake over old coals. The sooner the whole sorry episode was forgotten the better, but Mary, having come this far, wasn't to be deterred so easily. She pulled a large handkerchief from the pocket of a floral pinafore and wiped her round, glistening face as she stated firmly, 'Let me have me say, Rose. It ain't often I apologise, so make the most of it.' Drawing in a deep breath that seemed to swell her enormous breasts even more, Mary gave her nose a perfunctory swipe before continuing. 'The truth is, I can't remember much about that night, but I remember enough to know I said things to you that I'd kill anyone else for saying, an' for that I'm truly sorry. But I ain't changed me mind about the other business.' Her head up, she now looked directly into Rose's eyes. 'I stand by what I said about Jack. He's a decent enough bloke, and he's got guts standing up to me and Frankie like he did, but I still say he ain't good enough for you.' Rose's eyes took on a mutinous sheen and Mary heard her own voice rise in desperation. 'Now don't go getting all riled up just 'cos I'm telling you the truth as I see it. I know you'll do just what you want in the end, but that don't mean to say I can't have my opinion.' Her voice softened, lending a note of entreaty to her tone. 'I want to see you settled with somebody who can take care of you properly . . . I mean, who can support you so you don't have to work all your life, like I've had to. Now, like I've said, Jack's a likeable fellow, but he's never gonna amount to much, is he? Oh, now, don't look at me like that, love.' Rose had backed away, anger written over her features, and Mary knew she was beaten. Sighing heavily, her shoulders sagged as she muttered, 'All right, love. If Jack's the man you want, then I'll say no more. I just hope you know what you're doing. 'Cos marriage is for life. And, believe me, I've seen enough to know that life can seem bloody long if you're spending it with the wrong person.'

Rose clutched at Mary's hands. 'Jack's the right person for me, Auntie. I've known it for a long time, I just couldn't see it until now.'

Mary sniffed loudly. 'Yeah, well, you'd better not keep him waiting, then.'

Anxious for something to do, Mary barged her way back to the sink and plunged her arms deep into the rapidly cooling water. 'Go on, then,' she said, gruffly. 'I'll finish the washing-up. You get yourself off. Oh, and I suppose you'd better bring him back home with you. If he's gonna be related to me, I'll have to get used to having him around. Just don't expect me to fall on his neck, that's all. I ain't never been one for toadying to people, and I don't plan to start now. He'll have to take me as he finds me.' Then she jerked her head towards Rose and added tersely, 'Still, there's no great rush, is there? I mean, you ain't thinking of getting hitched straight away, are you?' The underlining meaning of the words wasn't lost on Rose and her cheeks reddened. She lowered her eyes and murmured, 'No, Auntie. There's no great rush.'

Mary's great body seemed to deflate as she cried shrilly, 'Course, there ain't. I never said there was, did I?'

But her tone couldn't quite hide the note of uneasiness in Mary's voice. And Rose, knowing the reason, held Mary's gaze boldly, until the older woman turned back to the sink in confusion. 'Well, what you waiting for? A bleeding brass band to see you off? Go on, get out of me way. If we're having company tonight, I'd better see about cooking something for tea.'

'Thanks, Auntie.' Rose, subdued now, was busily tying the ribbons of her best bonnet under her chin. The simple task complete, she tiptoed across to the woman at the sink and kissed the smooth cheek, saying lightly, 'I'll be back about five, all right?'

A few minutes later Rose let herself out of the house and breathed in the warm summer air, then expelled a heartfelt sigh of relief. Lord! That had been hard going. And it wasn't going to get any better either.

The sound of a door opening brought her head round to greet her neighbour. 'Good afternoon, Mrs Thorpe. Lovely day, isn't it?'

Mavis Thorpe, a quiet, unassuming woman in her mid-forties, glanced at Rose and smiled. Pulling her door to, she answered cheerfully, 'You look pleased with yourself, love. Going to meet your policeman friend, are you?'

Rose smiled wryly at the inquisitive woman. 'Yes, I am, Mrs Thorpe. We're going to hear the band play in the park, then come back here for tea. Aunt Mary's already getting out her baking trays.'

The woman fell in beside Rose as they walked down the narrow road into the high street. 'Any chance of hearing wedding bells in the near future, Rosie love? We ain't had a wedding in the street for years. It'd be nice to have something to celebrate for a change. We could all do with a bit of cheering up since the old Queen died, Gawd rest her soul. Mind you, I never expected you to marry a copper, not with you being so close to Frankie, 'cos—'

'There's no immediate plans, Mrs Thorpe,' Rose said sharply, annoyed at the woman's presumptuous manner. It wasn't as if Mavis Thorpe was a good friend of either her or Mary. They were merely neighbours, who exchanged a few words when they met by chance.

'Oh, I'm sorry, Rosie. I didn't mean any harm.' The woman was instantly contrite. 'Only I was just wondering out loud, that's all. You ain't offended, are yer, love?'

Chastened, Rose touched her arm and said apologetically, 'No, it's me that should be saying sorry, Mrs Thorpe. I didn't mean to rude, but I don't want everyone in the street thinking I'm getting married. But if there's any news in that direction, my aunt will let you and the rest of the neighbours know.'

At mention of the fearsome Mary Miller, the timid woman said hastily, 'Of course, love. I ain't a gossip, you should know that by now.'

And it was true. Mavis Thorpe wasn't one for spreading rumours, unlike some of her neighbours, Mary included.

They parted at the top of Mare Street, and as Rose ran to catch the tram that would take her nearer to the park, Mavis Thorpe shouted after her, 'Remember me to Frankie, will you, Rosie? Tell him I was asking after him.'

Sinking down on to the slatted bench on the tram, Rose's face fell. Everyone wanted to be remembered to Frankie. Everyone wanted to be his friend – even shy, unassuming Mavis Thorpe.

Except Jack, of course. And the entire London Constabulary. Yet if Frankie was to be believed, even some of the blue-uniformed men weren't averse to hobnobbing with the local villain! She spent the short journey in deep thought.

CHAPTER NINE

Alighting at the stop opposite the chemical firm Bush, Boake & Allen, Rosie walked leisurely down tree-lined streets until she came to the gates in Victoria Park Road. She saw Jack immediately, sitting on a bench under a sprawling oak tree, his nose buried in the *News of the World*. She took off her shoes to let her feet savour the feel of the lush green grass as she made her way towards the preoccupied figure. Creeping up behind him, Rose placed her hands over his eyes and bent to kiss him. 'Guess who?' she whispered into his ear.

Jack reached up and took her hands saying, with a grin, 'Susie!'

'I'll give you Susie, you cheeky devil.' Rose chuckled and flopped down beside him. She held up her face for a welcoming kiss, then snuggled close to his side, delighting in the new intimacy they now shared. 'Anything interesting?' She nodded towards the newspaper lying in his lap. 'Aunt Mary won't have that in the house. She says it's a wicked piece of scandalmongering that no decent person would be seen dead reading.'

'How does she know if she's never read it? And how can someone be caught reading if they're dead? Sounds double Dutch to me.'

Rose nudged him none too gently in the ribs. 'Don't be clever. You know what I mean. Anyway, speaking of Aunt Mary, I've got some good news. She's come round, at last, thank goodness, and you're invited for tea, so you'd better be on your best behaviour and start using that charm you keep telling me about to get in her good books.'

Jack's eyebrows rose in delight. 'Blimey! How did you manage that? I thought after that bust-up, I'd never be able to put me head round the door again – well, not and come out in one piece.' He cocked his head to one side, his eyes appraising her.

Rose laughed softly and snuggled closer. 'I didn't do anything. I was too frightened to bring the subject up in case it started her off again. But suddenly she just said sorry, then we had a good talk, and she asked me to bring you back home for tea.'

'And that's it? Everything's back to normal, just like that?' The grey eyes stared down at her, perplexed. 'You sure it's not just a trick to get me in the line of fire? I mean, she ain't gonna be waiting for me with a frying-pan, is she?'

Rose gazed at the top button of Jack's white shirt. She hadn't told him the whole truth about the reception Mary had given her that night. To do that would have meant repeating the dreadful words and accusations levelled at her in a drunken rage. But it was more than that. Something deep inside Rose refused to admit to the nasty side of her aunt: it would seem like an act of betrayal. So she had told Jack that Mary was angry that she had walked out on her and Frank, and for staying out so late. Which was all true, to a point. And, as far as Rose could see, there was no good to be had in relating the whole gory incident.

'I promise I'll protect you, *Constable*.' She grinned up at him. 'You just concentrate on buttering her up.'

Jack bent to kiss the freckled nose. 'Anything you say, darlin'. She'll be so buttered up by the time I've finished with her, she'll be able to slide between a two-inch gap without touching the sides.' Jack gave her an affectionate cuddle, folded his newspaper and drawled, 'Well, come on, then, lazybones. Get your shoes back on if you want to go to the bandstand, otherwise they'll be packing up before we get there.'

'I'll leave them off, thank you. I hate wearing shoes. I'd much rather go about barefoot, especially on grass. You should try it, it's a wonderful feeling.'

Tucking her arm through his, Jack remarked, 'It won't be so wonderful if you step in some dog's muck – unless you think that's a sign of good luck.'

Undaunted, Rose pulled a face at him, and they strolled lazily across the wide expanse of parkland.

Ten minutes later they were sprawled on the grass, enjoying the musical effort of the uniformed brass band. All around them, couples and families sat or lay, contentedly savouring their day of leisure.

Young children raced in and out of the throng of adults, earning sharp rebukes from their parents, yet they were not deterred from their games. For many, Sundays in the park were a blessed relief from their everyday existence, and they relished their brief sojourn with undisguised relish.

When the sun became too hot, Jack helped Rose to her feet and they went in search of some refreshment. Forsaking the lure of the stone drinking-fountain, they strolled to a nearby pub and sat outside with their drinks.

Resting her elbows on the wooden table Rose looked across at Jack, a gentle smile tugging at her lips. 'Well, come on, out with it. You've had something on your mind all afternoon. You'd better tell me before you burst with the effort of keeping it to yourself.'

Jack stared at her in comical dismay. 'Is it that obvious?'

'It is to me.' Suddenly wary, she asked, 'It's not bad news, is it, Jack?'

Jack took a sip of his beer, his face and actions abruptly taking on an air of sheepishness.

'No, no, there's nothing wrong. In fact you could say it's good news. I wasn't gonna say anything until it was certain, but I'm in line for promotion and . . .'

Rose squealed in delight. 'Jack! Oh that's wonderful, darling. For goodness' sake, why didn't you say something before? How long have you known . . . ?' Her voice began to rise in excitement.

'Whoa, slow down, love.' Jack cut in hastily, his eyes darting to the other customers, who had begun to stare at the young couple. His cheeks reddening in embarrassment, he added quietly, 'I haven't got it yet. There's half a dozen of us all chasing the same job.'

A shadow of disappointment fell over Rose's face. 'But you deserve to be promoted, Jack. You've been in the police force since you left school.'

Jack laughed ruefully. 'That's not how it works, love. Look at my dad. He was still a constable when he died. Though he never wanted to be promoted. All he wanted was to keep the streets safe and help people. Much good it did him.' A note of deep anger entered his voice, causing Rose's heart to flip painfully in sympathy.

She had never met Jack's parents, yet she felt she had known them through Jack's constant reminiscences about his past life.

William Adams, a cheerful, friendly man had died violently on the streets he had walked for over thirty years. Knifed to death by a drunken labourer one Saturday night, over five years ago. Jack had been at home asleep at the time, after just finishing a ten-hour shift. Two plain-clothes officers had come to break the news, their faces drawn in sympathy, and a dark, brooding anger against the drunken lout who had cold-bloodedly murdered one of their own.

Jack had been devastated. He had loved and admired the gentle, fair-minded man who had been a friend as well as a father. But on hearing the dreadful news his first thoughts had been for his mother. He had fought valiantly to control his grief in order to be strong for her. Yet in the end it was she who had comforted him. Gertie Adams had been a remarkable woman. After her husband's death, she had thrown herself whole-heartedly into helping others less fortunate than herself, and there were many. It was during one of these missions, while helping a harassed doctor during a difficult birth, that she sustained a simple cut on her hand that had subsequently become infected. She had contracted a fever and died less than a week later. It had all happened very quickly. There had been nothing the doctors could do to save her.

The loss of his mother so soon after his father had nearly destroyed Jack. The only thing that had kept him going was the memory of his mother's enormous courage. Not once after her husband's death had Jack ever heard her complain, and not once had she asked her only son to give up the profession he loved, even though it had been that same profession that had taken her beloved husband's life. Such was her tremendous character that her strength lingered on after her death, helping Jack to cope on his own and come to terms with the double blow that life had so cruelly dealt him.

Jack finished his beer with a long swallow. Both his parents had been remarkable people. He had been lucky to have had them. Hardly a day passed when he didn't think of them and feel the pain of their loss.

'Are you all right, Jack?' Rose's voice was soft with compassion. She had never known her father, and had no recollection of her mother, so she couldn't empathise with Jack over his parents' deaths. Yet the idea of anything happening to Aunt Mary was unthinkable. To Rose, the gruff, recalcitrant, plain-speaking woman had always been both father and mother to her; she couldn't imagine life without her.

Giving a lop-sided grin Jack rose to his feet. 'Yeah. Just get a bit sentimental now and then. Right! I'm ready when you are.' He tucked her arm into the crook of his elbow, then bent and kissed her cheek. 'Mind you, though, I think I might drop in at the station. I'd feel better if my sergeant knew my last known whereabouts – just in case!'

Ducking the blow aimed at his head, Jack caught Rose's hand and, with a shout of triumph more in keeping with an ebullient schoolboy than with a police officer in line for pro-motion, the young couple ran, hand in hand, their delight in each other's company obvious to all who saw them.

Mary lifted a large baking tray from the oven, shuffled painfully to a nearby wooden surface and thankfully put down her heavy burden. Wiping her perspiring face with the hem of her floral pinafore she leaned back against the sink for support. Gawd! Her legs were killing her. But she'd baked a nice batch of scones and a jam sponge for their tea. All she had to do now was make some sandwiches, then she could put her feet up for a while. She'd found over the years that an hour's rest with her legs raised on the stool usually helped the swelling subside. She remembered that young doctor Frankie had brought round once when her legs had first started to swell. Bloody quack he'd been. Gout, he'd said she had. Well, she'd told him right enough. Gout was a whore's disease. She knew all about gout. Look at old Henry VIII. He'd suffered from gout, and everyone knew what a randy old sod he'd been, and a drunkard into the bargain. This last thought sobered her, bringing with it memories of last week. Her head drooped with shame and she banged her swollen knees with her fists. If only she could go back in time and change what had happened.

What was worse was the suspicion that still lingered in her about Rose. Why was she suddenly so anxious to get married? All that time she'd been going out with Jack Adams, she'd always insisted he was just a good friend. And then, out of the blue, she goes and says she's thinking of marrying him, then stays at his rooms half the night. Well, what was a body supposed to think? Rose wouldn't be the first young girl to be caught out and, if that was the case, then the sooner Jack Adams made an honest woman of her the better. She didn't like the prospect of him becoming part of the family, but what could she do? As for Frankie – he'd go berserk if Rose married the copper. Worse still, he'd expect Mary to side with him in opposing the marriage. She felt as if she was being torn in two: no matter which way she turned, whatever she did or said, she was going to hurt one of the two people she loved more than life itself.

The minutes ticked by slowly as Mary sat deep in thought. When the mantel clock struck four, she stared at it as if seeking guidance from it. She had long feared that the day might come when her loyalties would be divided. Now it had arrived, and she knew where her allegiance rested. Frankie would blow his top, and maybe even turn against her for what he would surely see as an act of betrayal, but that was just too bad. Because, after all was said and done, Frankie was a grown man with a life outside this house she knew nothing about – and didn't want to know about either!

Her mind raced on. No matter what happened, Rose would always be there for her. Despite what Mary had said about Rose's mother, she knew deep in her heart that her niece had a strong sense of loyalty and inner strength that her poor departed mother had sorely lacked. And Rose, dear kind-hearted Rosie, would never leave her invalid aunt to care for herself.

Whereas Frankie! A heartfelt sigh escaped her lips. He had been good to her, oh, yes, he had, no one could say otherwise. He'd been like a son, still was for that matter, but she had to admit she couldn't depend on him as she did on Rose. Look at this past week. Neither sight nor sound of him, and she might not see him for weeks ahead either. Then he would turn up suddenly, a grin on his handsome face and an armful of presents. He was a character, was her Frankie, but he wasn't what you could call dependable.

A sudden niggle of guilt attacked her. Dear God! What was she thinking of? Herself. Weighing up who was more likely to look after her. A sick feeling of shame rose in her throat. 'But I'm not just thinking of meself,' she appealed to the empty room, her thick fingers anxiously plucking at the folds in her serge skirt. 'I think the world of both of 'em, only . . . But it's natural I should worry about me future, ain't it?'

The silent room offered no solace, but when, from the corner of her eye, she caught sight of herself in the mirror on the far wall, slumped in dejection, she sat up straighter and jutted out her chin resolutely. 'Bugger this,' she announced fiercely. 'It don't matter what happens to me. As long as my Rose is happy, that's all that matters. And sod what anyone else thinks – including Frankie.'

Her brave words hung heavily in the air. Yet despite them she knew that if a rift came about she would be heartbroken.

'That was lovely, Mary, thanks. I can't remember the last time I had such a smashing tea.'

Mary fidgeted on her chair. Ever since they had arrived home, both Rose and Jack had been friendly, especially Jack, who seemed to be going out of his way to ingratiate himself into her good books. Yet in spite of his smiling face and warm words, Mary sensed that he was making the effort for Rose's sake, and in this she could sympathise with him.

She, too, was finding the visit hard work, for despite her best intentions it was impossible to change the way she felt overnight. Yet if she wanted harmony between her and Rose, she would have to get on with her prospective nephew-in-law.

That didn't mean she had to sacrifice her principles by fawning all over him, but it wouldn't kill her to be civil. With this in mind she replied cordially, 'Thank you, Jack. It's nice to be appreciated.'

Painfully aware of her aunt's feelings, Rose looked to Jack for approval before she said, 'Auntie, we know this is difficult for you, and we'd like to say how grateful we both are that you're trying so hard. And we want you to know that we'd like you to live with us after we're married and—'

'Oh, no. No, I'm not having any of that, me girl,' Mary cut in brusquely, cheeks reddening. 'You won't want an old woman like me hanging around after you're married. I ain't gonna be a burden on you, Rose, so you can get that idea out of your head right now.'

'But, Auntie—' Rose began, but Jack forestalled her.

'You won't be a burden, Mary. I really would like you to live with us after the wedding. I know you're not happy with Rose's choice for a husband, but I love her very much and the only thing that matters to me is making her happy. That's something I can't do without your help.'

'I ain't asking for charity, lad. And I ain't gonna live with someone on sufferance. I've still got me pride, whatever else I've lost.' Mary bristled, her inherent independence temporarily overriding the fear of being left on her own.

Rose looked at Jack imploringly, and he, knowing he had his work cut out, pushed back his chair and went to Mary's side. He dropped down on his haunches, looked up at her and said simply, 'I know it ain't gonna be easy, Mary, for any of us. But I'm willing to give it me best shot if you are. I don't expect you to suddenly welcome me into your arms like a long-lost son. All I ask is that you give me a chance. So what d'yer say, Mary. Will you at least think about it?'

Mary moved uncomfortably on the hard chair and sniffed.

'All right, I'll think about it, but I ain't promising anything,' she answered, grudgingly. 'After all, you ain't exactly given me much time, have you? I mean to say, up till a week ago I never knew Rose was even thinking about getting wed. It came right out of the blue. So you can't expect me to be cock-a-hoop about it, now can you?'

'No, no, of course not.' Rose and Jack spoke simultaneously, then broke off and smiled across the table dividing them.

Mary saw the loving look they exchanged and all the fight went out of her. She dropped her gaze to her lap where her hands were twisting restlessly, and muttered, 'All right, I'll give it a try but, like I said before, I ain't making any promises.' An immense tiredness was creeping through her limbs, and she felt a great desire to lay her head down and weep.

Jack's next words brought new life into her. 'Thanks, Mary, that's all we ask.' Then he gave a shaky laugh. 'Anyway, it's not like we're planning to get married tomorrow, is it?' He glanced at Rose for confirmation. 'It'll be a year at least before we can save enough for the big day. I told Rose today I've got a chance at promotion and that'll mean more money, but nothing's settled yet. In the meantime we're gonna be looking round for a bigger house . . . That's if it's all right with you, Mary?'

Mary's head jerked up, her tiredness vanishing as if by magic. 'You ain't getting married right away?'

Rose looked at her in puzzlement. 'No, of course not, Auntie. Why should we rush into it? Ooh . . . oh, Auntie!' Mortified, Rose stared at the older woman as the truth of what Mary had feared became clear. She came slowly round the table and took her aunt's hands. 'We're not getting married because we have to. We're getting married because we love each other.' Relief oozing from her every pore, Mary clutched wildly at Rose, her eyes bright with unshed tears. 'Oh, Rose, Rosie love. Oh, I'm sorry, love. I'm sick to me soul that I could've thought such a thing about you. I should've known you wouldn't do anything underhand. You're a good girl, Rosie, always have been. I could cut out me tongue for what I said to you. You'd never get yourself into trouble – you ain't the type . . . Oh, Rosie love, can you ever forgive me?'

Jack shuffled to his feet and stood awkwardly back from the emotional scene. So that was the real reason behind the rift between Rose and Mary. He'd had a suspicion that there was more to it than Rose had admitted. Moving forward he laid a hand on Rose's shoulder. 'I'll leave you two alone, love. It's all right, I'll let meself out.'

Rose nodded absently, her whole attention given to comforting the older woman, and when Jack paused by the door and looked back, he experienced an uncomfortable sense of isolation – of being left out. He had had the same feeling last week, until Rose had turned up on his doorstep. Now it was back with a vengeance, and as he left the terraced house he wondered bleakly if he would ever be included in the close bond that Rose shared with Mary Miller. Or whether she could ever love him like she loved Mary – and the other one!

When no answer came, Jack, his hands thrust deep into his trouser pockets, walked home dejectedly, all the happiness of the day evaporating into the warm summer-night air.

CHAPTER TEN

''Scuse me, Guv'nor. Sorry to disturb you, but you said to remind you about the time, only it's getting on for five, an' you . . .' The nervous man stood in the centre of a large, overly ornate room, his gaze studiously averted from the small group of scantily dressed women who were lazing around on plush upholstered chairs and sofas. A few men were sprinkled around, some looking relaxed, others, like himself, uneasy in their surroundings.

Frankie Buchannon seemed at home on a green velvet couch, one arm draped familiarly around the shoulders of a blonde. He glanced up at the man who had addressed him and appeared to do a double-take, then threw back his head and gave a hearty bellow of laughter. 'For Gawd's sake, Fred, sit down and have a drink. You look like you've just caught yer missus with the milkman.'

The man called Fred put one hand to the collar of his starched white shirt in uncomfortable confusion. His three-piece checked suit, like the shirt, was second-hand but good quality, and Fred Green wasn't used to such finery. But if he wanted to remain on Frankie Buchannon's pay-roll he would have to get used to wearing clothes like these. And he wanted to remain where he was. There was hardly a man alive in the East End who wouldn't want to be in his shoes. Fred had been with Frank for over five years now, a goodly proportion of that time having been spent in prison. His last stretch, eighteen months for demanding money with menaces, had finished four months after Frankie's sentence. The man himself had been waiting outside Wandsworth when Fred had emerged from the Judas gate. Frankie Buchannon was a good governor to work for, even if some of the tasks assigned were not for the faint-hearted. He was generous to his men and their families, and a reasonable man, provided you did as you were told and didn't ask any questions.

Aware of the amused eyes of the women present, and especially those of his governor, Fred felt his cheeks burn and cleared his throat. 'No, thanks, Guv'nor. I don't wanna go home with me breath smelling of drink. Me old lady would kill me.'

Frankie's smile broadened. 'Come on, Fred. You ain't scared of your missus, are you? Besides, I asked you to have a drink with me. Now, you ain't gonna let me down in front of all these lovely ladies . . . are you, Fred?' The handsome face was a picture of benevolence, yet there was no mistaking the sinister note in the seemingly innocent request.

Fred swallowed noisily. 'Yeah, all right, Guv'nor. Thanks, I don't mind if I do.'

'That's it,' said Frankie. 'You fill your boots . . . and I don't just mean with the drink, eh!' Another gale of laughter followed, eliciting a sickly grin of strained mirth from the ill-at-ease Fred.

Frankie picked up a glass from a green onyx table at his side, threw back the contents with one gulp and got to his feet. 'Don't worry, Fred. I'll let you off this time. But, Gawd blimey, you should've seen your face.' Turning to the blonde woman still sprawled on the couch he grinned disarmingly. 'See you soon, Mabel. Next time I come I'll make sure I've got more time to spare!' He gave her a broad wink and strode through heavy rose-coloured damask curtains into an equally plush lobby and headed for the exit, his henchman close on his heels.

Out on the street, Frankie looked sideways at the silent man and said tightly, 'What's up with you?'

Coming hastily to attention, Fred mumbled, 'Nothing, Mr Buchannon. I was just worried about you missing your appointment with that estate-agent bloke. Only you said it was important.'

Frankie took out a gold pocket-watch, looked at it and nodded. 'We've got plenty of time. It don't pay to let these people think you're too eager, know what I mean? Then again, I don't want to miss him. Look, there's a cab. Quick, Fred – on your toes, man! What you hanging about for?'

Eager to please, Fred ran out into the road, his arm waving furiously to attract the black, horse-drawn cab. 'Grantham Avenue, Bow. D'yer know it?'

'Course I know it. I'm a cabbie, ain't I?' The Cockney driver grinned from his perch.

'Number sixteen. And get a move on. I'm late already.'

'Right you are, Guv.'

Frankie climbed into the cab, leaned back and thought about his journey – and the reason behind it.

It was just over a year since his release from prison, but it seemed a lifetime. In that relatively short time, Frankie had expanded his small empire almost beyond recognition. Gone were the small-time protection rackets, and in their stead had grown a large organised profit-raking enterprise that extended to the West End. The two poky sweatshops had grown to ten, and brought in a weekly sum of money that hitherto Frankie had not made in six months. All of these new industries had been financed by a string of bank robberies, so well planned and executed that, although the police had been suspicious, they had been able to do nothing. The first thing Frankie had done was to hire two first-class book-keepers, who exerted their expertise to account skilfully for all of their new employer's worldly goods. Yet still the police kept sniffing round, hoping to trip him up. They'd have a long wait: Frankie had been planning the bank jobs for years. Years of spying out the land, making sure that the men involved could be trusted, going over minute detail again and again. The untimely prison sentence had been unforeseen *and* unfortunate. Yet even behind bars he had continued to plan for the future, and the time he had spent inside had fuelled his desire to be out of reach one day of the law.

Over the years he had become expert in covering his

tracks, learning, often the hard way, from his mistakes. And now, with a small but select few of the local police force and judiciary in his pocket, he didn't anticipate any major problems in the future.

Lighting up an expensive cigar, Frankie inhaled deeply and with much satisfaction. It had been a long, often frustrating haul, but he had planned well and bided his time and was at last reaping the rewards. Now it was time to take a further step up the ladder to respectability.

For years he had lived in hotels and boarding-houses, preferring not to tie himself down to one place so that he could move quickly when the need arose. Those times were now in the past, and Frankie was on his way to see a vendor's agent with a view to buying a house.

The traffic was heavy at this time of day, the rush-hour, and it was another forty minutes before they reached their destination. Waiting anxiously to greet them was a small, dapper man in an ill-fitting striped suit and bowler hat, a pair of gold-rimmed spectacles perched on the end of a bulbous nose. 'Mr Buchannon?' He strode towards Frankie, his hand outstretched.

'I ain't got much time. Let's get on with it, shall we?' Frankie moved past the man to stare at the house before him, and came to an abrupt halt. The property in question was grander than he had envisaged and, for a brief moment, he felt overawed. The detached three-storey house stood in splendid isolation from its neighbours. The heavy oak door was flanked by two white stone pillars on either side that held up the porch roof, with three red-stoned steps leading down to an attractive, diamond-patterned tile path through the middle of a good-sized lawn, bordered with flower-beds and shrubs. Frankie raised his eyes to the top of the house, to the attic storey, which was adorned with prominent eaves and elaborate brackets that formed a horizontal band of stone projecting from the outside wall. Below this were three large windows, with intricate surrounds that matched the two on the ground floor at either side of the porch. Frankie felt his heart begin to race. This was the kind of house he had dreamed of in his youth, after a long day scavenging for food to bring home to his mother, and during all those years when he'd been forced to make money in any way he could. There had always been something inside him that had made him want to pay his own way: at night when he had crawled into bed, bone weary yet triumphant at having brought home some contribution to his upkeep, he had longed for a place like this. He had always known that he would make it some day, and now that day had arrived.

Conscious of the other men's curiosity, he pulled himself together. It wouldn't do to appear too eager. 'Have you got the key?' he asked the agent.

The little man, sensing a sale, brought all his experience to the fore. 'Of course, sir, of course. I wouldn't have asked a gentleman like your good self to travel all this way for nothing. Please, follow me.' Preceding Frankie and the open-mouthed Fred, he clicked open the wrought-iron gate and led the way up the tiled path.

'Bleeding hell, Guv'nor. It's a bit on the posh side, ain't it?' Fred muttered.

Frankie turned on him. 'What d'yer mean? You saying it's too good for the likes of me?'

Fred shrank back in alarm. 'No, Guv'nor, course I ain't. Not for you. I was talking about meself. I ain't never seen a house like this, never mind gone inside one. It's smashing, ain't it?'

Mollified, Frankie aimed a light punch at Fred's shoulder. 'Yeah, it ain't bad. Ain't bad at all. In fact, it might be just what I've been looking for.'

'Mr Buchannon, sir, if you'd like to follow me?' the little man called anxiously.

Beneath his breath Frankie mimicked, 'To the ends of the earth, darling.'

Fred snickered, then at a warning glance from Frankie, was silent.

Once inside the house they were both quiet as the man took them round fussily. 'You'll note the marble surround of the iron grate, Mr Buchannon, and the moulded skirting.' He was proudly showing his client the main reception room. 'These are indicative of all the grates in the house. And, if you'll look up, you'll see the beautiful plasterwork on the ceiling.' Both men's heads turned upwards in response. 'The rose design is central only to this particular room, but each room has its own individual design of ceiling mouldings.' The man bustled round, eager to show off his knowledge. When they had seen all of the downstairs rooms, the agent said importantly, 'Now, if you'd like to accompany me upstairs, gentlemen?' As they followed him, Frankie ran his hand along the curved balustrade in wonder. They examined the four large bedrooms, with Frankie maintaining an air of aloofness, even though his heart was hammering inside his chest. Yet when the agent, his plump face etched in triumph, announced, 'Here, sir, we have the *pièce de résistance*, the bathroom', and threw open the mahogany door, the sheer opulence before him caused even Frankie's breath to catch in his throat.

The gleaming white walls were tiled from floor to ceiling. In the centre of the room stood a huge claw-footed bath with gold taps and hand-rails, the like of which he had never seen before. The equally impressive wash-basin was framed by gilt-edged mirrors and a long, sweeping tiled ledge. In the far corner, discreetly concealed by a gold plush curtain, was the very latest design in indoor WC, looking far too grand for its functional purpose.

'If you'll allow me, sir?' The agent, beaming with pride as if he'd designed the whole house himself, pulled at the wooden panelling beneath the sink to reveal a ceramic sink-like object, explaining effusively, 'This is a bidet, sir. The very latest innovation for personal hygiene. The entire bathroom was designed by George Jennings, who also, may I add, won a gold medal at the Paris Exhibition in eighteen eighty-nine.' At Frankie's side, Fred Green's open face was filled with undisguised awe. 'Bleeding hell, Guv'nor. It's too good to shit in!'

Frank whirled round and barked, 'That's enough. Wait downstairs!'

Fred, downcast, murmured, 'Sorry, Guv'nor.'

'Downstairs – now!'

'Yes, Guv. Sorry, Guv.'

It was almost an hour later before Frankie left the house, his mind formulating ideas.

'Did I mention the Italianate style, sir?'

Jerked from his reverie, Frankie said abruptly, 'You what? I mean, pardon?'

'The style of the external part of the house, sir. It's Italianate, derived from the Renaissance palaces of Venice, Rome and Florence. It was established by Sir Charles Barry, most notably at—'

'I'll take your word for it.'

The agent waited patiently, not at all taken in by his customer's studied indifference. 'If you're not satisfied with this house, sir, I have many more I can show you.'

'What? Oh, no, I don't want to see any others just yet.' Standing back a pace, Frankie looked hard at the house, his face impassive. 'Before I make me mind up, I want to show me family. See what they think of it.'

'Certainly, sir, certainly. And what time would be convenient for them, Mr Buchannon?'

Frankie considered, then threw back his shoulders and said confidently, 'How about tomorrow? About eleven. I can have me family here then.'

'Capital, sir, capital.' The agent beamed delightedly, already spending the commission he would earn from the sale. 'We'll say tomorrow, then, at eleven o'clock. Good day to you, Mr Buchannon, and you, sir.' He inclined his head towards Fred.

'Right little arse-licker, he was, wasn't he, Guv'nor?' Fred said cheerfully, after the departing figure. But Frankie, absorbed in his own thoughts, didn't hear him.

CHAPTER ELEVEN

'So, when's the wedding, then? Or has your intended put it off again?'

The sneering tone in Sally's voice set Rose's already frayed nerves further on edge. Concentrating on the task of cutting thick slices from a large crusty loaf, she replied tartly, 'Why? Will you miss me when I leave, Sally?'

They were in the kitchen at the back of the Red Lion, taking advantage of a lull in trade to prepare the food for the evening rush.

Sally laughed brashly. 'Yeah, I'll miss you, like me arse'd miss piles,' she said coarsely.

Rose winced but said nothing. In truth, Sally had hit a raw nerve. She had expected to be married by now, or at least to have a definite date for the wedding, but Jack refused to make any commitment until his promotion came through, even though his advancement to sergeant was assured. A pessimist by nature, he wouldn't believe his achievement until the sergeant's stripes were firmly on his shoulders. Then there was the business of him wanting a transfer out of London: he argued that they could have a better life away from the East End streets. But Rose suspected that Jack's main reason for wanting to flit was to get her away from Frankie's influence. Mary had been horrified by the idea and stated loudly and often that there was no way in the world she would ever leave her birthplace. But there was another, more pressing

worry on Rose's mind, which was growing with each passing day.

After that awful scene with Mary last year, Rose had
refused at first to spend any more time at Jack's flat. He
had been sorely disappointed at first, but had agreed,
reluctantly, to wait until they were married. It had been
easy enough to make such plans in the cold light of day,
but on the rare evenings when Jack persuaded her into his
home temptation always proved too great. The last time
had been over a month ago when Rose, her aunt's drunken
accusations still haunting her, had resolved not to take any
more risks. Only it was looking as if the last time might well
have been one time too many.

'You look a bit green. What's the matter, Rosie? Ain't you
feeling too good?'

'Oh, shut up, Sally, and mind your own business,' Rose
snapped, which only served to exacerbate Sally's teasing.

Widening her eyes in mock horror, the older woman
exclaimed, ''Ere! You ain't up the duff, are you? Not you.
Not Miss Cast Iron Drawers—'

Rose turned on her. 'Just shut your filthy mouth, Sally,
or by God I'll shut it for you.'

Sally leaped back at the ferocity in Rose's voice, any more
taunts silenced by the fury in the flashing blue eyes boring
into her own.

As Rose stormed out of the kitchen, Sally watched her
departure with quizzical eyes. 'Bleeding hell! She has. The
silly cow's gone and got herself caught. Well, well, well!
Now ain't that a turn-up for the books.'

Out in the passageway, Rose leaned against the wall,
fighting a rising sickness in her throat. 'Please, God! Don't
let me be pregnant. I promise I'll never do it again. Just
don't let me be pregnant.'

An irate figure burst into her line of view. 'What the
bleeding hell are you two playing at out here? I only
asked you to make some sandwiches, not cook a bleeding
four-course meal.' Henry Dixon glared at Rose. Then his
expression changed to one of concern at the sight of her
stricken face. ''Ere, what's up, girl? Ain't yer feeling well?'

Swallowing hard Rose strove to put on a normal front.

'No, I'm fine, thanks, Mr Dixon. Just came over a bit flushed. It's hot out in the kitchen with the pies cooking in the oven.'

Dixon's face cleared. 'Well, if that's the case, then get out into the bar and start serving.' Looking past her he shouted, 'And that goes for you, too, Sally. Get your arse out here now, unless you've come over all hot and bothered as well.'

Sally sauntered into the hallway, her face alight with merriment. 'All right, all right, Henry. There's no need to shout, I ain't deaf.' She pushed past Rose and ambled into the bar, her mouth spreading automatically into a wide smile for the punters.

When Frankie arrived at the pub just after nine o'clock, Rose had recovered her composure, managing to put her fears at the back of her mind for the remainder of the evening. When he saw her, Frankie headed towards her, leaned one arm on the bar and called, 'How about some service, darlin'?'

Sally began to make her way down the bar to him but Rose reached him first. 'Hello, Frank. What can I get you?'

'The usual, please, Princess, and the same for the boys.' He jerked his head at the two men standing behind him. 'Then I want a word with you, in private.'

Rose looked worriedly over her shoulder to where the landlord was putting some money into the till. 'I don't know, Frank. I've still got another hour until my shift ends. I don't want to take liberties.'

Frankie gave a loud guffaw. 'Don't be daft. Henry won't mind – will you, me old mate?' he added, as Dixon came to join them.

'Mind what, Frankie?' he asked warily.

'If Rose takes a few minutes to have a little chat with me.' He glanced down the crowded bar and added, 'You and Sally can manage without her for a bit, can't you?'

'Frankie!' Rose interrupted. 'Not now. You can see how busy we are.'

'Rubbish.' He waved dismissively. 'I only want to borrow you for five minutes. Now, that ain't asking much, is it, Henry?' His eyes lifted to the stony-faced publican.

'It don't seem like I've got much choice, does it?' Henry said, his voice steely.

Anxious to avoid any arguments, Rose led Frankie quickly to a nearby table. 'I won't be long, Mr Dixon. And I'll make up the time at the end of my shift.'

Henry's face relaxed. 'That's all right, love. You've only got an hour to go and Rita'll be here soon.'

Rose sat down, flustered. 'I wish you wouldn't do this, Frankie, I . . .'

'Do what, Princess?' He looked puzzled. 'Can't I have a word with me best girl when I want to now?'

'Not when I'm working, Frank,' Rose replied, harassed. 'You seem to think I'm playing some sort of game here, instead of trying to earn a living.' As Frankie's face darkened, Rose sought to appease him. She was feeling particularly fragile at the moment and unable to deal with any more bad feeling. Laying a hand on his, she said softly, 'I'm sorry for sounding sharp, Frank. I – I haven't been feeling too good today. I shouldn't have taken it out on you. Forgive me?'

Immediately Frankie became solicitous. 'You should've said, darlin'. Hang on, I'll have a word with Henry, get him to give you the rest of the—'

'No, no, it's all right, Frank, I don't want to make a fuss. It's just . . . Well, you know, women's problems.'

Frankie's face cleared. 'Oh, that. Listen, Princess, I've seen a house.' He pulled his chair further under the table and leaned nearer to her, his eyes bright with excitement. 'You should see it, Rose. I've seen some nice places in me time, hotels and places like that, but—' He broke off to take a swallow of his drink. 'It's like something out of a book. Well! That's why I wanted to talk to you. I want your advice. I was thinking that maybe you and Mary could come back there with me tomorrow – you know, give me your opinion.'

Rose gazed at the animated face, and found herself grinning at his infectious enthusiasm. 'This is a bit sudden, isn't it? But I'm pleased, oh, I am, and so will Aunt Mary be when I tell her. It'll be nice to know exactly where to find you after all these years. But why do you want us to come with you for a look? You must know if you want it or not.'

'I do, but I still want your opinion. You know me, Rose. Normally I just want somewhere to eat and sleep, but it's different now. It's time I settled down.' He winked and smiled broadly. 'It's not like I'm gonna have to do a runner if the police come calling. Those days are gone for good.'

Rose squeezed his hand tightly. 'I'm glad, Frank.'

'Me too. So! Will you come and have a look at it with me? I told the bloke I'd come back tomorrow with me family. Well . . .' He hitched up his shoulders in a rare moment of self-consciousness. 'You and Mary are me family, though I expect the feller's expecting me to turn up with a couple of kids and a wife in tow.'

Rose felt a warm glow settle over her. 'Of course I'll come with you. I don't know about Aunt Mary, though. How far away is it? Only, you know, she doesn't go out much any more.'

Frankie expelled a loud sigh of relief and got to his feet, pulling Rose with him. 'Don't you worry about Mary, Princess. I'll have a cab waiting on your doorstep in the morning. Mary won't have to walk a step – except round the house, of course.' Pleased with himself he walked Rose back to the bar and kissed her cheek lightly. 'You'd better get back to work then, before old Henry has a bleeding turn. Sorry I've gotta dash off, it's business. See you tomorrow, Princess, about tennish . . . 'Ere, everything all right, is it? I mean with you and Constable Plod? Only I ain't had me invite to the wedding yet.' He bent over her and kissed her again. 'I am invited, ain't I? After all, who else is gonna give you away?'

Rose tried to look annoyed, but it was impossible to be angry with Frankie when he was in this mood. She gave him a friendly shove. 'Everything's fine, thank you very much. Now clear off, I've got a job to get back to.'

'See you tomorrow, Rose.'

Rose lifted up the barflap and slid back behind the counter, humming a popular tune under her breath. It was amazing how Frank had taken the news of her engagement. They had all expected him to go mad but instead he had been as nice as pie, even offering to lend them the money for the wedding. Of course, that was out of the question –

Jack had nearly had a fit at the very thought. Still, it had
been nice of him to offer. When she looked back at all the
fuss and worry she and Mary had suffered at the thought
of breaking the news to him, she felt a little foolish. Taking
out two glasses from beneath the bar she filled them with
ale for the waiting customers, ignoring the inquisitive look
Sally was casting in her direction.

Of all the people to have guessed her secret, Sally was
the last person Rose would have chosen. Still, Sally *was*
only guessing and, besides, she wasn't sure herself if she
was pregnant. She was only a few weeks late. There could
be any number of reasons for that and she wasn't going to
start panicking until she knew for sure. If the worst came
to the worst, then she and Jack would just have to get
married straight away. It wasn't as if she'd gone with any
old Tom, Dick or Harry. Jack would stand by her, of that
she was certain. So, really, she had nothing to worry about.
Whichever way the wind blew, she was safe.

'A house! What sort of house? Frankie ain't said nothing to
me about buying no house.'

Rose was busy laying the table for supper. Jack had said
he would come when he had finished his shift, and Rose
wanted to talk to him. It seemed ages since they had last
had a good heart-to-heart. Lately it had been just work,
saving and . . . Yes, well, that was what she wanted to talk
to him about. These past few weeks had been terrible. And
even if she wasn't pregnant, the worry she was living with
now wasn't something she wanted repeated. Tonight she
was going to get Jack to set a date for the wedding, even
if she had to tie him to a chair to do it. They had wasted
enough time as it was.

'You gone deaf or something, Rose? I asked you a question.' Mary's belligerent tone cut across Rose's troubled
thoughts.

'I'm sorry, Aunt Mary, I was miles away.'

Mary frowned at her niece. 'I said, Frankie didn't tell me
anything about buying a house. He was here a few days ago
and he never mentioned it then.'

'I don't think he knew then, Auntie.' Rose tried to placate

her. 'From what he told me, he only saw it for the first time today, and now he wants our opinion.'

'Humph. Well, I'm glad someone's settling down. Which is more than I can say for your Jack. Not that I'm rushing you.'

'Auntie,' Rose began patiently, 'I've explained it a dozen times to you. Jack wants to get a bit of money behind us before we get married, and a bigger place to live.'

Mary grunted. Swivelling round to face Rose, she wagged a reproving finger at her niece. 'Bigger place my arse. There's families living ten to a room round these parts, so don't go giving me that old malarkey about this house being too small fer us all. Now, I know I wasn't keen on you two getting wed at first, but I've got used to the idea, and it's about time it was sorted out properly. And it ain't just me what thinks so either. Frankie was saying exactly the same thing the other day, so you have a word with Jack about it, and don't let him keep putting you off. He's dragging his feet, me girl. So if I was you, I'd do something about it. Otherwise you're gonna end up an old maid like me. An' I want to see some little 'uns around me before I pop me clogs.'

It was an unfortunate speech in the circumstances, and Rose felt herself growing hot. 'You're only fifty-four, Auntie. Don't go putting years on yourself. Anyway, Jack'll be here soon so don't go getting at him the minute he puts his nose around the door.'

As if her words had conjured him up, the front door opened and Jack called merrily, 'Hello. You both decent, or am I out of luck again?'

Rose rushed to meet him and fell into his open arms. 'You're early. I didn't expect you for another half-hour. Supper's all laid out. You sit yourself down with Auntie, and I'll get the kettle on.'

Jack gave Rose a gentle squeeze, released her and grinned at the woman in the armchair. 'Evening, Mary. How've you been?'

Scratching at a warm spot below her ample breasts Mary snorted. 'If you was to come round more often, you'd find out, wouldn't you?'

Rose sighed. 'I'll get the tea.'

Leaving Jack and Mary alone, Rose made the large pot of tea, her ears straining to catch the muted conversation from the parlour.

As she carried the large tray into the room she said, 'Tea's made.'

The supper of crusty bread, cheese and pickles was eaten in comparative silence. Jack cleared his throat several times as if about to speak, then smiled inanely before carrying on with his meal.

Finally, as if the words were being wrenched from his tongue he blurted out, 'Listen. There's something I need to talk to you both about.' Both women looked at him expectantly. He picked up his knife and began to run the edge distractedly over the tablecloth.

Rose noted this and felt a stab of alarm. When he added, hesitantly, 'I've found a place for us to live. It's ours if we want it,' apprehension settled in the pit of her stomach. But these were the words she had been waiting for, so why was she suddenly so frightened?

'Where?' The word came out so quietly that Rose wasn't sure that she had spoken aloud, until Jack began to fidget uncomfortably, refusing to meet her eyes.

Busy with her food, Mary was unaware of the sudden tension in the room. 'Bleeding hell! Now, ain't that a coincidence? First Frankie finds a place to live, and now you two.'

Jack glanced up absently. 'Frankie?'

'Yeah, he's taking us to see it tomorrow, ain't he, Rosie?' Mary looked to her niece for confirmation, but Rose's attention was fixed on Jack. There was something very wrong here.

'What's the matter, Jack?' she asked quietly. 'You seem a bit on edge. Just where is this house you've found for us?'

Almost shame-faced, Jack stammered, 'Now look, Rose . . . and you too, Mary. Just listen to what I have to say before you jump down me throat!' Growing ever more flustered, Jack threw down the knife and leaped to his feet. He brushed a heavy lock of hair back from his face. 'I've been offered me own station. There's a house to go with it, three bedrooms, so there'll be plenty of room for all of us. There's other blokes who'd kill for a chance like this, but the Inspector offered it to me. This afternoon it was, just after seven. I'd popped back on me late break and he'd left a message for me. The only snag was, I had to give him his answer straight away. Like I said,' he appealed to the silent Rose, 'it's a chance of a lifetime to have me own station at my age, so I had to say yes, didn't I, love? I mean, I'll never get another opportunity like it. I—'

Rose pushed back her chair and went to stand behind Mary, her hand gripping her aunt's shoulder as if to prepare her for a shock. 'Where is it, Jack? *Where exactly is this marvellous place?*'

Her face was stony, and Jack, seeing the angry suspicion in the bright blue eyes, felt his anger take hold. He clasped his hands tightly behind his back and rocked on his heels. 'It's a small village, just outside Southampton. My transfer's been approved by the Inspector, and I'll be able to move in at the end of the month.'

'*Southampton!*' Mary screeched, her large body jerking in panic. 'Why the bleeding hell did you want to go and ask for a transfer there?'

Fighting to keep calm, Jack said patiently, 'I didn't ask for a transfer there, Mary. It just came up, and I'd've been a fool to turn it down. It . . .' But neither woman was paying him any attention.

Struggling to get off the chair, Mary's face was beginning to turn an alarming shade of purple. 'Well, you can forget about me, mate. I ain't gonna go and live in some godforsaken hole. Oh, no, lad. Not on your nelly.' Then she glared up at the stricken Rose. 'Did you know about this, girl? 'Cos if you did, then it was a bleeding nasty trick. You know I'd never move outta London – I said it all along, didn't I?' Stabbing a finger at Jack, she raged, 'Or is that why you've arranged to move to the other side of England, so as you won't have to take me along with you?' She shrugged off Rose's hands and breathed heavily. 'Well, don't you worry about me, I can take care of meself. And I hope you'll be very happy, the pair of you.'

Rose was stunned to the heart of her being. How *could* he?

How could he have done such a thing without consulting her first? Or was Mary right? Had he arranged it all behind her back? It seemed strange that a young officer like Jack would be given the chance of his own station on the spur of the moment. Things like that normally took months, years, to arrange. Oh, no. No, he couldn't do a thing like that. Not Jack. Yet he had taken up the transfer. Even knowing how upset Mary would be, and that she would never move out of London, he had accepted the move to Southampton. A place that would seem like the other side of the world to someone like Mary Miller.

An icy numbness gripped Rose. 'I think you'd better go, Jack.' She heard the chill in her voice and was surprised to find how calm she sounded. 'Aunt Mary's right. It was a nasty trick to pull. But if you're set on moving away, then you'll go by yourself.'

Jack made to move towards her, his hands outstretched. 'Rose . . . Rosie, love. I know it looks bad but I swear I knew nothing about it until this evening, I—'

Rose shrank away from his touch, her lips trembling with passion. 'Get out, Jack. The wedding's off.'

Jack's face blanched, then he tried to laugh, but succeeded in uttering only a hoarse croak. 'That's a bit melodramatic, ain't it, Rosie? Look, I'll come back tomorrow, after you've had time to think it over and—'

With an anguished cry Rose lashed out at him. The unexpected blow sent him reeling backwards, and as he stretched out a hand to steady himself, Rose came at him again, her fists pummelling at his face and shoulders. *'Get out! Get out of my house, you bastard!'* She was scream-ing, unable to control herself as she saw her world being blown apart.

Jack tried to catch the flailing arms, but it was hopeless. Ducking another well-aimed blow, he backed out of the room, his arms shielding his face and head. When the key Rose had given him fell out of his pocket, he tried to pick it up, only to have it snatched from his grasp.

'And I'll have that back as well!' Rose shrieked.

Jack staggered back, his hand fumbling for the doorknob behind him, then he was in the hallway and at the front door, and finally, dazed and shaken, he reached the safety of the street.

At the sound of the front door banging, all the fight oozed out of Rose. She stumbled blindly across the room and collapsed, sobbing, into the armchair.

Mary, her own voice near to breaking, tottered over and sank into the opposite chair, mumbling tearfully, 'I can't go all that way, love. Not at my age. You do understand, don't you, love? I ain't just being awkward.' When Rose continued to sob, Mary felt tears begin to course down her own cheeks. 'Don't cry, Rosie, please. You'll make yourself ill. Come on, girl, give over. We're better off without him, Rosie love. We're better off without him.'

But Rose was inconsolable.

CHAPTER TWELVE

'Well, what d'yer think, Mary?' Frankie was acting like a small boy showing off his favourite toy. The eagerness in his face and voice pierced through Rose's wretchedness, bringing a faint smile to her lips.

The three were in the reception room of the house in Grantham Avenue which, although it came under the jurisdiction of Hackney, was just on the borders of Bow. They had been all over the house and now he was waiting for the approval of the two most important women in his life. For once in her life, Mary was lost for words. Her eyes gravitated to the ornate ceiling and the tinkling crystal chandelier, then moved slowly over the embossed wallpaper and marble surround of the iron grate, then dropped to where her swollen ankles sank into the deep red carpet. She was glad she'd suffered the agony of wearing her best shoes, yet even in her Sunday-best blue two-piece, she felt out of place in a house like this.

Rose pulled herself out of her gloom, drew her arm through Frankie's and hugged him affectionately, determined not to let her misery overshadow his excitement. 'It's lovely, Frank, really lovely. If I were you, I'd snap it up quick before someone else buys it.'

'You really think so, Princess?' Frankie's handsome face was alight with enthusiasm.

'Yes, I, do,' she said firmly. 'You like it and you say you can afford to buy it, so why wait?' Then she grinned up at him mischievously. 'All you'll need to make it perfect is a wife!'

Frankie looked alarmed. 'Leave it out, Princess. One wedding in the family's enough, so don't try any match-making. I ain't ever met anyone I'd want to spend the rest of me life with yet. Besides, how could any woman compete with you and Mary?' The older woman was still standing as if mesmerised so he said, 'Did you hear that, Mary? Rose is trying to get me married off.' When she didn't answer, Frank disengaged himself from Rose and walked across to her. 'What's the matter, Mary? Don't you like the place? I thought you'd be pleased. You've been on at me for years to settle down. Is it 'cos it's too posh?'

Mary shifted painfully from one foot to the other. Then she said, drily, 'It's a far cry from where you was born and raised, lad, but I'm pleased for you. It was just the surprise, like. I wasn't expecting anything so grand. It's not the sort of place I'd be comfortable in, but if this is what you want then you go ahead and buy it, and good luck to you. Though why you want a house with four bedrooms, I don't know, I'm sure. Still . . .' she drew herself upright '. . . I ain't got to live here.'

Frank's face fell. 'I was hoping you might one day, Mary. I mean, if things don't work out with Rose and Jack, I thought it would ease your mind knowing there was somewhere else for you to go. But if you're dead set against it . . . Well, I'll have to have another think, won't I?' As he spoke, he looked directly into Mary's eyes, his high spirits dampened by her open, and hurtful, comments.

Mary met the commanding gaze squarely, then flinched as she saw the joy leave his dark brown eyes. Wetting her lips, she gulped. Gawd Almighty! What was the matter with her lately? All she seemed to be doing was upsetting those she loved most. First Rose and now Frankie. Blinking furiously, she looked at her niece for support, but Rose was staring out of the large bay window, her mind clearly elsewhere – and it wasn't hard to imagine where.

Frank, too, had turned away, and as Mary watched him rest an arm, crestfallen, on the marble mantelpiece, a tumultuous surge of emotion swept over her. Desperate to make amends she shuffled over to him and laid a pudgy hand on his arm.

'It was thoughtful of you, lad,' she said, 'and don't think I ain't grateful, 'cos I am. But you don't have to worry about me living with Rose and Jack 'cos the wedding's off. We're both staying right where we are, ain't that right, Rosie, love?'

Frank spun on his heel, his face alert. 'Is that true, Princess? You're not gonna get married after all?'

Rose saw the delight flare in his eyes and turned back to the window. She didn't know how to answer, nor could she trust herself to speak. Everything had happened so suddenly: this time yesterday she had been full of plans for the future with Jack, and now, less than twenty-four hours later, her life seemed to be in ruins. Added to her heartache was the gnawing worry that she might be pregnant. Her monthly show still hadn't appeared, and she didn't know what to do. Her safety net had been snatched from beneath her so abruptly that she still hadn't taken it in properly. She knew Jack wanted to marry her as much as ever, but she couldn't forgive him for the way in which he had behaved. Even if the unexpected transfer had happened as he had said, there was still no justification for him accepting it when he knew the unhappiness it would cause Mary. For that alone Rose couldn't forgive him.

A shudder ran down her back and her arms came up around her shoulders. She had promised Mary faithfully that she wouldn't go back on her decision to remain in London, and there was no chance that she and Jack might get back together – even if Jack changed his mind about the transfer, the damage had been done. He had betrayed her trust and, in doing so, had killed something inside her, something that could never be replaced.

Yet still her tortured mind raced on blindly.

If only Frankie had found this house sooner, had offered Mary the chance to move in with him, maybe Jack's announcement wouldn't have come as such a blow. Then Rose wouldn't have minded where she lived, as long as she could visit Mary regularly and have her to stay for holidays. But, as Mary had stated, this house, lovely as it was, wasn't the type of home she was used to. Yet you never knew with Mary. Maybe if Rose had supported Jack in the proposed move, she might have changed her mind. Goodness knows, her aunt loved Frankie as if he were her own son, and in time, perhaps, she would have adapted to her new surroundings.

A dry sob caught in Rose's throat.

All that was conjecture now. She had made her decision and now she must stand by it. But it was going to be hard. Loving Jack as she did, and dear God, how she loved him, it was going to be hard to get used to life without him. But love wasn't always enough. You had to have trust, too, and Jack, in the one sneaky act she had ever known him commit, had destroyed that.

She felt Frankie come up behind her and continued to stare out of the window, afraid to speak in case she gave way under the strain. But when his arms came round her she folded into the familiar, comforting embrace and let her tears flow.

Holding her close to his chest, Frankie stroked the copper curls tenderly, all the while murmuring soothing words. Yet even as he spoke, he couldn't stop the powerful surge of exultation that was raging through him. It was just as well Rose couldn't see his face, for she would have seen the triumph blazing in his eyes, perhaps questioned it: it went much further than the situation warranted.

Frank clasped the slender body even more tightly. He would look after her, see that she wanted for nothing. And in time he would find someone for her. Someone better than the gullible bastard she had fallen for. His Rose was worth more than that, and he was going to make sure the next man in her life was one of whom he, Frankie Buchannon, approved.

CHAPTER THIRTEEN

'Rita, have you got a minute, please? There's – there's something I want to ask you.'

'Yeah, course, Rosie love. What can I do for you?'

The two women were having their dinner break in the kitchen, much to Dixon's annoyance. Sally's shift wasn't due to start for another hour, and there had been an unexpected rush of customers. At the moment he was running the bar with only the elderly potman's help.

Casting a wary look over her shoulder to make sure no one else was listening Rose felt her face begin to burn and her hands tremble as she asked, hesitantly, 'Do you know of anyone . . . anyone that . . . that gets rid of unwanted pregnancies?'

Rita's jaw dropped open in amazement. The thick-cut sandwich she'd been holding fell from her fingers. 'Gawd, blimey! I thought Sal was just being a cow, but you are, ain't you? You've gone and got yerself into trouble. Aw, Rosie . . . Oh, I am sorry, love. But what about your feller? He'll stand by you, surely. He's mad about you, love – I've seen the way his eyes follow you whenever he comes in here: I wish someone'd look at me like that.' She wiped her hands on her skirt, and added, 'Look, I know you've had words – bleeding hell, who doesn't? Oh, don't look so surprised, Rosie, you can't keep much secret round here, but to try and get rid of a baby . . . Does Jack know about it?'

Rose shook her head tiredly. 'No, I didn't tell him. There wasn't any point, not now.'

'*No point?*' Rita almost shouted, then quickly lowered her voice, 'Listen to me, love. If there's a chance of you getting married, then bloody well grab it with both hands. There's plenty of women with your problem – believe me, I know. But not many have the chance to marry the father. Most of 'em don't even know who the father is. Now, I don't know why the pair of you quarrelled, but I'm telling you, Rosie, compared with what you're thinking of doing – well! Even if you don't love him no more it don't matter. There's plenty who'd run up the aisle with a monkey in your condition, and your feller . . . Well, I wouldn't kick him out of bed.' She studied Rose's ashen face, and sighed. 'Was it really bad? Was he knocking you about? Is that why you called off the wedding?'

Rose reared back in horror. '*No!* No, of course he wasn't,' she said, rushing hotly to Jack's defence. 'He never laid a finger on me.'

Rita leaned back in the upright wooden chair and smiled wryly. 'Yes, love, if you say so. But it ain't his hands what's got you into trouble, not on their own, anyway.' Rose's head drooped and Rita stared at the copper curls in sympathy. 'All right, it ain't none of me business why you don't wanna marry him, though I still think you're barmy – Yeah, all right, I won't say anything else about it,' she added, as Rose made to rise. 'Sit still, an' let me think a minute, will you?' Drumming her fingers on the table, she asked quickly, 'Have you tried hot baths and gin? That sometimes works.'

Rose pushed back a strand of hair. 'I've nearly scalded myself and I've got through a bottle of gin, but nothing happened.' The smile wobbled and disappeared, then, with tears blurring her vision, Rose implored the other woman, 'Oh, Rita, please, you've *got* to help me. I don't know anyone else to turn to.'

Unable to bear the girl's despair, Rita got to her feet and paced the small room, deep in thought. 'I don't know, love. I've known women die at the hands of those butchers. It just ain't safe. Look, won't you try and make it up with—'

Rose's face was set against any further argument. 'I couldn't now even if I wanted to. He's gone – Jack's gone to Southampton. He left last week and, from what he said, I don't expect him back.'

Her lips trembled as she recalled their last meeting. He had been waiting on the doorstep the day she and Mary had returned with Frankie after seeing his new home. The usual insults had been traded between the two men, resulting in Jack marching away, only to return that night to plead his case once more. Rose had kept him on the doorstep: Mary was still in a volatile mood, and Rose, weary of endless arguments, had finally closed the door in Jack's protesting face.

But Jack wasn't a man to give up easily, and for the next two weeks he had turned up at the house, in the pub, had waylaid her in the street, dogged her every step in a desperate attempt to win back the woman he loved. And every time she had felt herself weaken, there were her aunt and Frankie reminding her of what Jack had done. The pair of them went on and on at her, keeping up the pressure to persuade her to forget Jack and get on with her life. And with the extra worry of finding herself pregnant she'd hardly known what she was doing any more. Yet when she had realised Jack had taken her at her word and gone to Southampton she had been stunned. Because, somehow, even though it had been she who had demanded that he leave her alone, she had never thought that he would. The noise from the bar was becoming louder as the customers began to get tired of being kept waiting for service. Over the din Rose could hear Henry Dixon calling for them to get a move on.

'Mr Dixon's calling us, Rita,' she said numbly.

'Let him bleeding well call, then,' Rita said harshly. 'I ain't leaving here till I get you sorted out. Look, love,' she came to Rose's side and took her hand, 'have you thought about keeping it? I know it won't be easy, what with you not being married. But you won't be the first girl to have a baby without a ring on her finger. And it's not like you're all alone, is it? You've got your aunt and Frankie to help you out—'

'*No*. No. They can't find out. Look, leave it, Rita. I'm sorry I asked. I shouldn't have put you on the spot. I'll find somebody myself and . . .' She trailed off in a soft moan.

'Where you gonna find somebody like that, love?' Rita asked scornfully, although her face had fallen into lines of compassion at the look of desolation in Rose's eyes. She was so young – so vulnerable. Rita thought swiftly: it was obvious that her young friend was determined to find someone to get rid of the unborn child and if she, Rita, couldn't stop her, then she had to make sure Rose went to someone respectable – that is, as respectable as you could get in such a sordid business. She made up her mind, then asked sharply, 'How much money have you got?'

'Not a lot. I mean, I don't have any savings of my own. Jack was seeing to that side of things. I couldn't save anything on what I earn. Why?'

'Because it'll cost you.'

Hope sprang into Rose's eyes. 'You'll help me, then? *Oh*, Rita, thank you. You'll never know how much I appreciate it.' A great sigh of relief escaped her dry lips.

'Don't go thanking me yet, love. And, like I said, you'll need money. The sort of person you're looking for don't come cheap – not a good one, anyway. Couldn't you ask Frankie for a loan? He's not short of a few bob, is he? You could always say you needed it for something special. You don't have to tell him what for.'

Hastily Rose stammered, 'I couldn't do that, Rita, it wouldn't be right. I got myself into this mess, so it's up to me to get myself out of it.' She drew a deep breath. 'How much will I need?'

Busying herself with cleaning crumbs off the table, Rita said diffidently, 'I ain't sure. I'll ask around, but you'll probably need about five pounds, maybe more. Can you get the money if I find someone? You can't wait too long, you know. How far along are you, anyway? About three months? Or is it more?'

Rose nodded. 'Just on three months.' Suddenly she felt curiously detached from the situation. It was as if she was looking in on the conversation instead of being a part of it.

'And don't worry about the money. I know how I can get hold of it.'

Rose turned towards the bar and walked in ahead of Rita. She took Henry Dixon to one side and said calmly, 'About what you asked me a while ago, Mr Dixon. You remember. About me showing a bit more tit behind the bar.' Before the astonished man could reply, she added, 'Well, you give me a rise in pay and I'll show as much tit as you want.'

'Remember I told you I was going to be home a bit late tonight, Auntie?'

Mary glanced up from the cardigan she was knitting. 'Yeah, I remember, love. Look, are you in any trouble, Rose? Only you've been acting strange lately. You don't look too good neither.' Laying down her knitting she said gently, 'You know you can always talk to me, don't you, love? What I mean is, if there's anything troubling you, you would tell me, wouldn't you?'

'Yes, of course I would, Auntie.' Rose felt the strain of trying to smile. 'But there's nothing for you to worry about. I'm just feeling a bit down. You know, what with Jack and everything.'

Mary's mouth softened into an understanding smile. 'Ah, I thought it might be that. I said to Frankie it were probably that 'cos he's noticed you ain't been yourself lately, too. He don't miss much, don't Frankie.'

Gathering up her bag from the table Rose answered flatly, 'No, he doesn't, does he?'

As she went to leave, Mary hesitated then said awkwardly, 'Now, don't get angry, love, but I told Frankie you was working extra shifts, and he wasn't too pleased. I told him we don't need his help, even though we're grateful to know he's offered if we was to need it. But you know what he is. He's never liked you working in that pub, and I agree with him there. Rose, love, I've been thinking. Now, I ain't gonna say we can do without your wages, especially with me not being able to earn – though for all the extra time you've been putting in, you don't seem to have much to show for it. But that's beside the point. Like I said, I've been having a chat with Frankie, and now he's settled in his new house . . . Well, you don't have to worry about me being on me own so much. You could leave the pub and start looking for a decent job. You could even try and get your old job back. You was getting on well there, before you gave it up to take care of me. 'Cos, like Frankie said, we know where to find him now he's not wandering round all over London. So if I needed anything while you was at work, I could always go to Frankie's.'

Rose snapped her handbag shut. 'And how would you manage that, Auntie? Grantham Avenue is a good half-hour away by tram. And while the neighbours wouldn't mind coming to fetch me from the pub in an emergency, I doubt if they'd be happy to go all that way even if they could be sure of finding Frank in.' A sudden burst of impatience shot through her. 'Look, Auntie, I'm in a bit of a rush and I'll probably go straight to bed when I get in, so we'll have a chat tomorrow.'

Wounded by Rose's offhand manner, Mary turned back to her knitting, but not before Rose had seen the hurt in the pale blue eyes. Instantly contrite, Rose threw her arms around the fat neck and said softly, 'Lord, I've been a trial to you lately. But things will be different soon, Auntie, I promise. I've just got to get myself sorted out.'

Mary brightened. 'That's all right, love. I ain't always a bundle of fun meself, now, am I?'

Kissing the smooth cheek, Rose gave a small laugh. 'You said it, Auntie. Now, remember, don't wait up for me and I'll see you in the morning. 'Bye.'

She picked up a paper bag, which held her new working clothes, and glanced back at the placid figure, sitting so contentedly by the empty grate. She had a sudden wild urge to run back into the room, throw herself into Mary's ample lap and unburden herself. But she checked the impulse: she knew better than anyone else how swiftly her kindly aunt could change into a cruel, vicious harridan.

Pausing in the hallway she closed her eyes, terror draining every drop of energy from her. With an effort, she pulled herself together and made for the door. Then she looked back once again. This time, though, she didn't see the benevolent Mary seated quietly in her armchair, she was confronted by a bloated, drunken woman, her red face filled with rage, and heard again the savage, hateful words that had been flung at her that ill-fated night.

'Don't you come crying to me if you suddenly find yourself up the spout, 'cos I won't lift a finger to help you.'

'It'll be either your fancy man or the workhouse. And he might not hang around now he's got what he wanted.'

'. . . wouldn't the neighbours have a field day to see me pure, innocent Rose come waddling down the street with a bastard bulging in her stomach.'

'I won't have it, Rose . . . D'yer hear me? . . . I said . . . D'yer hear me . . . ?'

Rose's stomach churned but she lifted her chin, swallowed hard and left the small house quickly.

After Rose had gone Mary sat quietly, her thoughts returning to a conversation she'd had with Frankie a couple of days ago. He'd asked if she and Rose would like to move in with him. Oh, he'd joked about being lonely on his own, but Mary thought that was nearer to the truth than Frankie would admit. She hadn't mentioned it to Rose yet, because she wasn't sure how she herself felt about leaving her home. She had been prepared to move if Rose and Jack had found a place nearby, even though she hadn't been happy about sharing a house with Jack Adams. So, she had reasoned, if she had been willing to do that, why wouldn't she consider moving in with Frankie, a man she thought of and loved as if he was her own flesh and blood?

Because, as she had said when they went to see the place, she would feel like a fish out of water in that massive, posh house. She wasn't used to such luxury. Oh, Gawd! She didn't know what to do for the best. She'd have to wait until Rose was in a better frame of mind before she broached the subject, although Gawd only knew when that'd be.

Mary picked up her knitting once more, but her fingers remained idle.

'I never thought I'd live to see the day. Miss Goody Two Shoes, all dressed up like a tart just to rake in more money. I hope you'd jump in me grave as quick. I've only been off for a couple of weeks, stuck in me bed with a lousy cold, and you've already took me place, ain't you? You little two-faced bitch.'

Rose swept past the irate Sally to take an order from a young man who ogled her plunging neckline.

'I'm talking to you, you stuck-up cow.' Sally nudged Rose sharply in the side, which brought forth a cry of pain from her victim.

Rose had opened her mouth to fight back when she felt herself grabbed roughly from behind. Her head spun round and her eyes widened in shock at seeing Frankie, angrier than she'd ever seen him, glaring at her. 'So this is why you've been trying to stop me coming in for a drink. All that bollocks about wanting to be left alone for a while, I should've known something was going on. Well, you can get your things, right now. You ain't stopping here looking like that. You look like an old slag.'

Dumbfounded, Rose could only stare at him, her heart beginning to beat wildly. Tugging to release herself, she cried, 'Let go, Frank, it's nothing to do with you. Go away, I don't want you here.'

'Well, that's just too fucking bad, girl. 'Cos I'm here and I'm taking you home.'

The bar had fallen silent, all eyes and ears on the couple struggling across the bar.

Holding Rose's wrists in a vice-like grip, Frankie snarled at the publican, 'This is *your* doing, Dixon. I warned you what would happen if you took any liberties with her. I'll be back to deal with you later. As for you, you stupid little cow, get yourself from behind that bar and no fucking arguments. I ain't in the mood.'

Rose felt as if she was being suffocated. As well as the pain Frankie was inflicting on her wrists, she felt over-whelming humiliation and struggled even harder to free herself.

Then, an unexpected ally came to her rescue. Sally, her face troubled, stepped forward. ''Ere, come on, Frankie, let the girl go. She ain't doing any harm – just trying to earn a few extra bob like the rest of us. She—'

Frankie lifted his free arm and brought the back of his

hand down viciously across the barmaid's face, sending her
reeling back against the bottle-lined shelves.

A united gasp went up from the crowd, but none dared
interfere; not when Frankie Buchannon was involved.

Rose watched in horror as Sally crashed to the ground.
Then, all the pent-up anger, fear and frustration that had
been building for weeks were suddenly let loose. She
snatched up an empty bottle from the bar and waved
it in Frankie's face, screaming hysterically, 'You bastard!
There was no need for that. She was only trying to help me.
And take your hands off me, or I swear I'll brain you with
this. I mean it, Frankie. I've had enough of people telling
me what to do. *I've had enough.* Do you hear me, Frankie?
I've had enough, *I can't take any more.*'

Slowly Frankie released her, the anger dying from his
face. Looking behind Rose to where Sally was stumbling
to her feet, and then to the strained face of Henry Dixon,
he snarled, 'You ain't heard the last of this, Dixon.' Then
he was gone, leaving a trail of destruction in his wake. In
the hushed bar, Henry Dixon shook himself into action. He
was badly shaken, but he'd never admit it. In his position
to show any sign of weakness would be fatal. He'd stood
up to Buchannon, and others like him, for years. He wasn't
going to start crumbling now. He cast a scornful eye over
the crowded bar as he roared, 'What's the matter with you
lot? Seen enough, have you? Well, the show's over so you
can all stop gawping and get on with what you were doing.
And you, Bill,' he shouted down the bar, to where the frail
potman was attempting to comfort the weeping Rose, 'get
your arse down here and sweep up these bleeding glasses
before I fall over 'em and cut me throat.'

The white-haired old man gave Rose an awkward pat on
the arm and shambled off to do as he was bidden.

Dixon poured himself a large whisky. Both of his barmaids looked as if they were about to keel over. His eyes
swept over Rose and a sense of outrage filled him at the
thought of the way in which Frankie had treated her. Poor
little cow. Something was bothering her – else she wouldn't
have offered to pull in the punters by showing her wares.

Frankie's parting words reverberated in his mind, and he

poured himself another drink. He must have been mad to
take Rose up on her offer: he'd known there would be hell to
pay once Frankie found out. But this was his livelihood, this
pub. It was up to him to decide who served behind the bar,
not Frankie Buchannon or anyone else. Besides, once Rose
had made the offer, what could he have done? Admit he was
afraid of upsetting Frankie and turn her down? Never!

The whisky had settled in his bloodstream, giving him
courage and helping to blot out the threat hanging over
him. He strode down the bar, replenished his glass and
poured one extra which he held out to Sally. ''Ere, you
look like you could do with it. What about you, Rosie,
love? D'yer want me to pour you one an' all?'

Weakly, Rose shook her head. She was trembling all
over and felt as if she was going to be sick. In all her
life she had never seen Frankie behave like that – and
the language he'd used! She shivered, hugging herself for
comfort. He had been like a stranger and it had frightened
her badly. If he could behave like that at seeing her in a
low-cut blouse, what would he do if he found out she
was pregnant? Dear God! It didn't bear thinking about.
She had to get out of here and do what she'd planned.
Rose clenched her sweating palms and appealed to Henry,
'Can – can I leave early, Mr Dixon? My shift's nearly over
and . . .'

Fortified by the amber spirit, Dixon nodded, his voice
strong and decisive for the benefit of his customers. 'Yeah,
you get off, Rosie. Me and Sally will manage till Reet gets
in, won't we, Sal?'

Rose looked at the woman who had always had it in for
her, bewildered at why she should risk Frankie's wrath for
someone she didn't like.

Sally's face still bore the imprint of Frankie's hand, but
she shrugged indifferently. 'Yeah, I suppose so.'

Mumbling her thanks, Rose went into the back to get her
bag, her legs wobbly. On her way out she stopped by Sally
and said shyly, 'Thanks, Sally. It was good of you to try to
help me like that. I'm very grateful, and I'm truly sorry for
what Frank did to you. I feel ashamed for having brought
it on you. I'm sorry.'

Embarrassed by the fulsome speech, Sally muttered self-consciously, 'Yeah, well, I'd've done the same for any woman 'cos no other bugger will.'

Rose gave a tremulous smile, understanding the other woman's brusqueness. Just because Sally had tried to help her didn't mean that they had suddenly become good friends. The bickering would probably start all over again, once this episode was forgotten, but she was grateful, and she wouldn't forget how Sally had put herself at risk to help her while others had stood by and done nothing. She checked the clock over the bar: her appointment with the doctor Rita had found was in an hour's time.

A rush of bile rose in her throat, sending her stomach into a lurching wave of renewed fear. But there was no turning back now. Any idea she might have had about changing her mind had been washed out by Frankie's murderous rage.

Head held high, Rose passed the curious men and women who had witnessed the altercation between herself and the proclaimed Lord of the Manor, and let herself out of the pub.

It was a lovely August evening. Warm, clear and sunny. An evening when it felt good to be alive. And she was on her way to murder her unborn child.

Trying to calm the nervous fluttering in her stomach she walked grimly away from the pub. With each step she took she murmured to herself, 'I'm sorry, I'm so sorry, but I don't have any choice. I'm sorry, little one. You're never going to see the beauty of this world, nor the cruelty and pain. I'm sorry, love . . . Please, please forgive me . . . please . . .'

CHAPTER FOURTEEN

When Rose arrived at the address Rita had given her, instead of going straight in, as she had planned, she hurried by, her head hanging low as if her intention was clear to everyone who saw her. She was in turmoil as she tried to drag up the courage to return to the innocuous-looking end-of-terrace house on the corner of Graham Road. Now that the time had arrived, she wasn't sure she could go through with it. Wandering aimlessly, Rose tried again to think of other ways out of her predicament, but there were none.

'Come on, girl. Don't lose your nerve now. This time tomorrow it'll all be over and then you can get on with your life,' she said to herself, as if she were talking to another person. 'Just take a deep breath and get on with it. The longer you hang around out here, the harder it's going to be.'

She turned round and retraced her steps. As she drew nearer to the house, a steel curtain seemed to drop over her eyes, blocking out all further thoughts. Then she was knocking on the green-painted door and being ushered inside by an elderly, nervous-looking woman, who glanced quickly up and down the road as if making sure no one was watching. She showed Rose into a shabby but clean parlour, talking all the while. 'Now don't you worry about nothing, darlin'. You're in safe hands here. Me husband's a doctor, so he knows what he's doing.'

Rose stared numbly at the sparrow-like woman, who was now looking at her impatiently. 'Well, come along, dear. Haven't you got something to give me?' As Rose continued to stare blankly, the woman added, 'The money, dear. You *have* brought the money, I hope? Only my husband takes a great risk helping you young girls out of trouble and he can't afford to do it for nothing.'

Rose fumbled at the clasp of her handbag and her nerveless fingers extracted the agreed sum. On seeing the folded notes, the woman became more amenable, clucking over Rose as if she were a dear family friend. The money disappeared into the palm of one hand, and with the other she steered the silent girl into another room off the parlour, talking cheerfully as if Rose had just popped in for tea. 'This is me husband's surgery. You just slip your things off, love, and I'll get you ready. There's no need to look so frightened, dear. He knows what he's doing. Not like some of these back-street butchers you could've ended up with.' As she talked, she was deftly helping Rose take off her skirt and undergarments. Rose let herself be led to a long, high leather couch, too traumatised to offer any resistance, wanting only to have the whole sordid business over and done with.

The room reeked of disinfectant and bleaching agents, but it was the trolley, bearing a row of unfamiliar and wicked-looking instruments, that struck fresh terror into Rose's heart. Closing her eyes she lay back, trying to erase the sight from her mind. 'Will . . . will he give me something to knock me out? I . . . I don't want to be awake while he . . . he . . . Oh, dear . . . I'm sor – sorry.'

'Now don't you worry your pretty little head about nothing, love.' The woman darted around Rose, making motherly sounds. 'You'll get the same sort of treatment here as you'd get in any fancy hospital. You wait and see . . . Oh, here he is.' A large, shambling man had entered the tiny room. Rose felt a rush of air as he whipped the bleached sheet unceremoniously off her quivering body. Then rough hands were forcing her legs apart and she felt cold steel touch the inside of her thigh. With a startled gasp she tried to sit up but was roughly pushed down again.

'Now, now, we'll have none of that, dear. Me husband ain't got all day. So the sooner we get this dealt with the better for all of us.'

Rose looked wildly at the bearded man looming over her. A strong odour of whisky wafted over her face and she retched. Hitting out blindly at the hands prising her legs apart, she tried to sit up again. 'Bleeding hell! What you playing at, girl?' The woman was breathing heavily as she tried to stop Rose from clamping her legs together. 'If you'd kept your legs shut in the first place, you wouldn't be here now. Look, the doctor's gonna give you something to make you sleep. When you wake up it'll all be over. Come on, girl, breathe deeply, that's it . . .'

Rose felt a damp cloth being pressed over her nose and mouth, and her struggles became fainter. A great darkness descended and behind her eyelids tiny red spots danced erratically. Yet the chloroform didn't work quickly enough. Rose went into shock as a razor-sharp pain ripped through her body, tearing her insides apart, and she felt a sudden rush of warmth between her legs. Then the bird-like woman started screaming – the shrill sounds of panic becoming fainter and fainter until they faded away completely.

'You expecting someone, Rita? Only that's the fourth time you've looked at the clock in the last five minutes.'

The dark-haired barmaid jumped guiltily as her companion, a livid dark bruise already forming down the left side of her face, eyed her quizzically. 'No, no, I ain't expecting anyone.'

Sally remained unconvinced. Sidling up to her workmate she nudged Rita and winked. 'Go on, tell us. Who's the lucky feller, then? Is it someone you've met in here?'

Rita turned away irritably. 'I ain't waiting for anybody, Sal. I was just seeing what time it was, that's all.'

Sally shrugged. 'Please yourself, Reet, It ain't no skin off my nose – oy, watch what you're doing, mate. You nearly had me fingers off then. What's up with you tonight?'

Sally pulled her hand away quickly from the cash drawer and looked at her friend in annoyance. 'I'll be glad to get home tonight. First I get clobbered for trying to help out Rose, an' now you try and chop me bleeding hand off.'

'I said sorry, didn't I? Don't go on at me, Sal. I ain't in the mood for your larking about tonight.'

A frown knotted Sally's forehead. In all the years she'd worked with Rita, she'd never known her friend to be offhand or touchy. She was normally a laugh a minute, was Rita. Shoving a pint of beer across the counter to a waiting customer, Sally moved to where Henry Dixon was chatting to some of his regulars. ''Ere, d'yer know what's up with Rita, Henry? She's been like a cat on hot bricks since she came in.'

Dixon broke off his conversation to glare at his senior barmaid. 'How the bleeding hell should I know what's wrong with her? Why don't you ask if you're so worried? It ain't – Aw, shit! What the bleeding hell's she done now?' he roared as the sound of breaking glass rang out for the second time that day.

Quickly Sally diverted her governor's attention. 'It's all right, Henry. I'll see to it. You carry on having a natter.'

She moved swiftly to where Rita was crouching on the floor over a smashed glass and hissed, 'Look, Reet, are you gonna tell me what's wrong or not? I might be able to help if you'll let me know what's up.'

Rita's eyes were shimmering. 'It's Rosie, Sal. I should never have let her go on her own but she said she wanted it that way. Oh, Sal . . . if anything happens to her, I'll never forgive meself.'

Sally's eyes narrowed as a glimmer of suspicion sprang to her mind. She grabbed Rita's arm and said roughly, 'What you talking about, Reet? Where's Rose gone? An' what's it got to do with you?'

When Rita didn't reply, Sally let out a loud exclamation of fury. 'She's gone to get rid of the baby, ain't she? The stupid little bitch. And you helped her, didn't you? Well, *didn't you?*'

A small group of men were clamouring for service, and without stopping her tirade Sally deftly pulled the pints, slopping the contents over the counter, and took the money from outstretched hands.

Beside her, Rita moaned softly and moved over to the doorway behind the bar. 'Don't you go at me, Sal. I was only trying to help the poor little cow. I did me best to talk her out of it, but she wasn't having any of it. If I hadn't found her someone, she might have ended up with some old witch and a pair of knitting needles.'

'Yeah, yeah, all right, Reet.' Sally stood still for a minute, lost in thought, then asked, 'Where's she gone, then?'

Rita looked round to make sure no one was listening, then whispered, 'Old Dr Lewis, you know. The one in Graham Road, opposite the Hackney Infirmary.'

Sally let out a mirthless laugh. 'That's a bit of luck then, ain't it? If anything goes wrong, she won't have far to crawl for help.'

Sally's thoughts raced as she deliberated whether or not to ignore the piece of news that Rita had dropped in her lap. Ten minutes passed, then, uttering an angry oath directed at herself, Sally marched up to Dixon and declared, 'I'm off, Henry. Something important's come up. You can dock me wages later.'

Dixon choked on his drink and spluttered, 'Oh, no you don't, madam. I've had enough of you women pissing me about for one day. Now, get yourself back serving or don't bother coming back at all.'

Sally laughed harshly. 'All right, Henry. You know you can't replace *me*. Don't worry, I'll make it up to you.'

As she pulled up the bar flap to leave, Rita caught at her dress, demanding, 'Why are you so bothered about what happens to Rose all of a sudden? You can't stand the sight of her, so why should you care if she's in trouble?'

Sally shook her off. 'I don't! But if anything happens to her, who d'yer think Frankie's gonna blame? Eh?'

As Rita blanched, Sally added, 'Anyway, she's only a kid. Look, I'll come back later and tell you what happened.' Then she was gone, leaving Rita to fret alone.

CHAPTER FIFTEEN

When Sally arrived outside the address Rita had given her, she was wondering if she was doing the right thing by interfering. After all, if Rose had made up her mind to get rid of the kid, who was she to stick her nose in? Besides, it would all be over by now. Rose's appointment had been for six o 'clock and it was gone seven now. People like the ones who lived behind this door didn't hang about: they did what was asked of them, took their money and got rid of the unfortunate woman. Some of the better ones, and there were a few, let their clients rest for a few hours afterwards, but most bundled them straight out of the door.

For Gawd's sake, woman, Sally urged herself, if you're gonna knock then get on with it. She rapped on the peeling front door, waited a few minutes, then knocked harder. The house remained quiet. Puzzled, Sally chewed her bottom lip while she thought what to do next. It was obvious no one was in – or if they were, they weren't going to answer. Still she hesitated. There was something not right here. The house seemed too quiet, unnaturally so. It had the air of desertion.

Oh, stop it, she chastened herself. A house was a house. Maybe she'd got the wrong address – Rita wasn't the brightest woman Sally had ever met. Even so . . . Bending down Sally lifted the flap of the letterbox and peered through it. The tiny hall was empty, the two doors leading off it closed. Feeling rather silly she called, 'Hello! Hello?

Is anyone in?' There was no reply. She hadn't really been expecting one: if she'd had any sense she would have tried Rose's house first. After all, she lived just ten minutes' walk from the pub. Instead, though, she'd walked all this way on what now seemed to have been a fool's errand. She straightened up and shrugged. Well, she'd tried. There wasn't much more she could do here. Rose was probably tucked up at home with some aspirins and a hot-water bottle, while she, Sally, had wasted time and lost a couple of hours' wages into the bargain.

'They ain't in, you know. Did a flit about half an hour ago. Saw them meself, him and his wife, charging out of there like the place was on fire.'

Suddenly apprehensive, Sally walked to where a scruffy-looking woman was standing on her doorstep.

'You sure they was doing a runner? I mean, they might have just been in a hurry to get somewhere.'

The woman laughed unpleasantly.

'I know a flit when I see one. Loaded up a barrer they kept out the back and took off. Bloody good riddance an' all. Why?' she asked. 'What's it to do with you anyway? They friends of yours, were they? I ain't never seen you round these parts before. Or was you looking for a bit of help in getting rid of something? If you know what I mean.'

Sally's face was grim. 'Yeah, I know what you mean, but that's not what I'm here for.' She looked up and down the street warily. A few children were playing in the road outside open doorways, and now and then a voice could be heard raised in anger. A typical London back-street, nothing sinister here.

She needed to know if Rose had been here – but could she trust this skinny woman, who was watching her with shrewd, sharp eyes?

Sally moved closer. 'Look, a mate of mine was suppose to come here this evening. Well . . . she ain't exactly a mate, just someone I work with. But she's only a kid, and I was worried about her, so I thought I'd make sure she was all right – know what I mean?'

The neighbour replied, with a loud snort, 'Oh, yeah, I

know what you mean, all right, and I don't hold with it. But I mind me own business and—'

Impatiently Sally cut in, 'Yeah, I'm sure you do, love. But did you see me mate come here? About an hour ago, it would have been. You couldn't miss her. She's young with a load of bright browny-red hair, all curls and—'

'I saw her. That is, I saw her go in as I was nipping round to see me mum. I didn't see her come out again.'

At the growing alarm in Sally's face, the woman softened. 'Look, you can cut through my back yard into theirs, if that's any help.'

'Oh, yeah, thanks, love,' Sally answered gratefully.

Five minutes later, she was standing outside a grimy back window, her face pressed tight against the cool pane. Then she reeled back in horror. *'Oh, my Gawd!'* she breathed. She couldn't see any sign of Rose, but she could see the blood. It was everywhere. Up the walls, over the floor – everywhere.

Frantically, now, Sally hammered on the back door, which immediately fell open almost sending her flying into the damp scullery. 'Rose, Rosie, where are you? You silly little cow! Where are – Oooh . . . Rosie, oh, Gawd help us.'

There, lying in a bloodied heap by a closed door, lay the young woman Sally had come to find. Heedless of the gore surrounding the inert body Sally dropped to her knees, her hands shaking. Rose's face was as white as fresh-fallen snow.

Behind her Sally heard someone come into the room. 'Oh, shit! Is she dead? Oh, Gawd, I'm not staying here.' The neighbour woman backed fearfully away from the awful sight, then screamed for her husband. 'Quick, Bert, get the police. There's been murder done next door! Hurry up, you lazy sod. Get your arse round to the nick, and fetch 'em back here sharpish!'

Sally remained kneeling by Rose's side, and surveyed the carnage surrounding her. It was all coming back. All those memories she'd tried to bury. All the heartache, the pain, the indescribable sense of loss. Like an avenging angel of doom, the walls of the small, bloody room closed in on her as she found herself transported back down the years to a time she had hoped never to face again. Sally felt her eyes dim as shadows from the past continued to assault her. Ten years ago, it had been. Ten years of silent suffering, of wondering . . .

The commotion next door was getting louder as the frightened neighbour continued to berate the reluctant Bert to fetch the police. Galvanised into action by the din, Sally relinquished her hold on Rose's limp hand and raced from the room, her feet slipping in a pool of blood. She burst into next door's parlour. 'Hang on! Don't go getting the law involved – she ain't dead. Look, you don't want the coppers sniffing around here, d'yer? Besides, by the time they get here, the poor little cow probably *will* be dead. Look, you've got to help me!' The man before her was dishevelled and bleary-eyed, had obviously just woken up. She begged him, 'Please, could you help me get me mate over to the infirmary. She's in a bad way. We've got to get her to a doctor, she—'

The woman pushed Sally away roughly. 'He ain't going nowhere except to fetch the coppers. I feel sorry for the poor cow, but she ain't nothing to do with us. We—'

Desperate now, Sally cried, 'You can't just leave her lying there! 'Cos I'll tell you this much for nothing. If she pegs out, it won't be the coppers you'll have to worry about. That girl in there is a relation of Frankie Buchannon's, and if she dies, he's gonna be round here wanting to know why no one did anything to help her. And I wouldn't like to be in your shoes then.'

Breathing raggedly Sally waited – but not for long. At the mention of Frankie's name a change came over the couple. Sally saw the fear in their faces. But, uncertain that she was telling the truth, the man blustered, 'Frankie Buchannon ain't got no relations. Everyone round these parts knows that . . . Well, only that old girl what helped bring him up.'

'Well, that's where you're wrong,' Sally shouted. 'That girl in there's his niece,' she lied. She didn't have time to explain Rose's relationship to Frankie and every minute that passed brought Rose closer to death. She must have been convincing, though, because the man's expression

changed suddenly to one of eager determination. He pushed
aside his fretful wife and said, 'Shut your gob, Bessie, and
leave this to me,' squared his shoulders and nodded at the
hovering Sally. 'Righto, miss. I'll carry her to the infirmary.
You just lead the way. We wouldn't want anything to
happen to Mr Buchannon's niece, would we?'

But his resolve faltered when he saw the bloody form
lying in next door's parlour. He would have turned tail
and run if Frankie's name hadn't been mentioned – but
it had and it had instilled in Bert a powerful incentive
to push aside his misgivings and set to work. Averting
his eyes from the splattered walls, he gently lifted the
blood-soaked body, cradling it to his muscular chest. As
easily as if his burden was a child, he carried Rose from
the house, followed anxiously by Sally.

News of the unfolding drama had quickly spread around
the street, and when the trio stepped outside the front door
they were met with a dozen curious pairs of eyes and many
questions. Sally ignored them all, leaving the explanations
to Bessie, who was now recovering from her fright and
relishing her new-found importance.

The odd trio made their way up Graham Road and into
Homerton high street, attracting the attention of all they
met. Fortunately, none of the passers-by were in uniform.

When Rose was handed over to the medical staff at the
infirmary, Sally mumbled her thanks to the man who had
helped her and numbly followed the stretcher down a long,
grey corridor.

Behind her the burly man watched the corpse-like form
disappear from view. He had done all he could and felt
pleased with himself. There was no need to fear any repris-
als from Frankie Buchannon for he, Bert Young, had done
his best to help the unfortunate young woman. If she
survived, maybe Frankie would come to thank him. The
thought brought him a tremor of delight. Glad to be out of
the grim building, Bert Young returned home – his good
deed done, hopefully to be recognised and appreciated
some time in the future.

It was several hours later before Sally was allowed in to

see Rose. When she entered the ward and saw the still shape beneath crisp white starched sheets, her skin almost blending into them, a wealth of emotion engulfed her. She felt so tired, both physically and mentally. If there had been an empty bed in the ward she might have been tempted to climb into it, but she still had one more task to complete before she could go home. And that task filled her with more dread than the rest of the day's events.

She hadn't expected Rose to be awake, and was surprised to find her so. Sally hauled out a small bench from under the bed and eased herself down on to it.

Rose stared at her with glazed eyes, her lips trying to form questions, but she hadn't enough strength.

'It's all right, mate,' Sally said kindly, 'Don't worry about anything. I just wanted to make sure you was all right before I got off home.'

Through parched lips, Rose whispered painfully, 'Why did you come?'

Sally looked into her eyes and answered tiredly, 'It's a long story, Rosie. Let's just say I went through the same thing once. Only I had to do it on me own. It was a long time ago, but it's not something you ever forget. Besides . . .' she lifted her shoulders in resignation '. . . someone had to make sure you was all right. I'd have done the same for anybody.'

Rose closed her eyes and Sally, thinking she had fallen asleep, was about to leave when Rose's voice, barely aud-ible, halted her once more. 'Thanks, Sally. It was kind of you . . . That's twice you've helped me today. Sally . . .' Rose tried to moisten her dry lips, but the effort was too great. She was so tired. All she really wanted to do was sleep. Sleep for a very long time and wake up to find it had all been a terrible nightmare. But there was one more favour she had to ask of Sally. 'Will you . . . go to see my aunt, please? Just tell . . . her I'm all right . . . and . . . I'll be home tomorrow. Don't let her know what's happened, Sally . . . I don't want her to know . . . Please, Sal . . .'

Sally squirmed on the hard bench. 'Yeah, it's all right, mate. Look, you get some rest. I'll make up some story to tell your aunt. Don't worry, I'll see to everything, you just get some kip.'

Rose fought valiantly to remain conscious. There was something else she had to say, something important. She summoned all of her rapidly dwindling strength and murmured fretfully, 'Get Frank for me, Sally. I want Frank here. I need him. He'll take care of everything. Tell Frank, Sally, tell Frank I need him . . .'

Awkwardly patting the cold hand lying outside the sheet, Sally nodded wearily, 'I was gonna get him anyway, Rosie,' but Rose had fallen back into a drugged sleep.

Feeling like an old woman, Sally left the ward, avoiding any official figure who might start asking questions.

Once outside the grim walls she took lungfuls of the crisp night air, trying to clear her nostrils of the sickly hospital smells. Sighting a cab she hailed it. It was a luxury she seldom availed herself of, but at the moment she felt she deserved a little pampering.

Resting her head against the upholstered seat, Sally rehearsed what she was going to say to Frankie.

CHAPTER SIXTEEN

As she did not know her former lover's new address, Sally ordered the cabby to take her to the Red Lion. On the short journey, she tried to order her thoughts. First of all, she'd have a couple of drinks to fortify herself, then go round to Mary Miller's and spin some kind of story to stop the old girl worrying when Rose didn't come home tonight. While she was there, she would try and wangle Frankie's address out of her – though from what she'd heard of Mary Miller, she wasn't going to be easy to hoodwink. Sally knew that if her plan failed, she'd have no choice but to tell the truth and let Mary sort things out with Frankie. Maybe, even, that would be the best for everyone concerned. She'd done her good deed for the day and now it was up to Rose's family to see her safely through her ordeal.

As the cab came to a halt outside the pub, a loud, rough voice told the driver to wait. Sally recognised Frankie's voice and her stomach lurched at the prospect of facing him with the news about Rose. Sally paid the driver and stepped onto the pavement, then turned to face the tall, dark-haired man coming towards her.

'Business must be good these days, Sally. I'd have thought you'd have had to drop your prices by now – after all, you're getting on a bit, ain't you?' Frankie loomed over her, his lips curved in a sneering grin. The two men with him laughed at their governor's malicious jibe.

The callous words, along with his look of distaste, brought

Sally's head up with a painful jerk. *'You bastard,'* she spat, tears of frustration stinging the backs of her eyes. After all she'd been through, these last few hours, his unjustified vituperative attack was the final straw.

Frank laughed nastily as he shouldered her out of his way. 'You should know better by now than to get on the wrong side of me, Sal, but I'll let it go this time. I've got more important things to think about than a slag like you.'

Sally's eyes were cold and bleak. 'Like your precious Rose, I suppose.'

Frankie paused, one foot on the cab's step, and looked at her contemptuously. 'Yeah, my Rose. She's worth a thousand of your sort, and you tried to drag her down to the gutter with you. Did she borrow those clothes off of you, Sal? They looked like the type you'd wear. A tart's clothes. Well, I've been back to sort Henry out and now I'm telling you. Rose won't be back, she—'

Quivering with fatigue and anger Sally shouted, 'You don't own her, Frankie, and she ain't the sort to be ordered about – and she ain't as innocent as you'd like to think neither.'

Frankie's lips tightened into a grim line. 'Don't push your luck with me, Sal, I'm warning you. And don't judge every woman by your own cheap standards. The only reason Rose got herself tarted up was to earn a few extra bob, 'cos she was too proud to ask me for help. But she won't be doing it again. Now get out of me way or else . . .'

Her eyes glittering dangerously, Sally moved a step nearer, then, her voice low, her words deliberate, she said slowly, 'And d'yer know why she needed a few extra bob, Frankie? Well, I'll give you a clue, shall I? It was the same reason I had to start showing me wares to get some money quickly. I didn't have any other choice at the time, d'yer remember? The only difference between me and Rosie is, I wasn't too proud to ask you for help, but you didn't want to know.'

Frankie stared down at her unblinking, awareness growing on his set face.

Sally uttered a shrill cry of triumph. 'You remembering now, Frankie? All coming back to you, is it? I was barely a kid meself at the time, but you always did like 'em young, didn't you? Oh, you were so charming, so full of yourself, and I fell for the oldest line in the book, didn't I? You was gonna take care of me, weren't you, Frankie? Gonna show me the world, you said. But all I ever saw was the inside of a back room where some old quack tore me insides out and left me to bleed to death. And I would've an' all, if some busybody in the street hadn't called the coppers.'

All the time she was talking, Frankie's handsome face might have been carved out of stone for all the emotion he showed. But Sally knew that her words were hitting home, knew without doubt that he had understood where they were leading, and the knowledge that she was hurting him spurred her on. Ignoring the danger in which she was placing herself, she continued to taunt him, out of control now. 'The penny dropped yet, Frankie? Well, I'll spell it out for you, shall I, Mr Lord of the bleeding Manor? Your precious Rosie went and got herself knocked up. But that ain't all we've got in common, 'cos her bastard of a bloke ran out on her the same as mine did. So how d'yer like that for poetic justice? Oh, I picked that bit of talk up from Rosie. Posh, ain't it? She was always one to talk posh, was our Rosie—'

Her words ceased as an iron hand closed around her neck. She could smell whisky on Frankie's breath as he hissed viciously, 'Shut your lying, stinking mouth, you little whore, or I swear I'll shut it for you permanently.'

'Guv! Guv! Give over, there's people watching,' Fred Green pulled at the furious man's arm. 'Come on, Guv, you can't believe anything she says. She's just trying to wind you up. Leave her go, Guv, she ain't worth getting nicked for.'

Slowly Frankie released her, his eyes murderous. He flung Sally away from him and stepped back, his fists hanging by his sides.

All her bravado gone, Sally clutched at her bruised throat, her breath coming in short, painful bursts. Knowing she had gone too far, she was seized by an urgent desire to run, to get away from the grim figure glaring down at her with loathing. But she had promised Rose she would get Frankie to her, and whatever else she did or didn't do, she always kept her word. She swallowed painfully and croaked, 'I'm telling the truth. I didn't know what she was up to, I'd be the last person she'd tell. But when I found out, I went looking for her. And it's a good job I did, 'cos the bloke she went to was as bad as the one I had. If I hadn't of turned up when I did . . . Look, Frankie. This ain't got nothing to do with me. I've done my bit. But she asked me to get you, and I have. She's in the Hackney Infirmary, and she's bad, Frankie, she's really bad. I don't know if she's gonna make it. All she kept saying was to get you and to tell her aunt she wouldn't be home tonight.' A dry sob caught in Sally's throat, and she cried bleakly, 'Won't be home tonight. Gawd Almighty! She'll be lucky if she ever comes home!'

She felt herself sway, but no hand came out to steady her. When her head cleared she was on her own. Sobbing quietly Sally trudged to the pub. She needed a drink. But when she tried to push open the doors they remained shut. Puzzled, she pushed harder.

Then Frankie's words came back to her. *'I've sorted Henry out.'* A new wave of fear swept through her fevered brain. Hammering on the heavy doors she screamed wildly, *'Henry . . . Henry, open the door! It's me, Sal! You all right in there? Henry! . . . Reet! You there, Reet? Henry . . . Henry . . . !'*

It was nearly three in the morning before Rose became fully conscious. When she turned her head to one side, there, slumped in an old wicker bath-chair, sat Frankie, his normally immaculate appearance rumpled, his perfectly groomed black hair sticking up on end. She kept still, her face buried in a pillow. Her eyes filled with tears as the memory of why she was here came flooding back.

She had killed her baby – Jack's baby – and no matter how many times in the future she told herself it had been for the best, she knew she would never forgive herself for what she had done. Maybe she should have died, too. It would have been fitting if the murderer had in turn been murdered.

She made no sound, yet somehow Frankie became aware that she was awake. He leaned forward, caught hold of one hand lying on top of the blanket and raised it to his lips.

'Hello, Princess. Welcome back to the land of the living. You
had me worried for a while. The doctors told me you might
peg out, but I told 'em, not my Rose.' He gazed down at her,
his dark eyes soft with love. 'Now, then, you've got to rest.
Here, look . . . I've had you moved to a private room. That
other place they had you in was like a bleeding morgue.'

'Frankie . . .' Stretching out a slender hand she mumbled,
'Drink, Frank . . . please . . . Get me some water.'

Frankie rose stiffly from the confines of the wicker chair,
fetched a small tumbler of water and held it to Rose's
cracked lips. When she had taken a few eager sips, he laid
her head tenderly back on the pillow. And when she gave
a weak smile he had to fight down a fierce urge to gather
her up into his arms for safe keeping.

Instead his hand reached out to the mass of damp,
tumbling curls that had fallen over the pale, beautiful face.
'You try and get some rest, Princess. The doctor said you
need plenty of sleep.'

A look of alarm crossed Rose's face. She grabbed at
Frankie's hand and wailed, 'Don't go, Frank. Don't leave
me here alone. I'm scared, Frank . . . I'm so very scared.'

'I ain't going anywhere, Princess. I'll be here when you
wake up, I promise. Go back to sleep, Rosie love, go back
to sleep.'

Rose's eyelids fluttered then gradually closed and her
breathing became even as she let herself drift off.

Frankie remained sitting on the edge of the hard bed until
he was sure she wouldn't wake, then gingerly eased himself
up, ready to return immediately if she should stir. But the
recumbent form was deep in the arms of Morpheus.

Crossing to a large window he stared out into the dark
night, his tired mind in a whirl as he tried to find a way
to make things right for Rose – and Mary. Mary, who had
been told that her beloved niece had been involved in a road
accident and who was now probably nearly out of her mind
with worry. Yet how much worse it would have been to tell
her the truth.

For now, Rose's secret was safe as far as her aunt was
concerned, but what of later? If that damned excuse for a
doctor had done his work properly, there wouldn't be any

need for further lies but the bastard had botched the job from start to finish. Frank ground his teeth.

If it hadn't been for Sally, Rose would probably still be lying in her own blood in a back-street room, unable to summon help. She had been left to die like a wounded animal caught in a trap. A surge of white-hot fury raced through Frankie. When he caught up with the man responsible, he would kill him. The man had hurt Rose, nearly killed her, and for that he would have to pay. A soft light from the corridor reflected Frankie's face in the window. A face drawn with anguish as he contemplated how near he had come to losing his Rose. Behind him, Frankie could see the outline of Rose's still body under a hospital blanket. It was a good job Sally had gone after her. Frankie's brows knitted in bewilderment. He still couldn't understand why Sally, of all people, had put herself out like that. It didn't make any sense – but then nothing did at the moment.

At first, Frankie had been filled with rage against Jack Adams. If the policeman had shown his face a couple of hours ago, he would surely have done for him. But he'd had time to think more rationally since then, and the truth was that, in spite of his animosity towards Jack Adams, Frankie knew that he would never have left Rose if he'd known she was pregnant. In a strange way Frankie had nurtured a sneaking admiration for the young copper. He wasn't a man to be intimidated, and the Lord knew, Frankie had tried, yet each time Adams had come back at him, matching word for word, insult for insult. If it had come to it, Adams wouldn't have hesitated to exchange blows, even with a man renowned throughout the East End for his prowess in street fighting. No. Jack Adams wasn't the sort of man to run out on a woman when she needed him. So for some reason Rose had kept her condition to herself. Why, Frankie wasn't sure. Maybe, just maybe, she had realised she didn't love Adams enough to spend the rest of her life with him, but Frankie didn't think that was right. He had seen the two of them together – and the love that had emanated from them. He sighed heavily and pressed his forehead against the cool pane of glass. He didn't hear anyone enter the small, dimly lit room, so when the soft voice cut into the silence he jumped. He spun round to face the intruder.

'Mr Buchannon!' A man in a black frock coat came towards him, his hand outstretched. 'My name's Dr Maitland. I was called in to help assist with your niece's case. We met briefly when I first arrived.'

Confused and disorientated by lack of sleep and anxiety Frank grasped the hand. 'I remember, Doctor.'

The doctor studied the man in front of him with interest. So this was the legendary Frankie Buchannon. Labelled a common criminal by some, he apparently had the power to order a high-ranking official from the medical governing body to summon one of the top doctors in London to save the life of a young woman who had placed herself in the hands of an abortionist – a crime in itself, and one that carried a severe penalty.

Thomas Maitland, a renowned obstetrician, surveyed the handsome, enigmatic figure, who had been instrumental in ensuring his presence here at one o'clock this morning, where he had found the young woman in question close to death. For the past two hours he had battled to save both the young mother and her unborn child, while Buchannon had paced the corridors of the infirmary like a caged animal.

Thomas Maitland was an experienced judge of human nature and he could see that here was a man who had been to the brink of despair and back. The cause of that despair was lying in the narrow bed behind them. The doctor walked over and looked down at his sleeping patient. 'Has she woken since you've been here?'

Frankie rubbed his face, trying to think straight. 'Yes. About half an hour ago. I gave her a drop of water – she was thirsty.'

The grey-haired man nodded. 'My colleague, Dr Ramsey, tells me you've been kept up to date with what's happening. Have you told your niece the news?' Now he was looking directly into the dark brown eyes, and Frankie, summoning inner resources to ward off his increasing fatigue, answered flatly, 'No, I didn't think she was ready to hear it.'

Lifting the limp wrist, the doctor felt for a pulse and monitored it without the aid of a watch. 'That, of course, is

your prerogative, Mr Buchannon. Though in my experience
it is sometimes better to impart unpleasant news as quickly
as possible. However, I must say, informing a woman that
her unborn child is still safe in the womb wouldn't be my
notion of bad news. But, then, my job is to save lives, not
destroy them.'

A flicker of anger banished Frankie's exhaustion. Meeting
the doctor's disapproving eye, he said, coldly, 'And it ain't
your job to make judgements without knowing all the facts.
People do terrible things sometimes out of sheer terror or
panic. My Rose has never hurt a soul in her life, so you
can wipe that sanctimonious look off your face. If you don't
think she's good enough for your attention, then I'll find
another doctor to look after her. Someone with a bit more
understanding.'

The elderly man stood his ground. 'Please forgive my
harsh statement, Mr Buchannon. You're absolutely right,
of course. But, like you, I am desperately in need of sleep.
I'm not seeking to excuse myself when I say that we are
all mortal and prone to human error. Please accept my
apologies.'

Now Frank looked more closely and saw the red-grained
eyes and tired lines in the other man's face. 'Yeah, all right,
Doc. It's been a bad night all round, ain't it?'

The hostility eased and the doctor inclined his head
towards the bed. 'Is there no chance the young man in
question will stand by your niece?'

Frankie followed the doctor's gaze. 'It's not quite as
simple as that, Doctor.'

'Very well. You will know the circumstances better than
I. Still, it would have made things much simpler if there
had been a father standing by. She's going to need an eye
kept on her over the remaining months, especially to make
sure she doesn't make another attempt. She was lucky to
have survived such an ordeal. Most women wouldn't have
been so fortunate.' He shot a look at Frankie. 'Has the nature
of your niece's condition been explained fully to you?' He
noted the fraught expression that crossed Frankie's face.
'No. We've all had our hands full these past few hours.
Look . . . It would be better if we could talk somewhere

more private, just in case Miss Kennedy should awaken unexpectedly. An office has been given over for my use and we can speak more easily there. It's just down the corridor,' he added as Frankie's eyes darted anxiously to the sleeping Rose. 'You need to be fully appraised of the situation if you are going to be able to help your niece.' Holding the door open wide, the doctor waited for Frankie to pass, and Frankie, with another worried look at the unconscious form, slipped out into the hallway.

Once in the roomy office, the doctor sank into a large leather chair, gesturing Frankie to another positioned at the other side of the large, walnut desk.

When both were seated, the doctor looked across the desk and steepled his fingertips beneath his chin. He thought for a moment then said formally, 'First, Mr Buchannon, may we be entirely honest with each other? Miss Kennedy isn't your niece, is she?'

Frank was astounded, but he collected himself and said, 'What if she isn't? I don't see as how that's any business of yours, Doctor.'

'I'm afraid it's very much my business, Mr Buchannon. When dealing with my patients, I like to know as much about the individual as is humanly possible, to ensure they have the best possible care. You see, Mr Buchannon, we doctors can only do so much. We can repair broken bones and sew up torn bodies, but ultimately, and especially in cases like Miss Kennedy's, a complete cure can only be achieved if the patient has the support of a loving family. Of course, there are exceptions. Some patients have the strength to take care of themselves after they leave here. And though that is an admirable trait, to my mind nothing can compare with the love of a family – and loyal friends. Which are you, Mr Buchannon?'

For an instant Frankie was tempted to tell this superior-looking bastard to mind his own business. Then he remembered the doctor's words: this *was* his business. In doing what she had, Rose had made her business known to this man, and if Frankie wanted his help, he would have to answer his questions.

Frankie had looked after his own affairs for too long to

need to confide in others, but there was something about the elderly gentleman, observing him patiently, that reached out to him and broke down his reserve. He cleared his throat and, in short, terse sentences, he told of his relationship to Rose Kennedy, and of how it had come about. The doctor listened intently, his lined face seeming to relax a little as he became aware of the real affection Frankie felt for the young woman patient who had been thrust into his care.

When he had finished, Thomas Maitland adjusted his half-moon spectacles on the bridge of his nose, intertwined his fingers and said softly, 'Thank you, Mr Buchannon. I appreciate your candour.' Now his voice and actions became more businesslike. 'With regard to Miss Kennedy, your charge, if I may refer to her as such, has a condition known as placenta praevia. It's quite rare. The last study, made in eighteen ninety-six, suggests that the condition occurs in roughly one in a thousand pregnancies. In Miss Kennedy's case, the placenta – or afterbirth, as it is often known – has become attached to a part of the wall of the uterus directly above the opening to the birth canal. This being the case, the slightest contact made with it through the vagina can result in copious bleeding, which is obviously what happened today. If the "doctor" in question had taken the time to conduct a simple internal examination, he would have been aware of the obstruction but, then, such men aren't renowned for their thoroughness. The moment the instrument to abort the foetus was entered into the vagina it came into contact with the placenta and the subsequent haemorrhage occurred.'

As he listened to the doctor, Frankie felt a sensation of faintness steal over him. It shocked and frightened him: he had been inured to life's unpleasantnesses from an early age. He sat up straighter in the chair, clenched his teeth and ground out, 'Spare me the gruesome details, eh? All I want to know is if she's . . . if Rose is gonna pull through this.'

He had expected a hearty reassurance and his heart began to pound at the grave look on the doctor's face.

'I won't lie to you, Mr Buchannon. Abnormal pregnancies of any kind can be life-threatening to both mother and child.'

Frankie felt faintness threaten again as fear clutched at his very soul. 'But you – you made me think she was gonna be all right. I mean, all that talk about wanting to know your patient so's she could get the best treatment. You made it sound like—'

'Mr Buchannon, please, don't alarm yourself.' The doctor was now leaning over the desk, his hands held out reassuringly. 'I would be failing in my duty if I didn't make you cognisant of all the dangers.' Thomas Maitland stroked the lower half of his face before continuing, 'Miss Kennedy has been exposed to danger by the loss of blood she has endured. This in turn increases the tendency to septic inflammation. As for the child – its life may have become endangered by asphyxia through the interference with the placenta, which may result in either prematurity or malpresentation – or both.' He got up, came round to stand in front of Frankie and perched on the edge of the polished desk. 'Please, Mr Buchannon, don't look so despondent. I've painted a pretty dismal picture, I know, but there is light at the end of the tunnel. Not so long ago, one in three mothers died from placenta praevia. Now, I'm pleased to say, with modern treatment, many more are saved . . . although the risk to the unborn child remains high.'

The muscles in Frankie's throat seemed to have seized up. Up until a few minutes ago, he hadn't cared if the creature growing inside Rose, for that's how he thought of it, had been destroyed. In fact, he had been stricken to find it still lived – Jack Adams's child. A bastard bred by a bastard!

But Frank knew, deep down, that if the child died, a part of Rose would die with it. And as much as he loathed the idea of seeing Rose raise Jack Adams's child, such was the intense love he had for her that he found himself praying for the child's survival. For only if it lived, would Rose ever become whole again – though if he thought for one moment that continuing the pregnancy would put Rose's life at risk, he would tear the child from her womb with his bare hands. A Rosie half alive would be better than no Rosie at all.

And what about Mary? Rose was her life. If anything happened to her, the old girl would simply give up. Oh, God! What a mess. Three lives hung in the balance, and all because Jack Adams hadn't been able to keep his trousers buttoned. Damn him to hell! Lights seemed to be dancing behind the backs of his eyes as Frankie strove to maintain a normal façade, but even his indomitable strength and tenacity seemed unable to aid him through this, his darkest hour. 'Look, Doctor. Just give me a straight answer, will you? The only thing that interests me right now is whether Rose is gonna pull through this. I don't care how much it costs. If you have to get another doctor in to help you, then get him. Money's no object. Not where Rosie's concerned.'

Thomas Maitland looked at the distraught man with pitying eyes. 'Money has nothing to do with this, Mr Buchannon. All that can be done will be done, you have my word. But I can't give you any cast-iron guarantee.'

Frankie stared at the doctor, his eyes beseeching. The awful fear that was tearing his body and mind apart had stripped away the tough, invincible surface that Frankie Buchannon presented to the world, leaving in its place a desperate, vulnerable man, who would do anything – anything at all – to save the life of someone he loved.

'You just do whatever it takes – get whoever's needed. Just – just don't let her die, Doctor. Don't let my Rosie die. Please.'

CHAPTER SEVENTEEN

The following forty-eight hours passed in a confused blur for Rose as she drifted in and out of sleep. During this fraught time, Frankie was hardly ever away from the small room where she lay.

A tearful, distraught Mary was now also keeping vigil over her unconscious niece, telling anyone who came within earshot that it was all her fault. She seemed to take a perverse comfort in berating herself publicly. And it was only after considerable effort, that Frankie persuaded her to be taken home for some much-needed rest.

He had ordered that no one on the medical staff should speak to either Rose or Mary unless he authorised it. He wanted the news of the baby's tenuous hold on life to be kept from both women for the time being. It was still early days. He didn't want to raise Rose's hopes until he was sure the baby would survive: it would be so cruel if Rose was told her child lived, only to lose it soon after.

Now, on the third day since Rose's admission, Frankie was again facing Thomas Maitland waiting to hear the doctor's prognosis. A small ray of hope glimmered in him at the sight of the expression on the weathered face.

'Ah, Mr Buchannon. Well, now, I won't keep you waiting any longer. I'm pleased to say that Miss Kennedy's condition has stabilised much more quickly than I at first expected. We doctors are often surprised at the resilience of some of our patients, and never more so than in Miss

Kennedy's case. The haemorrhaging has been checked and shows no immediate signs of recurring. If she is nursed carefully, and has the required rest, well . . . I have high hopes of delivering her of a healthy child in, say, five months' time. The birth must take place early before further complications can arise. Mr Buchannon! Are you all right, sir?'

Dazed, Frankie felt behind him for a chair and let himself sink down onto it. 'She's gonna be all right, then? Rosie's gonna be all right?' His voice sounded weak as he took in the news. Then, relief flooded through him, leaving him trembling. 'And . . . and the baby? Is it gonna live? I mean, I don't want to get Rose's hopes up if . . .'

Thomas Maitland's lips twitched into a thin smile. 'As far as I can tell at this moment, the child has a good chance of survival. But, as I told you before, there is always a danger of renewed haemorrhaging. Especially approaching the sixth month. But we are aware of the problem, and we will carefully monitor Miss Kennedy's progress. If you wish, I can arrange for a private midwife to be in attendance on her when she returns home.'

'What? Oh, yes, that'll be fine. Like I said before, whatever it takes to get Rose back on her feet.' Frankie got up unsteadily and shook the doctor's hand fervently. 'I don't know how to thank you, Doctor. If you ever need anything, well, you just have to ask.' Frankie began to leave, then stopped by the door.

'Yes, Mr Buchannon? Is there something else you wish to ask me?' Dr Maitland's genial tone sparked Frankie into life. Fiddling with the brim of the bowler hat he held between his fingers, he kept his gaze on the floor as he asked, 'Would she be . . . I mean, Rose. Would she be strong enough to get married? It wouldn't be anything special, I mean, no big fuss, or anything like that. Just a simple service. Would she be able to cope, or . . . ?'

Thomas Maitland's eyes widened at the unexpected request. Then his lips spread in a delighted grin. 'But that is excellent news, Mr Buchannon, excellent. It's just what Miss Kennedy needs at this particular time. Well, well, well. Oh, this is delightful. But I thought you said the father was . . .'

Frankie interrupted, 'The father doesn't come into it. It's me I'm talking about . . . that is, if Rose'll have me. I ain't asked her yet. Well! Is she up to it?'

Spluttering in confusion, the elderly doctor stared in amazement at Frank. 'Am I to understand that you plan to marry Miss Kennedy, and take responsibility for her child?'

Discomfited by the other man's open admiration, Frankie fidgeted, then his dark, brooding eyes locked with those of the physician. 'You could say that, Doc. Only don't go looking at me like I'm doing something noble. It ain't like that. If she'll have me, it'll be in name only. She's gonna need someone to look after her, and I ain't having anyone call her kid a bastard. So! What d'yer think, Doc? How soon d'yer think she'll be strong enough?'

The doctor was lost for words. Then he recovered himself. 'Good Lord! Well, this is certainly a surprise. As for your question . . .' He spread his hands wide in perplexity. 'Well, certainly not at the moment. Maybe in a few weeks—'

Impatient, now, Frankie butted in, 'Look, Doctor, all she's gotta do is say, "I will." Surely she'll be able to manage *that*.'

The doctor considered the tall, handsome man, with new respect dawning in his faded blue eyes. 'There is a small chapel in the hospital grounds, though I've never heard of a wedding being performed there. I daresay the chaplain would be happy to oblige if asked. It would make a pleasant change from the duties he is usually called upon to perform.' He went to the door and held it open. 'I shall make the necessary enquiries on your behalf, Mr Buchannon, but I must, in all conscience, point out that Miss Kennedy is in a very low state of mind and is not capable of making any major decisions. Of course, the news that her child is still alive may or may not ease her mind, bearing in mind what she tried to do.' The doctor saw Frankie's eyebrows draw together in anger, but he was not intimidated. 'You have said that the child is not yours, and that your relationship to Miss Kennedy is more in the line of close relative. And while I applaud your excellent motives, I think it would be unfair and unethical to impose such a momentous decision upon her while she is in such a low state. In all probability, she doesn't know what she is doing or saying at the moment. Her recent experience was harrowing, to say the least, and the medication she has been receiving has most certainly clouded her judgement. Surely it would be better if you waited until she was sound in mind and body before undertaking such a step? Even if it is for the best possible motives.'

Frankie swept past, his face set against all argument. 'You just do your job, Doc, and leave me to worry about Rose's welfare. And listen.' He paused outside Rose's room. 'I've done some things in me time I ain't exactly proud of, but the one thing I'd never do is hurt Rose. The only thing I want to do at the moment is give her me name and the security that goes with it. Once she's well again she can decide if she wants to stay married to me, but whichever way it goes, she'll still have me name, and her kid won't be born a bastard.'

'Very well, Mr Buchannon. You must do what you think best. But there is something you seem to have forgotten.' Barely able to control his impatience, Frankie darted him a look of enquiry. Undaunted, Thomas Maitland continued, 'You realise, of course, that I'll have to inform the police of this business. Abortion is illegal, as you know, and the man responsible must be caught and put out of harm's way as soon as possible. The next woman may not be as fortunate as Miss Kennedy.'

Frankie took a step away from the door. 'No! I mean, hang on. There's no need for that. I'll see to him, don't you worry about that. We don't need the police involved. We look after our own where I come from.'

'That may be so, Mr Buchannon. But where *I* come from we leave such matters to the proper authorities.'

Sensing that the man couldn't be swayed, Frankie took a deep breath and said, 'I respect your views. But is it really necessary to drag Rose into it? She's suffered enough. I already know where the man lived – I made it me business to find out. Look, if I give you his name and his last known address, will you keep Rose's name out of it – please?'

The doctor hesitated for what seemed an eternity then

nodded. 'Very well, Mr Buchannon. But only on the strict understanding that I receive the relevant information.'

'You have me word, Doctor.' Frankie saw the man's scepticism and felt a spark of anger. 'It's all right, Doctor. I may not be the kind of person you'd invite to dinner, but I'm a man of me word. You can ask around, if you like. I'm known round the East End and . . .'

The doctor surveyed Frank coolly, then gave a dry chuckle of amusement. 'I know who you are, Mr Buchannon, as do the majority of the staff. I'm sure they will give you all the assistance you require. Good day, sir.'

When Rose next woke, she was more lucid. As she took in her surroundings with a clear eye, and realised that it hadn't all been a terrible dream, hot tears welled up. Weakened from loss of blood, her fragile body shook feebly with suppressed sobs. Within seconds Frankie was at her side.

'Oh, Frankie. I killed my baby. I killed it. I'll never forgive myself – never. Oh, Frankie, oh, I'm sorry . . . I'm sorry. I didn't mean to hurt it, I didn't mean to hurt my baby.'

Frankie's arms went round her, one hand tenderly stroking the mass of hair. 'There, there, Princess. Give over. Listen to me, Rosie. Listen, will you.'

Rose stared at him with anguished eyes.

'It ain't dead. Your baby ain't dead. D'yer understand, Princess? It's alive. It must take after its mother, 'cos the little sod's still in there.'

Rose couldn't take it in. 'No, it can't be, Frank. The blood . . . There was blood everywhere. It couldn't have survived. It's just not possible.'

Frankie held her tightly and explained, as best he could, what the doctor had told him. He ended, 'You see, Princess? It's all right. Everything's gonna be all right.'

Rose sank back on her pillow, a smile tugging at her lips. 'You mean it, Frank?' she whispered. 'Really? You wouldn't just say that to make me feel better until I was stronger?'

Frankie kissed the pale forehead. 'Nah, I wouldn't do that to you, Princess. It's the truth, I swear it is.'

In an almost reverent movement Rose placed her hands over the small mound of her stomach. 'I can't believe it. I just can't believe it . . . Oh, Frankie.' Her eyes shone with new hope, but then a shadow crept over her face, dimming the brightness. Frankie saw the change, saw the look of fear, and knew the reason behind it. He was humbled. That Rose, of all people, should be in fear of him wasn't to be borne.

Abruptly he let go of her and went to the window. Standing with his back to her, he gazed out on to a dismal world, a bleak and lonely place for many. The view from the window was depressing, overlooking drab houses, poverty-stricken people. What kind of life would Rose have with a child to bring up on her own? Oh, Mary would do her best to help but she was getting on, and some days she could barely put her feet to the ground. Yet if he were to take care of them . . . If he asked, and Rose agreed to marry him . . .

For years he had known that something was missing from his life. He had laughed off enquiries about his lack of a wife but he had longed for someone with whom to share his life. Someone who would give it meaning, give him children and purpose. But such a woman had never crossed his path. Those with whom he mixed were unlikely to possess the qualities he was searching for – the qualities Rose had. Her modulated way of speaking, the way she carried herself, her independence, her spirit, her knowledge. Oh, yes, her knowledge. For Rose had been born with a capacity to learn, to educate herself, and the short while she had spent at the private school on which Mary had spent her savings had reinforced the natural ability she had been born with. Rose had class, for which Frankie had always yearned but which he was wise enough to know he would never possess – no matter how much money he had.

He would never find the woman he was looking for because he had already found her. She was here, watching him, waiting for him to speak, her lovely blue eyes filled with apprehension.

How would she react if he asked her to marry him? He gave a silent, mirthless laugh. She'd probably think he'd been drinking. And what if he asked and was refused? Could he bear it? Was he man enough to suffer rejection with dignity?

And what of the child – Jack Adams's child? Would he be

able to accept it as his own? To love it unreservedly. Because if he had any doubts, he mustn't ask Rose the question. He could never show the slightest irritation or dislike towards Rose's child, for she would be quick to notice.

'Frank!' His name had been whispered, almost fearfully.

He spun round and said shortly, 'Look, Rose, I've got to go out for a while. I won't be long, I promise,' he added hastily, at the look of alarm in her eyes. 'There's something I've gotta do. I'll be back in about half an hour, honest.' He needed a drink badly, and there was a pub at the corner where he could buy the Dutch courage he needed.

Rose watched his familiar figure leave the room, and as he went, so did her peace of mind. While he had been here with her she had felt a measure of safety. She was still afraid – afraid of what she would face on leaving here but mostly of the future for her child. Now that it was safe, she vowed it would never, ever come to any more harm, not while she was alive to protect it.

But how was she going to provide for it? She wouldn't be able to go back to work, not with Aunt Mary the way she was. A baby needed a strong pair of arms and legs to cling to during childhood, and Mary, bless her, couldn't provide that. But she would try. Oh, yes, her aunt would try her best – and hasten herself towards an early grave.

Fresh tears poured down her cheeks. Oh, Jack, Jack, you shouldn't have left me. But even as she thought it she knew she was being unfair. Before he'd left London, he had come round to the house every day and begged her – begged them both – but Mary had been adamant that she wasn't leaving her home. And Rose, faced with the choice, had chosen her aunt over Jack.

If she changed her mind now and wrote to him, what would the future hold? She would be for ever caught between the three people she loved most.

She must have dozed off, for when she next opened her eyes Frankie was once again by her side, his face wearing an expression she had never seen before. Before she could speak he said awkwardly, 'Look, Rose, I've been thinking. Now, it's not going to be easy for you after you leave here. I know Mary'll do her best, but it's still gonna be difficult for you to try to find work and bring up a kid. So, what I was thinking was—' He broke off, then went on, 'Look, maybe we can do each other a favour. I mean . . . Well, Mary's always on at me to get married and settle down, and you and the kid are gonna need someone to look after you, so what I was thinking was – Aw, shit! Help me out here, Rose, you must know what I'm trying to say?'

Rose could only gape at him in amazement. Yet even as she contemplated the absurdity of his proposal, a warm feeling of well-being was coursing through her. Ever since she was a child, Frankie had been on hand to protect her. She remembered how one day, at the tender age of eight, she had come home from school crying because her teacher had been picking on her. Frankie had taken her on his knee, wiped away her tears and said, 'You leave it with me, Princess, I'll sort it out.' And that teacher had never bothered Rose again. It seemed, on looking back, that he had always been there to 'sort it out', and now it seemed the most natural thing in the world to let him take control of her life. The desire to accept his offer was overpowering. To have Frankie with her always, to know she was safe and looked after. To have someone by her side who could tackle anything and anyone that came his way. Yet . . .

She said tenderly, 'Frank, it's good of you to offer, and I do love you, Frank, I always have . . . but – but not in that way.'

Eagerly Frankie seized her hands. 'I know, Princess, I know. But it'll be a start, won't it? I mean, like you say, we love each other. So it won't be the perfect marriage but you show me one that is!'

'But, Frank, what about . . . well . . . you know . . .'

A flush was rising steadily in her cheeks and he cupped her chin fondly. 'Gawd! Princess, I ain't never gone short of that. What I can't get elsewhere is a wife and a family – well, not the sort I want.'

Rose's head was spinning, but in the midst of her confusion she had made up her mind. Her child would have security – she owed it that much after what she had tried to do. But there was still one question she had to ask. Gathering her limited strength, she said imploringly, 'It's

Jack's baby, Frank. You know that, don't you? And after what I've done, or tried to do, I'll . . . I'll never let anyone hurt it. I intend to spend the rest of my life trying to make it up to my child – Jack's child. Do you understand, Frank? Think carefully at what you're planning to take on because it isn't going to be easy, not for either of us. And the baby mustn't suffer – it mustn't suffer any more.'

Limp with relief, Frankie stroked Rose's forehead. 'Ssh, Princess. It'll be all right, I swear – I'll make it all right.'

And Rose, weary and sick to the very core of her being, relinquished herself and her unborn child into Frankie's hands.

Ten days later, Rose, looking pale but determined, in a two-piece cream outfit trimmed with seed pearls and a large cream hat that almost obscured her face, stood before the hospital chaplain, holding Frankie's arm. She felt as if she were in a pleasant dream, comforting and reassuring. Beside her stood Frankie, looking more handsome than she had ever seen him in a black morning coat, black and grey striped trousers and a high hat. Seated in a bath-chair, thoughtfully provided by the hospital staff, sat Mary, resplendent in a new blue chiffon dress that she would probably never wear again, valiantly trying to cover her astonishment at the speedy turn of events. As she had told an amused Frank, everything had happened so fast she didn't know whether to have a shit or a haircut.

Explanations and discussions had been sidestepped by Frank, who organised, planned and executed all arrangements with such speed and dexterity that the two women had been swept along on a tidal wave of preparations. And such was the sheer force of his magnetic personality that questions had remained unasked and all doubts temporarily buried as the great day loomed nearer.

Now was the final reckoning, and as the chaplain asked Rose if she would take this man in holy wedlock, Frankie held his breath, praying that his efforts would not be thwarted at the last minute. To his left stood Thomas Maitland, who had agreed to be a witness, and he, too, found himself holding his breath. But neither men need have worried. So caught up in the whirlwind of events was she that Rose answered quietly but firmly, sure that she was doing the right thing by everyone concerned.

Then it was over. The little wedding party returned to the infirmary where Rose allowed the ward sister to help her remove her wedding finery, before she slipped back gratefully into the security of the narrow bed, tired but more content than she had felt in a long time.

Seated by the bed, Mary held her niece's hand, dabbing furiously at her brimming eyes with a large white handker-chief. Frank stood alongside her, his composure belying the overwhelming elation that filled every pore of his body. Rose was now his wife. After all these years, the three of them were a family again. A proper family this time, all legal and above board, and as he gazed down lovingly at the two women who were his life, he silently vowed that they would never be separated again.

CHAPTER EIGHTEEN

On a hot summer's day during the last weekend of August 1902, Jack was aboard a crowded, stifling train heading for Victoria Station. It was just six weeks since he had taken up his new position as sergeant in the small village near Southampton, and he was desperately missing Rose.

The job was all he had hoped for. The quiet village of Hemerly, its population numbering a mere 123, was a world away from the grim, dark back-streets of the East End. His three-bedroomed converted farmhouse was idyllic and peaceful, the perfect place to raise a family. But, for a man on his own, it seemed vast and mockingly empty.

Since his move he had written to Rose almost every week: apart from wanting to keep in contact with her, there was precious little else for Jack to do in the remote hamlet where crime was virtually unheard-of.

The only thing missing to make his life complete was Rose. Until a few weeks ago, she had answered all of his letters, reaffirming her intention not to leave London. Then, suddenly, the letters had stopped coming. Upset by her silence, Jack had redoubled his efforts to convince her – and Mary, of course – to join him. But the emotions he felt were too complex to transcribe on to paper: they needed to be spoken. So here he was, on his way to London, in a last, desperate mission to persuade the irrepressible Mary Miller to uproot herself and move away from her place of origin. He was certain that the formidable woman was the only obstacle preventing Rose from joining him.

He arrived at Victoria, sweating and rumpled from the journey, and immediately climbed into a waiting hansom cab. On arrival at Mare Street he paid the driver and stood, looking across the road at the Red Lion, which offered the tantalising prospect of a large glass of ale to wash away the dust of the train ride. It would also provide him with a shot of Dutch courage.

There was only a handful of customers in the bar so he didn't have to wait for the longed-for drink. He put a florin on the counter and said, to a startled Sally, 'Cheers, Sal. Bet you're surprised to see me back, ain't you?'

The blonde barmaid, normally ready for a laugh and a chat with any male customer, was strangely subdued. 'Yeah, you could say that, Jack. Come back to see Rosie, have you?'

Jack took a long, cool gulp of his drink, smacked his lips appreciatively and answered, 'Yep.' Then, he glanced round the pub and asked, 'She ain't here by any chance, is she?'

Before Sally could answer, Henry Dixon, a cloth in his hands, came to stand beside her. He picked up a beer glass and began to polish it.

Jack looked at him, then did a double-take at the fading bruises around the landlord's eyes. 'Bleeding hell, Henry! What happened to you? Those boys from Spitalfields been in here causing trouble again?'

Dixon avoided the question. 'Knows you're coming, does she, mate?' he asked, matter-of-factly.

Jack sensed an awkwardness in the pair and he lowered his glass. 'No. I thought I'd surprise her.'

Sally uttered a grating laugh. 'It'll be a surprise all right.' Then she flushed as Dixon gave her an angry, reproach-ful look.

Resting a foot on the bar-rail, Jack directed his gaze at the landlord. 'What's going on, Henry?'

The landlord gave a heavy shrug of his broad shoulders. 'Look, mate, why don't you just go back to where you came from and leave well alone? You're only asking for grief staying round here.'

Jack stared thoughtfully into space. What the hell *was* going on? He glanced around the pub, noted the way eyes fell before his searching gaze, and felt his stomach tighten.

'Frankie ain't gonna like it, Jack. Look, why don't—'

Jack spun away from the bar angrily, everything suddenly clear. So Buchannon had put out the word, had he? He, Jack Adams, was no longer welcome in these parts. His eyes raked over those present and he sneered, 'Look at the lot of you. All frightened of the big Mr Buchannon. You're all Buchannon's toadies, the whole cowardly lot of you. Well, don't worry,' he tossed back the remainder of his drink and slammed the empty glass on the counter, 'I'm off. I wouldn't want to put any of you in danger of being caught in my company. Huh! You all oughter be ashamed of yourselves.'

'Wait a minute, mate.' Dixon hurried after him, not knowing if he was doing the right thing in interfering but impelled to tell him the truth. Out in the street, he caught hold of Jack's arm. 'Look, this ain't easy to say, Jack, but I think you deserve to know what's been going on.'

Jack waited impassively, his grey eyes smouldering with quiet anger.

Scratching the back of his neck uneasily, Dixon searched for the right words to help ease the pain that would ensue from what he was about to say, but there were none. There was no kind way to say what had to be said.

'Hurry up, Henry, I ain't got all day. I've got to be back in Southampton by tonight.'

Dixon swallowed hard, lowered his eyes, then, his tone betraying his sympathy, he said flatly, 'Rose is married, Jack. Couple of weeks ago. I'm sorry, mate. I thought she'd have written to let you know.'

Jack was motionless. Then he knocked Dixon's hand from his arm. 'What you talking about? I only left her six weeks ago! She can't have got married so soon. What you playing at, Henry? You trying to cause trouble between me and Rose? Oh . . .' His eyes were blazing. 'Buchannon's put you up to this, ain't he? Told you to spin me a story if I came back!' He threw back his head and laughed mirthlessly. 'I thought you had more balls than that, Henry. I never took you for one of Buchannon's flunkeys.'

Anger mixed with compassion tore through the publican. 'I ain't one of Buchannon's boys, Jack,' he growled. 'Never have been, you should know that. You and me are about the only ones round these parts that ain't in his pockets. Now, I'm telling you straight. Rose is married, and there's nothing you can do about it. So get back on that train an' go home. There's nothing left for you round here – not any more.'

Jack stumbled back, his face ashen. He stared intently at Dixon and, with a growing sickness in the pit of his stomach, knew that he was telling him the truth. He looked beseechingly at the other man and muttered, 'Who? Who did she marry, Henry? My God, I can't believe it. Tell me before I knock it out of you.'

Like everyone else Dixon had been dumbfounded when he'd heard that Rose had married Frankie. No one had been invited to the hasty wedding, and rumours abounded that Rose had been in hospital, though no one knew why. It was a rum do and no mistake. Like everyone else he was bursting with curiosity, but you didn't ask too many questions where Buchannon was concerned. If anyone knew what was going on, it was Sally, but she was keeping tight-lipped about the whole affair. Then there had been Rita's sudden departure from the pub. No notice, no warning, just didn't turn up for work one day. She'd written him a short, untidy note saying she'd got a better job elsewhere, but there was something going on, and if Sally hadn't reassured him that Rita was all right, he'd have been more worried than he was.

Still, that was all done with. Now Jack Adams was waiting for answers and he wasn't going to go away until he received them. Dixon cleared his throat. 'Look, mate, I wish it wasn't me that had to tell you, but the truth is, Rose married Frankie. It was all a bit of a rush, an' everyone's as surprised as you are. But there it is.'

The words acted like a hammer blow on Jack's brain, and as the blood rushed to his face he shouted, 'I don't believe you! Where is she? Tell me, damn it! Where's that bastard hiding her?'

Dixon folded his arms across his chest and shook his head. 'I ain't got the address. All I know is it's somewhere over Bow way, some avenue or other . . . Genhan . . . Graham, something like that. I don't know the number, you'll have to ask around.'

Jack swore, then stalked off in search of a cab. Dixon watched the departing figure with sympathy, glad that he wasn't going to be present when the two men finally met up. If he had to make a bet on who came out the winner, though, his money would be on Buchannon.

Rose was lying in a hammock with a pillow under her head in the spacious garden at the back of her new home in Grantham Avenue. Nearby, seated in a wicker garden chair, was a young nurse, hired to watch over her patient during the day. Another older woman would come in later for the night.

Fanning herself, Rose looked out over the landscaped garden, her eyes curiously dimmed. Her treatment included sedation with a mild opiate drug to ensure complete rest during the remainder of her pregnancy, and sometimes it seemed to her that all she ever did was eat and sleep, yet she was content in a detached sort of way.

In the house she could hear Mary's voice, and smiled. Dear Aunt Mary. She still hadn't grown accustomed to living in such grandiose surroundings, and seemed to take comfort from berating the servants on the flimsiest of excuses. It was as if she was constantly striving to prove the worth of her existence in her new home, and had taken it on herself to oversee the servants and the running of the household.

Rose let herself swing from side to side, the muffled sounds of her aunt's strident voice echoing in the background.

Then another, equally familiar, voice penetrated her somnolent state. Rose attempted to swing her legs over the side of the hammock. The clumsy action brought the nurse swiftly to her side. 'Now, then, Mrs Buchannon. You know we mustn't try to move by ourselves.'

Irritated, Rose snapped, 'I want to go into the house. If that's all right with you, of course?'

The sarcasm slid over the earnest young woman's head. 'I think it's time for your medicine, dear. There you are. Just lean on me and I'll soon have you inside.'

Too weak to argue, Rose allowed herself to be led, like a docile child, across the luscious lawn, protesting feebly, 'I don't want any medicine. I feel half dead as it is . . . What's that noise? I—'

The voices from the house were getting louder and, sensing trouble, and perhaps danger to her patient, the nurse called for help. One of Frankie's men came running from the bottom of the garden.

Then the back door of the conservatory burst open and an irate man, his eyes seeming to bulge from his head, bounded towards Rose.

'Jack!' Rose struggled to free herself from the nurse's iron grip but she hadn't the strength. Frustrated, all she could do was gaze at the dishevelled figure, who was now only a few feet away.

Then Frankie's man sprang forward, blocking Jack's way, his arms in a pugilistic pose. 'Stay where you are, mate, or I'll knock your bleeding block off. Now, I'm warning you . . .'

Jack fended off the blow, and his own fist connected with the jaw of the other man, who dropped like a stone. Almost before he'd hit the ground, the nurse screamed and, as if out of thin air, two more men appeared, grabbed Jack roughly and forced him to the ground.

'Rose, Rose,' Jack cried, but Rose could only watch helplessly as Fred Green and his brother-in-law, Joe Perkins, now joined by the man Jack had knocked down, dragged the resisting figure away.

Then Mary was at Rose's side, her mouth working furiously as she ordered the men to throw Jack out.

'What's the matter with you, Rose?' Jack shouted wildly, as he was dragged unceremoniously away. 'Rose, Rose! For God's sake, what's happened to you?'

Rose stared at the tormented figure, her eyes brimming with helpless tears. There was so much she wanted to say to him, but the words were frozen at the back of her throat. Twice she tried to speak, but each time no sound came. It was as if she had been struck dumb.

'That's enough of that, Jack Adams.' Mary positioned herself in front of him. 'She's married now, lad. You had your chance and you threw it away. So don't come round here starting trouble 'cos I won't let you go upsetting Rose. I mean it, Jack. I ain't gonna let you hurt her again. Now . . . you gonna behave yerself, lad? Or do I get you thrown out on your arse? Come on, answer me. You gonna behave or not?'

Jack ceased struggling and jerked away from the men who held him. At a word from Mary they stood back, but stayed ready to pounce. Shooting them a look of loathing, Jack dusted down his sleeves and looked at Rose, who was now trembling in a large wicker chair.

'Jack,' Mary said warningly, but she knew him of old. He wasn't the kind of man to go meekly without a good explanation, so she would have to be convincing. 'Come here . . . No, not there,' she barked, as Jack moved in Rose's direction. 'Over there, where I can keep me eyes on you.' She indicated a canvas chair, a good few feet away from her distressed niece.

'Really, I must protest. Mrs Buchannon mustn't be exposed to this kind of disturbance, not in her—'

The nurse was rudely shoved aside as Mary stopped her from revealing Rose's condition. If Jack Adams knew the truth, there was no way Rose would ever be rid of him. Besides, she was married now: there was no point in raking over old coals. Mary had to get rid of the angry policeman before anyone present let slip the real reason behind the hasty wedding.

She placed a protective arm around her niece and strove to manage the volatile situation. 'Look, I know it's come as a bit of a shock, Jack, but there it is. There's no point in you coming here shouting the odds 'cos you can't change what's happened. Now, then, why don't you . . .'

But Jack was enraged at the sight of Rose surrounded on all sides, effectively shutting him out. 'Oh, I can see why you don't want me hanging around, Mary. It's all making sense now. You never intended Rose to marry me, did you, you spiteful old cow? I bet you didn't tell Frankie he'd have to wait till she was twenty-one, did you? Oh, no. I'll bet when he asked, you couldn't get Rose up to the altar quick enough, could you, you scheming bitch? God! You must think you've died and gone to heaven, 'cos this,' he threw out his arms wildly, 'this is what you always wanted, ain't it? Just the three of you, all tucked up cosy under the same roof!'

Panting, Jack glared at the woman who, in his mind, was at the root of all that had happened. He had known from the start that Mary had been against Rose taking up with him, but he had never for one moment imagined that she had been saving her niece for Frankie Buchannon. It was sick. Because apart from the pair of them having been brought up practically as blood relatives, Frankie was a good fifteen years older than Rose. God! He couldn't believe Mary had been so devious – and bloody vindictive into the bargain! But Rose could have said no. She had a mind of her own, didn't she? So why was she just sitting there staring at him like that? 'Why can't Rose speak for herself? She been struck dumb all of a sudden?' Then, he lowered his voice and pleaded, 'Rose, what's the matter, love? What have they done to you? Look, just give me the word and I'll get you away from here. Don't be frightened, darling. I don't know what Buchannon and this old witch have done to make you like this, but I'll make it right, I swear to you, Rose. All you've gotta do is say the word, and I'll have you out of here quicker than you can blink.'

'I don't think so, Adams.' A cool, sardonic voice came from behind him, and in an instant he was facing his old adversary, his hands clenching into fists. Frankie saw the gesture. 'Come off it, Jack, I ain't gonna fight you, there ain't no point.' He strolled easily to Rose's side and placed a strong hand on her shoulder. 'I don't want no trouble, mate, not here, not anywhere. Those days are gone. I'm a respectable businessman now.'

Jack laughed scornfully. 'Don't give me that, Buchannon. You might have fooled most people, but not me. You're nothing but a crook. Always have been, always will be.

Underneath the fancy clothes and the smart talk you're still rotten.'

'I've been patient with you, Adams,' Frankie said quietly. 'Now I want you out of my house. You're upsetting my wife.'

His voice sent a shiver down Rose's spine. She lifted her eyes beseechingly to Jack and whispered, 'Please, Jack, don't cause any more trouble. Just go. I'm sorry things turned out like this, but it's for the best. Honestly, Jack, it's for the best.'

Jack spun to face Frankie and Mary. 'What've you done to her? She looks drugged up to the eyeballs. And why's that nurse here?' He assumed a dangerous stance, ready to fight tooth and nail to get to the bottom of the sinister situation. 'There's something fishy going on here. I ain't been gone more than six weeks, and Rose suddenly ups and married the man she always seemed to think of as an uncle—'

Mary started to speak, but Frankie, his hand on her arm, stopped her. 'I don't owe you any explanations, Adams. But if it'll get shot of you, I'll tell you what happened.' Glancing down at the copper mass of curls, he said, 'Rose was in an accident. She walked under a carriage. She's still not recovered, that's why the nurse is here with her. And you're right, she is taking drugs. But only what the doctor prescribed for her. It's to keep her calm so as she'll get better quicker. And that's all I'm telling you. The rest is none of your business. If it'll make you feel any better, ask her. Go on, Adams. Ask Rose if she's happy. If she says she wants to go with you, I'll drive you both to wherever you want to go. You have me word. Go on. Ask her.'

Jack stared at the united trio, sick with despair. He had only to look at Rose to know she didn't want him any more. But still, he had to ask. Just one more time . . . Just in case . . .

His hands clenching and unclenching, he caught Rose's dazed blue eyes and implored, 'Is he telling the truth, Rose? Are you happy? I mean, he ain't making you stay here, is he?' A low groan passed his lips. 'Please, Rosie, say something, please.'

Her heart nearly breaking, Rose tried to focus on Jack's

face, then, her voice low but clear, she said, 'I'm happy,
Jack. I'm where I want to be. I'm sorry I hurt you, but I'd
– I'd rather you left now.'

Triumphant, Frankie squeezed her shoulder. 'There! You
satisfied now, Adams?' Then he addressed the hovering,
frightened nurse, in a voice of command, 'Take my wife
indoors, Nurse, and see she's put to bed to rest. And just
to be on the safe side, you can go and fetch the doctor.
She's supposed to be kept quiet and peaceful, and I want
to make sure this commotion hasn't done her any harm.'

Jumping to obey, the nurse, with Mary hobbling beside
her, helped the unprotesting Rose into the house.

His eyes bleak, Jack watched them go. Watched his only
love walking away from him and out of his life. Defeated, he
straightened his jacket, lifted his head proudly and looked
Frankie straight in the eye. 'All right, Buchannon, I'm going.
But before I do, there's one more thing I want to know. Why
did you marry her? Why did you marry my Rose?'

Frank, his expression inscrutable, said flatly, 'I asked her,
and she said yes. That's all you need to know. Now if you'll
excuse me, I have to go and see if my *wife*'s all right. You
can find your way out, can't you, Constable? Oh, I nearly
forgot,' he snapped his fingers mockingly, 'it's Sergeant
now, isn't it? And I forgot to congratulate you.' The levity
in his voice disappeared. Moving closer until their faces
were only a few inches apart, he snarled, 'Don't come back,
Adams, 'Cos if you do, you'll be sorry. Now get away from
my house.'

Jack gave him a withering smile. 'You don't frighten
me, Buchannon. Oh, I'll go, but not because you told
me to, for Rose's sake. I'll be back though, from time to
time. Just to make sure she's all right. 'Cos you know
something, Buchannon, you're up to something. I don't
know what, but Rose wouldn't have just suddenly decided
to marry you – not without a good reason. And I'll find
out what that reason was. I'm very good at finding things
out – it's my job.' Clapping his hat firmly over his unruly
dark curls he sauntered from the garden and out into the
tree-lined street.

Once out of view of the house, his composure crumpled.

She was gone. His Rose was gone from him and, despite his brave words, there was nothing he could do about it.

Numb with grief he hailed a passing cab and asked to be taken to Victoria station. There was nothing left for him in London. Nothing but memories.

Back at the house, Frankie stood by the large bay window looking out on to the street from his study, a glass of whisky in his hand. Seated behind him in a brown chesterfield armchair was a large, jittery man. 'Bloody hell, Frank, that was close. If Adams had seen me here, he'd have put two and two together, and I'd have been—'

Frank rounded on him. 'And you'd have what, Mitchell? You're just having a a a drink with an old pal. There's nothing wrong with that, not unless you lose your nerve.'

Inspector Brian Mitchell, Jack Adams's previous superior, mopped his perspiring face. For years now he had done his utmost to keep Frankie out of prison, for a hefty inducement, of course, and it had been a profitable partnership. He was aware that many of his colleagues had their suspicions about him but, without proof, there was little they could do. Yet if Jack Adams had seen him here, under Frankie Buchannon's roof, it might have set him thinking about his hasty promotion and the unexpected new posting out in the backwaters of Southampton. And if Adams started to ask awkward questions . . .

Frankie looked at the sweat glistening on the fleshy cheeks and jeered, 'Bleeding hell! Look at the state of you, you spineless bastard!' Walking easily to a glass-fronted cabinet, he took out a crystal decanter and carried it over to a polished mahogany desk. Setting it down on a mat he prised out the stopper and poured himself another drink, adding harshly, 'I'll tell you something, Mitchell. I might have hated Adams's guts, but he had balls – which is more than can be said of you. Oh, bollocks! Here, take your money and get out.' He flung an embossed white envelope contemptuously on the table. 'Go on, Mitchell, piss off. In future, I'll get one of me boys to drop it off. Oh, don't worry,' he sneered, as he saw the Inspector's face blanch in sudden fear, 'I'll make sure they're discreet. Well! What you waiting for?'

The man made a hasty escape, silently cursing Buchannon but too scared to make any protest.

Left alone, Frankie remained staring out of the window on to the street below. He was glad Adams had been. He had known he would turn up one day. Now he had, and Frankie didn't have to worry about him any more. It was over, and he, Frank Buchannon, had won – as he had always known he would.

Raising his glass he made a silent toast to himself. To a new life. A new, respectable life. With a new, respectable family. A disarming smile lit up his handsome face, then, savouring his triumph for a few delicious moments, he threw back his drink and went in search of his wife.

CHAPTER NINETEEN

By the time Frank Buchannon was forty-two, he had achieved his aim to become one of London's top businessmen. The one-time petty thief, turned racketeer and extortionist, was no more. In his stead was a highly respected, and very wealthy, man. His fortunes had climbed steadily since he had stepped out from the prison gates for the last time, nine years previously. The steadfast resolution to rise in the world had intensified after his marriage. From that day on, he passed into a new phase of his hitherto stormy, chequered life.

His meteoric rise up the ladder to success was aided by his beautiful, intelligent wife who, with her husband, had slipped effortlessly into their dazzling new world.

They made an arresting couple. Frankie was now considered a pillar of society, hosting dinner parties for important men and their wives while Rose played hostess with a natural grace and wit that charmed all who came into contact with her. It soon became obvious that Rose Buchannon wasn't just a pretty face as she discussed business projects, money matters and world news across the elaborate dining table with her distinguished guests. Not for her the idle chit-chat so common among the women with whom she now found herself in company. It was Rose who had first initiated her husband into the world of stocks and shares, thereby greatly adding to his already substantial wealth.

Stories about Frankie's wild days in the East End were

openly told – in fact, the man himself actively encouraged such talk. For, after all, he was often heard to say, there was nothing in his past that he was ashamed of. He admitted to his former shady dealings, careful to omit the harsher aspects of his early days, speaking of those times in such a way as to invoke laughter, and even, on occasion, admiration and envy from staid, overfed men, who had never known danger or excitement in their comfortably dull lives.

During the years following the birth of his daughter, Frankie had slowly but determinedly shed every unsavoury link with his past. Thriving businesses now stood where there had once been stinking sweat shops. The vicious protection rackets were in the hands of former employees of Frankie Buchannon, given in lieu of severance pay by their former governor.

Those who had the astuteness and ability rose to greater things alongside the dynamic Frankie; those who didn't come up to scratch were left behind. Few dared complain.

A new clothing factory and various large offices and shops, all overseen by Frankie's boys, as he still called them, had created a multitude of much-needed jobs in the poverty-stricken East End, thereby earning Frankie Buchannon the undying gratitude of hundreds of men and women.

And what could make any man more popular than to see him so lovingly paired with his child? To say that Frankie Buchannon doted on his daughter would have been an understatement. From the moment Victoria Anne Buchannon could walk, her besotted father took her with him everywhere. He could be seen regularly taking the enchanting child on outings to the park, and in his carriage around the shops and streets of Bow and the surrounding area when Rose was busy elsewhere in her charity work with the less fortunate of Stoke Newington. It was a role she undertook with much pleasure and little recognition. And from time to time, her affluent husband dipped willingly into his own pockets, in answer to a plea from the beautiful wife he adored.

The angel-faced little girl, who was the spitting image of

her mother, was even allowed to accompany her prestigious father on his business rounds, where eager employees were allowed to down tools temporarily and coo over the copper-haired youngster.

On Victoria's fourth birthday, Frankie took his family to Paris for a month's vacation, the outcome of which was the birth of a son, Benjamin Buchannon, delivered eight months after their return. Many speculated that the arrival of the new baby would put the little girl's nose out of joint but, if anything, Frank showered his daughter with even more love and attention, as if anxious to ensure Victoria wouldn't feel slighted by all the fuss over her new baby brother. But he needn't have worried, for the engaging, strong-willed Victoria, who took after her Great-aunt Mary in temperament, was immediately captivated by her new sibling and took great pains to let everyone know that Benjamin Buchannon was firmly under his big sister's protection.

Those who were privileged to be invited into the family home in Grantham Avenue for social occasions spoke about their visit for days afterwards. Women gushed over the children and their charming hosts. And who could overlook the redoubtable Mary Miller, that tempestuous woman who seemed positively fearsome when it came to her East-End roots and voiced the most risqué and loud observations whenever possible, regardless of who might be visiting at the time. Yet the Buchannons openly adored her, and so, of course, did their guests. It seemed to those who knew them that the Buchannons had everything anyone could wish for – but life is never that simple, or that kind.

There were many who remembered the old days, people who hadn't been able to better themselves, and others who hadn't been offered the opportunity.

Such a person was Sally Higgins.

If life had seemed to smile on Frankie and Rose, it had overlooked Sally completely. The day she had learned of Frankie's marriage to Rose her world had collapsed around her. For years Sally had nurtured a secret hope that Frankie would come back to her one day and that things would be as they had once been. Even when he was openly hostile, and often violent towards her, Sally had clung to the forlorn hope, and when all hope was gone, her dreams irrevocably shattered, a part of Sally simply gave up. Gradually, she turned to drink, first for comfort, then to blot out a life that had become unbearable.

Her long-time landlord and friend, Henry Dixon, tried his best to stop her drinking, but when her craving reduced her to stealing from the takings and turning up for work blind drunk, he reluctantly threw her out.

Still an attractive woman, Sally plied her trade in the streets, implementing her earnings by picking the odd pocket when the opportunity presented itself. She made a decent living for a while, but the ravages of drink finally reduced her to prowling the gutter in search of men she would once have crossed the road to avoid.

During the lean, desperate years, Sally had followed Frankie's success avidly in the local newspaper. And when, one sickening, desperate morning, she awoke to find herself on a filthy mattress between two equally foul-smelling, lice-riddled men, she crawled out into the street and wept copious tears of shame and loathing that she should have been reduced to such depths of depravity. Her self-abasement was made worse by the knowledge that, come the evening, she would do the same again in return for a bottle of drink.

It was later the same day when a despondent Sally, having guzzled a portion of chips, was about to screw up the newspaper her dinner had come wrapped in, when a familiar name caught her bleary eye. Wiping greasy hands down the sides of a matted, ripped skirt, her eyes, suddenly alert, raked the article. It was nothing sensational, just a short passage concerning yet another new shop the East-End entrepreneur Frank Buchannon had opened, thereby creating half a dozen new jobs to add to his increasing workforce. Instead of throwing away the paper, Sally clutched it to her chest as if it was a prized possession, her alcohol-clouded brain, dulled by years of abuse, beginning to germinate a plan.

With a look of resolve that hadn't been evident for many years, Sally walked slowly along the litter-strewn pavement deep in thought. Up ahead a smartly dressed man was emerging from a run-down terraced house, as if anxious not to be seen coming from such a disreputable place.

Sally sneered at the departing figure. They were all the same: keen enough to get their leg over at night when they'd had a few too many, then up and running the next day when they found themselves in unfamiliar, squalid surroundings.

Quickening her step, Sally caught up with the man as he hailed a passing cab. With practised ease, she bumped into him, her slim fingers, although somewhat shaky, expertly extracting a leather wallet from the inside coat pocket. Then she slipped down a side alley to count her spoils. Her face crumpled in disappointment as a solitary sovereign stared up at her. Stuffing the wallet down the front of her dress to pawn later, Sally fought down the temptation to go to the nearest pub. With a monumental show of will-power, she trudged half a mile to a second-hand clothes shop and haggled over the price of a blue serge dress and a black woollen shawl, both of which had seen better days, but still seemed new when compared with the rags Sally was wearing. Her next stop was the Hackney baths, where, for sixpence, she was shown into a small cubicle containing a cast-iron bath half filled with warm water, and given a sliver of soap and a threadbare towel. Twenty minutes later, clean and tidy for the first time since she could remember, Sally asked directions to Grantham Avenue in Bow.

Once at her destination, she stood on the corner of the street, her throat raw for want of a drink, her heart hammering painfully against the breast of her newly acquired dress, wondering if the grand house opposite was the one she was looking for. Years earlier, the local paper had printed an article about Frankie, giving his address, which Sally thought she had remembered, but now she was here she wasn't so sure. She paced up and down the tree-lined avenue as she fretted over what course of action to take.

She had just made up her mind to come back another time when she heard women's voices, mixed with those of excited children, coming from over the road. Ducking behind an impressive oak tree, she looked furtively at the house. Then a cunning smile appeared at the corners of her mouth as she recognised Rose at the door of number sixteen, chatting amiably with two prim-looking women in charge of three small children. Five minutes later, another woman arrived and left with a small child in tow. It was obvious, even to Sally's muddled brain, that a children's party was in progress. Sally settled in to wait. Instinct had told her to bide her time to see if Frankie was at home.

Craftiness, inbred in most alcoholics, warned her that he wouldn't be pleased to see her. Oh, no! And she wasn't so pickled that she'd risk her former lover's wrath. She continued to wait with a grim determination not to falter at this stage of her hastily devised plan. If Rose turned her away, then Sally didn't know what she would do next. She had already hit rock bottom: there was nowhere else to go but the morgue.

It seemed to Sally that she had been waiting for hours, and she was beginning to worry that she was attracting attention from the occupants of the other salubrious houses that adorned the avenue, but she gritted her teeth and stood her ground. Finally, when her courage was about to desert her, the front door of number sixteen swung open and three men walked jauntily down the path and got into a waiting carriage. As it passed her, Sally turned away her head, but not before she had seen Frank, the front and sides of his dark hair now sprinkled with grey, at the window, and felt her whole being react to his appearance as forcefully as if she had been struck a physical blow. And still she waited in the growing dusk of the October evening, trembling, eyes bright with tears at memories of happier days. Perhaps she would have returned the way she had come, if an irate woman, her cultured voice ringing with superiority, hadn't enquired haughtily, 'I say, you there. I've been watching you for the past hour. Be off about your business at once before I send for a constable.'

Sally's head reared up, but she cautioned herself to stay calm. Gathering her shawl around her shoulders she turned to the woman and replied, grandly, 'There's no need for that, missus, I was just leaving. Sorry to have bothered you,' and the woman retreated indoors.

'Stuck-up bitch!' Sally swore at the closed door. Then, gathering up the dwindling remnants of her strength, she crossed the road to number sixteen.

Earlier that day, the garden of number sixteen had rung with the cries and shouts of numerous children as the Buchannons celebrated the third birthday of their son Benjamin. Rose had hired a magician and a lanternist to entertain the children. Both men had done their jobs admirably, but the festivities had turned sour when the lanternist, displaying his slides to the hushed children, had shown *Hop O' My Thumb*, a gruesome tale, which while it enthralled Victoria and her friends, had frightened the wits out of Benjamin and the younger ones, who had screamed for their mothers.

The terrified children had dashed to the security of Mary Miller's well-cushioned body, shuddering and pressing deep against the rolls of comforting flesh. Those who weren't quick or lucky enough to be enfolded into Mary Miller's plump embrace were comforted by a concerned Rose and Frank.

It was now four o'clock and the party was over, but from the kitchen, where Rose and Mary were enjoying a quiet cup of tea after the noisy afternoon, they could hear Victoria and Ben shouting excitedly, 'It's my turn, Papa. It's my turn! Lift me up, Papa. Give me a piggy-back, Papa. Come on, Papa!'

'Bleeding hell! They'll kill the poor sod, if they're not careful. Here, you two, leave him alone for five minutes.' Mary banged on the glass pane, and was rewarded by two pink tongues stuck out in defiance, followed by a squeal of laughter as the two over-excited children ran down the garden, their small legs pumping furiously, with the tall figure of Frankie in hot pursuit.

'Gawd help us! He's as bad as them, the daft bugger,' Mary said affectionately, as she waddled back to the enormous scrubbed table and eased her girth on to a stout wooden chair.

Opposite her, Rose, her shining curls flattened into a neat bun at the base of her neck, chuckled. 'You don't have to tell me, Auntie. Goodness! Can you imagine what his big business friends would say if they could see him now? And did you see his face when that lanternist was showing the slides? Honestly, I swear Frank enjoyed them more than the children.'

Mary gave a grunt of displeasure. 'Silly bugger. Oh, not Frank. I mean, fancy showing them pictures to the little ones! Gawd Almighty, I thought they was gonna die of fright, poor little mites.'

A twinkle of merriment sparkled in Rose's blue eyes. 'They didn't half run! I thought for one terrible moment they were going to stampede right out of the house.' Then she let her head fall back and laughed out loud.

Mary took a long gulp of tea and looked around at the debris lining the kitchen. Plates smeared with cake and jelly were stacked in the sink, while equal deposits of the sweet treats had been trodden underfoot on the tiled floor. Streamers tangled across the table and balloons floated inches from the ground where they had been left abandoned by the small guests. In the far corner of the room, gaily patterned wrapping paper, which had contained Ben's presents, now lay forgotten in screwed-up bundles, the contents strewn across the table and work-tops to be sorted out and put away later that evening.

'Gawd help us! What a bleeding mess!' Mary shook her greying head in dismay and blew out her fat cheeks. 'You'd think there'd been a hundred kids here, instead of ten. Well!' Using the table as a lever, Mary hauled herself up from her chair. 'This won't get things done, I'd better make a start.'

Rose looked exasperated. 'Don't start that again, Auntie. Myrtle and Jane will be back soon. They'll deal with it.' Myrtle Fisher and Jane Wilson were the live-in maids Frankie insisted on employing, much to Mary's annoyance. Even after all this time Mary couldn't get used to being waited on. Seeing the obstinate glint in her aunt's eyes, Rose sighed fondly. She had given Myrtle and Jane the afternoon off to placate Mary, who had insisted the party should be organised and run by the family. But enough was enough. If the two women came back to find everything done they would start worrying again about the security of their jobs.

'Please, Auntie. I've already had Myrtle complaining – well, not complaining,' she improvised hastily as Mary sat down in anger, 'more concerned, Jane too. The poor things are worried you'll do them out of a job.'

Appeased, Mary gave a loud grunt. 'All right, then. I'll just clear the table, though. I can't stand looking at a mess.' But if the truth were told, Mary was worn out and looking forward to putting her feet up for forty winks, but she'd never have admitted it. And when, some ten minutes later, the two women returned from their afternoon outing, Mary made a great show of reluctance at handing over the clearing up into their capable hands.

Rose and Mary were in the process of trying to coax the excited children in from the garden for their bath when Fred Green and Joe Perkins came to collect their guv'nor for their regular night out at Frankie's club.

Dragging him away from the two protesting children, so that he could get himself ready for his night out, Rose and Mary sought to restore order to the now overtired and fretful youngsters. An hour later, with Frank gone, the children bathed, fed and fast asleep, Rose left Mary resting with her legs up in the living room, and went into the library to read.

Selecting a slim volume from the well-stocked shelves she settled herself by the window, but let the book lie unopened in her lap as her mind happily replayed the events of the day. She couldn't believe Ben was three already. Where did the years go? As normally happened when Rose started thinking of her son, she remembered the trip to Paris and a soft smile curved her full lips. She didn't know who had been the most surprised when Frankie had ended up in her bed after a late night's drinking and dancing at one of Paris's elegant night-clubs. For the previous four years of their marriage, they had, by unspoken agreement, maintained the relationship they had always enjoyed. Rose had her bedroom, and Frankie had his. If the servants had thought the arrangement odd, they had never made any comment, and Mary had wisely kept her own counsel. However, on that morning in Paris, when she had come bursting into Rose's room and found Frankie lying alongside her niece in the sumptuous four-poster, her face had spread into a grin of pure delight before she tiptoed out of the room.

Idly fingering the spine of the book, Rose stared lazily out over the garden. Her life hadn't worked out as she had once expected, but she was happy and contented. Frankie was a wonderful father to both their children, and if at times Rose's mind wandered to Jack, she firmly shut down on such thoughts. Everything she had she owed to Frankie, and not even in thought would she ever betray him. The love she felt for him wasn't the wild, passionate love she'd experienced in her younger days, but it was a deep love nonetheless, which she would always cherish.

Rose was just starting on her book when there was a discreet knock at the door. 'I'm sorry to disturb you, Mrs Buchannon, but there's a woman asking for you. She says her name's Sally, madam.' Myrtle, a plain woman in her mid-thirties, stood in the doorway, evidently displeased at the arrival of the unexpected guest.

Rose's forehead furrowed. Could it be . . . Goodness, it'd been years. She closed her book. 'Show her up, please, Myrtle.'

While Rose waited for her unexpected visitor, she paced the library floor in nervous excitement. Surely it couldn't be Sally Higgins! Why, she hadn't seen or heard anything from her since . . . A shadow of pain flitted across her face, then she straightened and shook herself briskly. That was all forgotten now. Dead and buried firmly in the past. A sudden shudder rippled through her body and she felt a moment's fear, then Myrtle reappeared and behind her stood a stranger, a shabby, frightened-looking stranger. Then the woman spoke, eight years rolled away and it was like yesterday again. 'Wotcher, Rosie. How's life been treating you?'

Rose swept forward, her hands going out to grasp Sally's own. 'Hello, Sally. It's good to see you again after all these years. Oh, come in, sit down.' Rose indicated a green leather chair. 'Myrtle, bring up a tray, please. And put some birthday cake on it, and a pot of tea.' She hesitated and turned to where Sally was perched on the edge of the armchair. 'Unless you'd prefer coffee, Sally?'

Sally gave a small, harsh-sounding laugh. 'I'd prefer a drop of whisky, but tea'll do for now, thanks, Rosie. That all right with you, ducks?' She shot a questioning look at the hovering maid.

Myrtle Fisher sniffed disapprovingly and left the room. Left alone the two women made small-talk, both looking up in relief when the maid came in with a heavy tray. 'Shall I inform Miss Miller you have a visitor, madam?'

'What? Oh, no, Myrtle. No, leave Miss Miller to rest. She's had a tiring day.'

Sally glanced up, her eyes inquisitive. 'Miss Miller? That your old aunt?'

'Yes, Aunt Mary lives with us,' Rose replied briefly.

Sally nodded, her gaze wandering around the room. 'She's done all right for herself, ain't she? You both have. Mind you, Frankie always did say he was gonna make it to the top. And you know our Frankie, always gets what he wants, don't he? And Gawd help anyone who gets in his way.'

Rose said nothing. Cautioning herself to remain silent for the moment, she ignored the alarm bells ringing inside her head and busied herself with pouring the tea.

Under the pretext of helping themselves from the tray, Rose and Sally took the opportunity to take stock of each other. Sally saw a beautiful, self-assured woman, elegantly dressed in a navy velvet skirt and pale blue silk blouse, fastened at the neck with a small gold brooch. Rose saw a haggard, shabby woman with bloodshot eyes and flaccid skin, who bore little resemblance to the vibrant, attractive girl she had once worked alongside. She felt an overwhelming stab of pity for her former workmate, who had obviously fallen on hard times.

Stuffing a large piece of fruit cake into her mouth, Sally glanced up, then flushed at Rose's pitying stare. 'Sorry, Rosie. I ain't eaten since this morning. In fact, I ain't had a decent meal in a long while. Still, I suppose you already guessed that. You being educated an' all.'

Rose put down the china cup she was holding. 'No, it's me who should be apologising, Sally. It was unforgivably rude of me to stare. It's just . . . Well, I never expected to see you again. And you turning up like this . . .' She spread her arms wide in a gesture of confusion. Then, noticing Sally hungrily eyeing a crystal decanter on the walnut sideboard she rose quickly to her feet. 'Would you like a drink? I mean, a proper drink. In fact, I think I'll join you, it's been rather a hectic day.' Rose chatted on, aware that she no longer had anything in common with this woman, and wondering guiltily how long Sally was planning to stay. If Mary was to come in now! 'We had a party earlier on, for Ben's birthday. That is, my son, Benjamin. He was three today. The entire house was turned upside down for most of the afternoon.' Sally grabbed the proffered glass and swallowed the contents in one gulp, then held it out to Rose. 'Cheers, Rosie. I'll have the same again, if you don't mind.'

Rose refilled the glass then resumed her seat, trying to think of something to say.

Sally's nerves had been soothed somewhat by the whisky, and she gave a low laugh. 'Don't worry yourself, Rosie, girl. You don't have to keep up the chit-chat, I ain't planning on stopping.'

Rose felt ashamed. She hadn't realised how transparent her feelings were. Wanting to make amends she said hurriedly, 'Don't be silly. You're welcome to stay as long as you like.'

Sally stared fixedly at the earnest face and grinned wryly. 'Always the lady, eh, Rosie? And what'd yer husband say if he came home and found me here?'

Rose took stock of the situation. Then, squaring her shoulders, she said firmly, 'I don't know what Frank would say, Sally, but as he isn't here, we won't worry about it.' More briskly now, she asked, 'How are Rita and Henry? Are they both well? I often think about them and—'

'Huh! Don't make me laugh, Rose.' Sally's voice had turned bitter. 'I bet you ain't given them a minute's thought since the night you left the Red Lion. Oh, don't bother denying it,' she added quickly as Rose started to protest. 'I don't blame you. I would've been quick to shake off the past if I'd been in your shoes. Still, seeing as you asked, I'll tell you.' Fast becoming easier in her surroundings, Sally walked over to the sideboard and poured herself another drink. 'As a matter of fact, good old Henry threw me out of the pub a couple of years back.' She winked broadly. 'Caught me with me fingers in the till. Oh, I ain't denying it. I was caught bang to rights. I needed the money you see, Rosie, to pay for me drinking. Your old mate's turned into a soak, but then you've only got to look at me to know that, ain't you? And, as far as I know, poor old Reet might have gone down the same road 'cos I ain't seen her for years.' As the whisky worked its way through her system, Sally became aggressive. 'In fact, I ain't seen her since the night after your dear *husband* beat the shit out of Henry for letting you show your tits in public an'—'

'No! I don't believe you.' Rose's angry cry cut across the room. Her cheeks flaming, she glared up at the shabby figure.

'Oh, he did, all right. Poor old Henry couldn't see straight for weeks afterwards. Frankie nearly killed him. And as for Rita . . . Well, she got such a fright when I told her how I'd found you, she did a runner. 'Cos if Frankie ever found out it was her who found you that old butcher, she'd have gotten a lot worse than Henry did. She upped and legged it. She sent Henry a note saying she'd found a better job, just in case Frankie came asking after her. No, I ain't seen hide nor hair of the poor cow since then. For all I know Frankie caught up with her, and if he did . . . well! Poor old Reet won't be telling any tales now, will she?'

Rose faced the smirking figure, her blue eyes suddenly hard. 'That's enough, Sally. Frank hasn't harmed Rita. He had no cause to. I never told him anything. So if that's all you've come to say, then you can go. I'm grateful for what you did for me, Sally, but—'

Sally whirled on Rose, crying, drunkenly, 'Grateful! I should bleeding well think you are grateful. If it wasn't for me, you'd be dead now. You and your bastard! I always said I was a fool to get involved and I was right, wasn't I?' Breathing heavily into Rose's stricken face, she went on, 'I thought you was better than that, Rosie. I know we never got on but you was always fair. Shit! You're just like all the rest, ain't you? When the chips are down, you don't wanna know. Well, I've got news for you, Rosie, girl. You owe me plenty, and I think now's a good time for you to start paying back the debt, don't you? I've kept quiet all these years but, like I said before, I ain't had a lot of luck lately. So, what d'yer say, Rosie? You gonna help an old mate out, or not?'

Pale but calm, Rose studied the intimidating figure with a confidence she was far from feeling and answered, 'You're right, Sally, I do owe you something. Although I didn't realise at the time that you wanted payment for helping me. If I had known sooner, I would have seen you were properly compensated.'

The quiet dignity in the cultured voice brought shame to Sally's worn heart. She sank back into the armchair and began to cry. At once, all bitterness left Rose and she dropped to her knees beside the distraught figure. 'Oh, I'm sorry, Sally. Truly I am. I didn't mean that. It was a terrible thing to say. And I should have come to thank you. I knew where you were. I have no excuse for not coming to find you, Sally. I thought Frank had seen you . . .' Her voice trailed off miserably. How stupid she had been. She should have known better than to imagine Frank going out of his way to thank Sally. He couldn't stand her. But what of Henry and Rita? Could what Sally said be true? Rose considered what to do next. Oh, Lord. She should never have agreed to see Sally. Yet what else could she have done? As Sally had so forcefully pointed out, Rose owed her a debt of gratitude, and now that debt was being called in.

A feeling of lassitude stole through Rose's slender body. She had been extraordinarily lucky over the years. She had two healthy children, neither of whom she had dared hoped for following the trauma of Victoria's birth. Then had come Ben, a child the doctors had warned her she would never be able to conceive after the botched abortion. Oh, yes, Ben had been a miracle in more ways than one. A tired old cliché that Mary was fond of repeating sprang to Rose's weary mind: 'Count your blessings.' Well, she was counting them at this very minute. She had her children, a husband who adored her and a beautiful house with servants to do her bidding. Yes, she had been lucky. But one always has to pay a price.

Shuddering, Sally looked up at Rose, her eyes brimming

with tears. 'You always was a lucky cow, Rosie. But what about the baby? How'd yer manage to wangle Frankie into bringing it up?' A derisive note had crept back into her voice. 'D'yer have to keep it quiet while Frankie's about? You know, keep the kid out of his way. 'Cos I can't see Frankie taking some other feller's kid on. Not even for you. He might act like a good father when there's company, but what about when you're all here on your own? What's it like then, Rosie? Go on, you can tell me.'

The eager, almost gloating note in Sally's voice brought Rose's hackles up once more. 'Victoria is Frank's daughter, Sally. There has never been any doubt on that issue.'

Sally's eyes stretched wide. 'Well, I'll be buggered! Who'd have believed it? The great Frankie Buchannon getting lumbered with another man's bastard and bringing it up like his own. Well, don't that take the biscuit?'

'Frank *is* Victoria's father. And I'd strongly advise you against mentioning the subject again, Sally.'

The two women's eyes locked as the tension in the room rose, then Sally dropped her gaze.

Rose left the room and went into Frankie's study. When she returned a few minutes later she took Sally's rough hand and pressed two large white five-pound notes into the coarse palm.

Sally's tears stopped instantly. She wiped her eyes with the edge of the woollen shawl, looked down at the notes and gave a watery smile. 'Thanks, Rosie. Thanks a lot. Oh, look, I'm sorry if I was a bit nasty, I didn't mean any harm. You know me, Rosie, always did have a mouth on me.' The hostility had been replaced with oily gratitude, and Rose's stomach lurched with distaste.

Sally was preparing to leave, her effusive thanks over-whelming. 'You don't know what this means to me, Rosie. Thanks, mate, I really appreciate it.'

'It's all right, Sally. It's the least I can do,' Rose replied dully.

A short time later, Rose watched dispassionately as Myrtle showed the unwanted guest out.

Sally's harsh voice carried up to Rose. 'Cheers, darlin'. 'Ere, you want to see a doctor about that, ducks.'

Myrtle looked down her nose at the blowsy woman, her disapproval evident.

'And what might that be, madam?' she enquired politely.

'That poker you've got stuck up your arse. I'd see about having it out if I was you.' The crude remark was followed by a raucous laugh. 'Well, I'll be off, then. But don't worry, I'll be coming back. Me and Rosie have got a lot of catching up to do. Ta-ta.'

On the landing Rose's fingers curled around the banister until her knuckles turned white.

CHAPTER TWENTY

'What's up, Princess? You're miles away. Got anything on your mind that I should know about?'

Rose's head jerked up guiltily. 'No, of course not, Frank.' Rose smiled at her husband. 'As a matter of fact, I was thinking about what to buy the children for Christmas. It's only a couple of weeks away, and I haven't a single thing yet.'

Frankie's face relaxed. They were seated in the living room on this Friday evening in December, Frankie sprawled easily on the dark red chesterfield, waiting for Fred and Joe to arrive for their weekly visit to a reputable gaming house in the West End. Rose was anxious for him to be gone in case Sally turned up unexpectedly.

In the three months since Sally had first reappeared in Rose's life, she had taken to calling once a week, always when Frankie was absent, and always leaving much better off than when she had arrived. The strain of keeping the visits secret from Frankie was beginning to tell. The servants had been sworn to secrecy.

But while Rose could control Myrtle and Jane, trying to keep Mary quiet was a different matter entirely. That rumbustious woman was incensed at what was happening behind Frankie's back, and lost no opportunity to tell Rose what a fool she was being in handing over large sums of money to a woman whom Mary described as, 'no better than she oughter be'.

And now Frankie was becoming suspicious, as well he might. He had always given Rose a generous allowance, as well as access to the wall safe in his study, but until recently Rose had rarely taken advantage of the liberal funds available to her.

Leaning back on the chesterfield now, he contemplated his wife lovingly. There was at least fifty pounds missing from the wall safe, and if she hadn't spent it on the children, then it was a reliable guess that she was planning a Christmas surprise for him. He reached over and fondled her knee, saying good-humouredly, 'Why don't you take a cab up to the West End one day next week? You could spend the day browsing around the shops and have dinner out. It'd make a nice change for you, instead of standing out in the cold dishing out soup in Stoke Newington, or stuck at home all day with the children . . . and Mary!' He made a face of mock horror, and Rose laughed despite her private worries.

Rose put down the evening newspaper she had been pretending to read and laid her fingers over the strong hand clasping her knee. Her face soft, she said, 'You are good to me, Frank. And I think I might do just that. It's been ages since I spent a day by myself shopping.'

Frankie squeezed the slender fingers then looked up as the front-door bell chimed. 'That'll be the boys.' Standing up, he bent over and kissed the top of Rose's head, adding, 'I won't be too late, Princess, but don't wait up, eh?'

Rose giggled. 'Don't worry, I won't. The last time I did, I saw the dawn break.'

Frankie grinned at her then moved to the door. He paused, then asked, 'By the way, Princess, you ain't seen or heard from any old friends lately, have you? 'Ere, what's up, Rosie? You've gone as white as a sheet.' A steely note had entered his voice at the sudden change in Rose's demeanour. She looked scared to death.

Rose took a tight hold on herself and managed a bright smile. 'It's these headaches I've been getting. They come on so quickly it takes me by surprise. Look, you go on, Frank, I'll ask Myrtle to fetch me some aspirin. A couple of those usually do the trick.'

Frankie hovered by the door, not wanting to leave her if she was in pain, and not entirely convinced by her words. Then he seemed to make up his mind. His manner noticeably cooler, he said, 'All right, Rose. I'll send Myrtle up. See you later.' Then he was gone.

Rose stared at the open door, her face drawn with anxiety. Frankie knew something was wrong. He had always been quick on the uptake, especially where she was concerned. But how could he possibly have found out about Sally? No! That couldn't be the reason behind his change of manner. If nothing else, Frank had always been direct. If he had found out about Sally, then he would have confronted her with it straight away. So what on earth had he meant by that remark about hearing from old friends?

'Frankie says you've got a headache. That right, Rosie, love?' Mary, her homely face drawn in concern, came into the room carrying a glass of water and two flat white tablets. 'Here you go, girl. Get these down you.' Handing Rose the glass, Mary waited until her niece had swallowed the aspirins, then sat down in the spot Frankie had not long vacated, her expression troubled. 'You oughter tell Frankie what's going on, girl. You can't keep dishing out his money to that trollop without him finding out.' Seeing the pale eyelids flutter, Mary sighed. 'Gawd help us, love, I know this Sally woman helped you out once, but you've paid her for her trouble, ain't you? Why d'yer keep giving her money? It's blackmail, that's what it is, girl, blackmail, pure an' simple. If you keep on giving in to her, she'll bleed you dry.'

Rose sighed wearily. 'I know, Aunt Mary, I know. It's just . . . Well, she's down on her luck at the moment. I feel sorry for her. It's like . . . I've got everything I could want for, and she has nothing at all. If it wasn't for Sally . . .'

Mary gave an impatient grunt. 'Oh, don't give me that old story again, Rosie. All right, so she helped you out – saved your life, I know, but that don't mean you've gotta spend the rest of your life, and Frankie's money, paying her back. Now, you've already given her a fair old whack. If she was genuine, she'd have used that money to get herself back on her feet, but she ain't. And why should she, when she's

found a mug like you to support her for the rest of her life?'
Mary wagged a disapproving finger. 'Now, look here, Rosie,
I ain't never kept anything from Frankie in me whole life,
and I don't like lying to him not after all he's done for us.
You keep on talking about how Sally saved your life, well,
what about what Frankie's done for you? Gawd knows, how
we would've managed if he hadn't stepped in to take care
of us? He's been good to you, Rosie, now you can't deny
that, he's been a bloody saint. I mean, look at the way he's
brought up Vicky, like she was his own kid. He thinks the
world of her. Sometimes I think he loves her more than little
Ben, an' when you think whose kid she really is . . .'

Rose sprang up from the chesterfield. 'That's enough,
Aunt Mary. We agreed, all of us, that that subject would
never be mentioned. Victoria *is* Frank's child, and I don't
ever want to hear you talk like that again. Do I make myself
clear, Auntie?'

Offended, Mary struggled to her swollen feet. 'Yeah, I
understand all right, Rosie. Keep your place, Mary, that's
what you mean. Well, don't you worry, girl. I know where
I stand now. But I'll tell you this for nothing.' Mary hobbled
over and stood within a few inches of Rose's wan face.
'Don't expect me to lie for you any more, 'cos I ain't gonna
do it. If Frankie asks me what's happening to all his money,
then I'm gonna tell him. It's only fair. It *is* his money you're
chucking about, after all.'

Rose felt her knees buckle and caught hold of the irate
woman's arm. 'Please, Auntie, I feel bad enough as it is.
Look, I promise, the next time Sally comes, I'll give her
one last payment, and I'll make it clear there isn't going
to be any more. I promise, Auntie. Only – only don't tell
Frank, please. He would be so hurt that I didn't confide in
him . . . and angry too, terribly, terribly angry.'

Mary's features softened. If the truth be told, she still
partly blamed herself for Rose's past misfortune. It had
been hard for Mary to discover that Rose hadn't felt able
to come to her old auntie for help in the first place – had
been in such fear of her that she had risked her life at the
hands of a back-street abortionist rather than face her wrath.
And what made Mary's conscience trouble her even more

was that she couldn't say that she would have received the unwelcome news of her niece's pregnancy with kindess or understanding. Oh, Mary knew she'd have been all right later on, when she'd got over the first shock. Then she would have done all she could to help, and flattened anyone unwise enough to offer any critical remarks. What was clear to her, though, too, was her undying loyalty to Frankie, and with this thought uppermost in her mind, Mary said sharply, 'Look here, me girl, I've said me piece an' I ain't going back on it. I'll hold me tongue till after that trollop's next visit, but if you give in to her again, then I'm telling Frankie what's going on. I know you feel sorry for her, and there ain't nothing wrong in being kind, but there's a world of difference in being kind and letting yourself be walked over. I thought you had more gumption than that, Rosie.'

Mary's words hit home. It was true, Rose was trying hard to keep her life on an even keel. Everything was going so well and she was afraid to do anything to spoil it. But Mary was right: Sally's demands must stop. It would be unpleasant, for Sally wasn't going to take kindly to having her new-found source of wealth dry up, but it had to be done. Mary was right: she, Rose, had become soft. It was time to get the old Rose back.

Then the doorbell chimed, and Rose felt her courage slip away. She cast a pleading look at Mary, then waited.

Myrtle's disapproving voice rang through the house. There was no need to ask who the late-night visitor was.

'Now, don't you go backtracking, me girl,' Mary urged. 'Tell her straight. After tonight, there's gonna be no more. 'Ere, d'yer want me to come with you, love? I'll soon settle her, don't you worry about that. I—'

Rose stepped in front of her. 'No, Auntie. This is my mess. It's up to me to sort it out. But thanks.'

'Well, I'm here if you need me,' Mary called after her gruffly.

As on other occasions, Myrtle had shown Sally into the library. When Rose walked in, Sally turned eagerly to face her.

'Hello again, mate. Coo, it's bleeding tatties out there. I nearly froze me arse off waiting for Frankie to leave. Still,

I'm here now.' Warming her hands over the blazing fire, Sally laughed self-consciously and added, 'I was gonna leave it till nearer Christmas, but I thought to meself, Rosie'll probably be busy later on.'

Rose walked further into the room, and when she spoke there was no friendliness in her tone. 'You were here only two weeks ago, Sally. You can't have spent all that money I gave you so soon.'

Immediately on the defensive, Sally's face settled into hard lines. 'You've forgotten what it's like out there in the real world. By the time I've paid for me lodgings and food there's not much left.'

'You can still find the money for drink.' Rose looked at her scornfully. 'I can smell it on you, Sally. You reek of whisky.' At the look of shame that passed over Sally's ruined features, Rose felt herself weakening, as she always did. She reached out to touch Sally's arm, then flinched when it was rudely jerked away. Determined to say what must be said, Rose lifted her chin and said, 'Look at yourself, Sally. Take a good look at yourself. The Sally I once knew wouldn't have accepted charity. That Sally was proud and independent. Look at you now. Why, you're still wearing the same dress and shawl you had on the first time you came here, even though you could easily have afforded to buy yourself some decent clothes with the money I've given you over these past few months.' When Sally remained tight-lipped, Rose went on, 'Good Lord, Sally, it's the depth of winter. You'll freeze without a good coat, yet you spend all your money on drink. You haven't even tried to get another job, have you?'

Like a wild animal ready to pounce, Sally leaped towards Rose, forcing her to step back in alarm. Between clenched yellow teeth, she ground out, savagely, 'You make me sick! D'yer hear that, Rosie? You make me sick to me stomach. *"You haven't even tried to get a job!"'* she mimicked, then made a growling sound in her throat. 'Everything's so black and white in your little world, ain't it? You've never known what it's like to be on your own. You've always had Frankie to fall back on. Good old Frankie, always there when you needed him. He wouldn't have seen you starve, or thrown out on the streets if you'd lost your job. And you always knew that, didn't you? At the back of your mind, you must have always known he would be there to step in if things got too rough. Oh, yeah, good old Frankie. You never could see any wrong in him, could you? Even though it was staring you in the face, you could never see what he was really like.'

Her face carved into lines of stone, Rose said stiffly, 'I think you'd better leave, Sally. You're no longer welcome in my house. I'll give you one more payment, then it's over between us. You helped me once and I'm grateful, but I've paid you back handsomely for that one good deed, and I'm not paying any more.'

Sally feigned astonishment. 'Is that right, Rosie? Well, we'll see about that. *Sit down, lady. You're about to hear some home truths about your dear, kind husband.*'

Outraged, Rose prepared to leave the room, but with a swiftness that startled her, Sally bounded across the room barring her exit. 'Oh, no, you don't. You're gonna listen. You're gonna find out why I helped you that night.' Rose stared with growing unease into the wild, ravaged face before her. Unwilling to provoke a fight, she prepared herself to listen calmly to Sally's rantings.

Sally relaxed slightly, but she remained firmly in front of the door. 'I told you that night in the infirmary that I'd gone through the same thing once, d'yer remember?' Not waiting for confirmation, she gabbled on, 'Well, what I didn't tell you was that it was your precious Frankie's kid I got knocked up with. Oh, you can look surprised,' she said bitterly, as Rose's eyes betrayed disbelief. 'I was only nineteen, still wet behind the ears. I thought Frankie was gonna marry me and we was gonna live happily ever after. Only he didn't see it that way. What *was* his exact words when I told him?' She pretended to ponder the question, then clicked her fingers in Rose's face, forcing her to step back a pace. Sally followed her relentlessly, breathing whisky at her. 'Oh, yeah, I remember now. He said, "What you telling me for? It could be any one of a dozen other blokes'. Why don't yer put all their names in a hat and pull one out? Just make sure it ain't mine, 'cos you ain't saddling me with no bastard kid."' Dreamily now, as if talking to herself, Sally continued, 'Oh, he wasn't completely heartless, oh, no. He gave me a couple of quid, and told me to go and sort meself out. So I did. Only it all went wrong. And there wasn't any friend to come looking for me—' She broke off, tired suddenly. 'Anyways, that's all in the past. I ain't come here for a walk down Memory Lane. I survived. And when Rita told me what you was planning on doing, it all came back to me. And before I knew it, I was tearing up to Graham Road trying to stop you.' She lifted her shoulders hopelessly. 'It brought it all back. I wasn't thinking of you. I'd've done the same for anyone in the same boat. It – it was like I was trying to turn the clock back and save meself.'

Moved by the tragic story, Rose murmured softly, 'I'm sorry, Sally. Really I am. Look, I'll give you enough money to get you back on your feet again and . . .'

But Sally was staring blankly at the far wall as if in a daze. She wandered through the room, trailing her fingers over the expensive pieces of furniture and letting her eyes roam around, as if seeing it all for the first time. Inside she was thinking, with maudlin despair, This should have been mine. This room, this house, the nice furniture and all that went with it, this should have been my home, not Rosie's. It should have been me dressed in that cream and black satin outfit and all the other lovely clothes she's got. It should have been me with children growing up around me. Everything that Rosie's got, including Frankie, should have been mine. And now the smug-faced bitch is trying to get out of paying a few bob to help me out. Well, we'll soon see about that! Her face settled into hard lines of defiance and she hissed, 'Oh, no, Rosie. You ain't getting rid of me that easily. I've got used to being kept. It certainly beats working me guts out for a living. No! We'll keep to our arrangement and—'

Springing into life, Rose yelled, 'You're mad. Mad! I don't have to give you anything. I only helped you out because you helped me once, and because I felt sorry for you. But not any more. You have no hold over me, Sally. You can't hurt me, and I'll be damned if I'm going to let you bleed me dry. I'll tell Frank what's been going on.'

Sally's index finger was drawing a circle on the walnut bureau, and when she spoke again, Rose felt the blood drain from her face. Every bone in her body seemed to turn to jelly. 'Did you know that Jack's back, Rosie? I saw him the other day. Didn't recognise him at first in his posh new uniform. Inspector, I think he is now. Anyway, there he was, all togged up, going into Hackney police station, and I thought to meself, Hello, I wonder if he knows he's a father. I mean, he should be told, shouldn't he, Rosie? After all, I know you said Frankie's brought Jack's kid up like his own, but he ain't her *real* father, is he? Oh, Gawd! Is that the time?' Her eyes had darted to the wall clock. 'I'd best be on me way. If you wouldn't mind getting me *Christmas present* first.'

For a few moments, Rose was frozen to the spot. Then a wave of uncontrollable rage swept through her, and with a roar that surprised even herself she lunged at the unsuspecting Sally screaming, '*You bitch. You evil bitch. You're not getting another penny out of me. I'll see you in hell first. And if you tell Jack about Vicky, I'll kill you. Do you hear me, Sally? I'll bloody kill you.*'

Taken off gaurd Sally stumbled back. The heel of her worn-down shoe caught in the edge of the Persian rug and before Rose could move, she fell back heavily, hitting her head against the side of the bureau with a sickening thud.

Almost instantly the door to the library was flung open, and a grim-faced Mary charged into the room shouting, 'That's it. That's enough!'

Rose cried hoarsely, 'Don't, Auntie, don't. She's hurt. Help me get her up.'

But Mary bellowed, 'I'll help her up, all right. I'll give her me toe up her arse. Come on, you trollop, get up off the floor.' Standing over the dazed Sally, Mary was a formidable figure. And Sally, shaking her head groggily, decided wisely not to push her luck any more that day. There was plenty of time to get more money out of Rose.

She felt a rough, heavy hand jerk her to her feet, then she was being propelled along the corridor. The next thing she knew she was out in the cold, dark street with the solid door slammed firmly behind her.

Still dazed and feeling sick, Sally began the long walk home. In the high street, she stopped to rest against a lamp-post, fighting down a wave of nausea and faintness. When she felt a little better she put her hand to her head. She had a terrible headache. The pain went right round the top half of her head like a vice. Stumbling and cursing, she rooted in her bag to see how much money she had on her and sighed with relief when her fingers closed around two half-crowns and some loose change. It was enough to get home to Hackney, and for a couple of glasses of whisky.

In the back of the cab, Sally closed her eyes and felt worse. Bugger that bitch, and that fat old cow for interfering. Well, they hadn't seen the last of her. And if they wouldn't cough up, then a certain inspector would be only too happy to see her right.

The cab wheel rolled over a dip in the road, bringing a cry of agony from Sally's lips. Bloody hell, she felt rough. The sooner she got home and into bed the better.

CHAPTER TWENTY-ONE

The Black Hat Club was comfortably full, admission reserved to members only. Men in dinner jackets sat around green-baized tables, some with fat cigars hanging from nonchalant lips as they eyed the cards they held.

Over in the far corner of the ornate, smoky room, another group of men stood around a roulette wheel, some gambling for fun, others as if their lives depended on the outcome of the next spin. Frankie stared down at the red and black numbers, his fingers curled around the dice he held, his mind clearly elsewhere. Normally he enjoyed his nights at the gaming club. To Frankie, gambling was a sport he indulged in for sheer fun, and unlike many of his companions, he set himself a limit and stuck to it religiously, always quitting if and when his luck was out.

Tonight, though, his mind wasn't on the game.

'Are you playing, sir?'

Fred Green and Joe Perkins exchanged worried glances as Frankie continued to stare unseeingly at the roulette table. At an encouraging nod from Joe, Fred nudged Frankie gently in the ribs. 'Guv! You all right, Guv?'

Frankie started, his eyes going first to the hovering Fred, then to the waiting croupier. 'Sorry. Me mind's somewhere else tonight.' Giving the dice a thorough shake he threw them down, his eyes lighting up in pleasure as seven rolled face upwards. Collecting his winnings, he turned to his men.

'I don't feel like playing any more tonight, lads. You stay on if you want, I'm off home.'

The two men stood undecided, then Fred, his craggy face creased into lines of concern, asked, 'What's up, Guv? You've been quiet all night.' A few years ago, he wouldn't have dared be so familiar, but since Frankie had married, the former hard man had mellowed considerably. Not that he had turned soft, far from it, but he had become more approachable in later years. Except for the past few weeks.

As the two men followed the tall figure from the club, they looked to each other for explanation of Frankie's strange mood. Finding none, they hurried after him, a man they would protect with their lives if necessary. There hadn't been as much call for their services since Frankie had turned respectable, yet there were still people who would love to see him in a pine box. With this in mind, they shouldered their way into the foyer, keeping the compelling figure in clear view at all times. They had been with Frankie since their teenage years, ducking and diving the local constabulary in a way that was second nature to the cheeky, brash Cockney youths.

There had never been any doubt about accepting Frankie Buchannon as their leader. It had been clear, even at an early age, that Frankie was different from the other petty thieves that littered the East End. He had brains and cunning, and he wasn't afraid to take risks. Both men's earliest jobs had been to protect him from anyone nursing a grudge, and there had been many such people back then.

As Frankie had slowly climbed the ladder to success, Fred and Joe, related now by marriage, had clung to their governor's coat-tails with grim determination not to be left behind, like some of their former mates. Now they managed a thriving textile factory between them, with only Frankie to answer to. To both men their rise in fortune had been like a dream come true and if, sometimes, they hankered for the excitement of the old days, they comforted themselves by remembering that they were too old for such carryings-on now.

Dogging Frankie's rapid footsteps, Fred and Joe, their

movements edgy, fell into step either side of him. He
no longer asked for their services as bodyguards. It was
something they accepted as part of their vocation, and it was
a task they took on gladly. They might well be respectable
managers of a large business, but deep down they were
still Frankie's boys. Always had been, always would be,
and their loyalty to the man who had saved them from the
gutter remained fierce and unwavering.

'Oh, Auntie, I should never have given Sally all that money.
I should have known she'd keep coming back for more. But
I felt so sorry for her, and when I remembered what she did
for me . . .'
　'That's enough of that talk,' Mary cut in brusquely.
Pouring a large measure from a half-empty wine bottle,
she went on, 'I'm sick of hearing you go on about what that
trollop did for you. Never mind about giving her money,
she's asking for a smack in the mouth. If she hadn't found
you that night, someone else would've. Besides . . .' Mary
lowered her voice in case the two maids, dismissed for the
night, might somehow be listening in to the conversation
taking place in the large, comfortable kitchen that Mary
thought of as her domain. 'Whatever she did for you in
the past, she's been bleeding well paid for it.'
　Peering over a cup of cocoa, Rose looked across the
kitchen table with appealing eyes. 'I know, Auntie. But
I still feel bad. I can't help it. Even more so now, after I
went for her like that. She was hurt, really hurt. I know you
think she was putting it on but you didn't hear that horrible
sound when her head hit the side of the bureau. It made me
feel sick.' Then another, more frightening, thought gripped
her. Putting down the cup with trembling hands she said,
shakily, 'Do you think she was bluffing about seeing Jack,
Auntie? What if she was telling the truth about him being
back in London? If she is, then she could tell him about
Vicky out of sheer spite. Oh, God! I couldn't bear it if he
found out. Not after all these years. I have a new life now,
and you know what Jack's like. If he—'
　'If Jack will what, Rosie?'
　Both women spun round on their chairs, their mouths

agape in shock at seeing the imposing figure lounging in the open doorway.

Rose was the first to find her voice. Pasting a smile on her lips, she cried, 'Frank! What are you doing back so early? I didn't—'

His eyes hard, Frank stalked across the kitchen, pulling off his heavy overcoat. 'Cut the crap, Rosie. I want to hear more about our old friend Jack. Been to pay you a visit, has he?' He hooked a foot around the leg of a chair and pulled it from under the table. Folding his long frame down he surveyed the two nervous women with a cold stare. 'I knew something was going on. You've been going round with a face like a smacked arse for weeks.' Reaching across the table for the wine bottle he put the neck to his lips and took a large swallow.

Rose's hand went to her throat in alarm. 'No, Frank. You've got it all wrong. I haven't seen Jack since that day he came here looking for me, I swear to you, I haven't.'

Frank's fist crashed down on the table and he bawled, 'Don't give me any of that old cobblers, Rose. I've just heard you talking about him. Christ Almighty!' Frank's free hand smacked against his forehead in growing anger. The sound caused Rose to wince as if that same hand had struck her instead. 'I can't believe you'd sit there and lie to me face. An' don't try and tell me I must have heard wrong, 'cos there's nothing the matter with me hearing an' . . .'

Stung by the recrimination in her husband's voice Rose could only stare at him in growing dismay as she braced herself to come clean and tell him what had been going on. But Mary retaliated first. Her initial shock at seeing Frankie home had faded and Mary's own considerable temper had begun to boil. Leaning her full weight on the table, she thrust a thick finger under his nose and roared, 'Well, it's a pity your brain ain't working so well as your bleeding ears then, ain't it, lad? 'Cos if it was, you'd know our Rosie would never go sneaking behind your back to another man. And if, by some strange miracle, she did start cheating on you, d'yer really think for one minute I'd sit back and let her get on with it? Gawd blimey, Frank, you should know better than that.'

Thrown by her fierce attack, Frankie lowered the wine bottle and sat up straighter, his handsome face taking on a look of perplexity as he realised he'd been wrong in his quick assumptions. Feeling like a small boy caught out in a minor misdemeanour, he looked guiltily at Mary's glowering face, then turned to the visibly distressed Rose. His eyebrows drew together in a questioning line.

'All right, so I was wrong about you seeing Adams,' he muttered, rubbing his chin in agitation. 'But something's going on here, and it's got something to do with him. So let's be having it, Rosie. What's going on?'

Rose swallowed apprehensively, her eyes on Mary for moral support.

'Well, go on then,' Mary urged persistently, 'Tell him. Or, by hell, I will, me girl.'

Rose said, breathlessly, 'I intend to, Auntie, if you'll just let me get a word in edgeways!' Then she fidgeted on her chair for a few seconds while she composed herself. When she started to speak, her voice sounded stronger than she felt as she began to unburden herself to her distracted husband. And as Frankie listened he felt a huge weight lift from his shoulders. For weeks now, ever since he had found out that Jack Adams was back in London, he had been filled with dread – of what, he couldn't put into words, it was just a feeling he couldn't shake off. And when Rose had begun to act strangely, he had imagined his worst fears had been realised. Then, to come home early and catch her and Mary talking about Jack! And all the time it had been that bitch Sally, blackmailing Rose.

The stupid bitch! The drink must have rotted her brain if she thought she could get the better of Frankie Buchannon, or any member of his family. Whatever good she'd done in the past had been wiped out in a single stroke by her underhand dealings. To try to cadge a bit of money to survive was one thing, but to threaten to tell Jack Adams about Vicky, the child that he, Frankie, had raised as his own and thought of as his own, that was something else. The spiteful bitch could blow his family apart if she wasn't stopped. A slow burning rage coursed through his lean, muscular frame. He'd see Sally dead before he let her destroy all he had worked for.

'Frank!' Rose was gazing at him with fearful eyes.

Pushing back his chair, Frankie strode swiftly to her side, dropped to one knee and put his arms around her waist. Looking up at the watchful Mary he asked, 'Give us a minute, will you, Mary?' And Mary, her bearing purposeful, nodded and left them alone.

Cupping the strong face in her hands Rose gazed tenderly into the dark brown eyes. 'How could you ever think I'd betray you, Frank? I'd rather cut my wrists than hurt you. You're everything in the world to me. Whatever Jack and I had was over the day I married you. I love you, Frank. In every way one can love, I love *you*.'

With a cry of shame Frankie caught hold of the slender hands and kissed them fervently. 'Oh, Princess. I'm sorry. But I promise I'll never doubt you again. On my life, I'll never cause you another minute's pain.' He gathered her up from the chair into his strong arms and buried his face in the luxuriant copper hair. 'I'd die for you, Princess. Without a moment's thought. I'd die for you.'

Rose murmured, 'There's no need for that, darling. As long as I have your love and trust, I won't ask anything more of you.'

They remained locked together for a few precious moments, then Frankie, feeling a growing urgency to settle things with Sally, drew away reluctantly. 'Listen, Princess, I've gotta go out for a while . . . No, it's all right. I'm not gonna do anything terrible,' he reassured her, as she pulled away in alarm. 'I just want to go an' have a word with Sally. Once she knows you've told me what's been going on, she won't give us any more trouble. I'll give her enough money to keep her mouth shut. 'Ere, hang on, I don't know where she lives, do I?' Frankie smiled down into Rose's worried eyes. 'Gawd blimey, Princess, don't look at me like that. I ain't gonna do anything to Sally, honest! Now, you tell me where I can find her. She did say where she was living, didn't she, Princess?'

'Yes, but, Frank—'

As Rose made to protest fearfully, he bent down and

kissed her lips. 'Trust me, Princess. Leave it to me to sort out.'

Filled with foreboding yet trusting him to keep his word, Rose reluctantly gave him Sally's address. 'She's living in that old tenement building down Morning Lane. It's number eleven, on the third floor, I think. Frank, I wish you wouldn't!'

Knowing Rose wasn't convinced of his intentions, Frank tilted her chin up. 'Look, Princess, I know I've let me temper get the better of me in the past, but I ain't gonna do anything to spoil what we've got. I ain't that stupid. Trust me, Princess.'

Eager to get away, he ran up to his study. Quickly he opened the wall safe, extracted six five-pound notes and stuffed them into his wallet. His eyes were cold with menace. The thought of giving that cow more money to keep her trap shut filled him with rage, but he had promised Rose. Still, accidents happen. He would give Sally the money as promised and he'd give her something else to remember him by too. By the time he'd finished with the filthy slag, she'd wish she'd never tried it on with Rosie. Remembering that he had said he would not harm Sally, Frankie's lips curved into a chilling smile. He was going to keep his promise to give her some money – and one out of two promises kept wasn't bad, was it?

'What are you doing, Papa?'

The sleepy child's voice surprised Frankie. In an instant he became the loving father. Scooping up the tousle-haired little girl into his arms he gently kissed the coppery curls saying lightly, 'What are you doing up at this time of night, you little horror? Your mother won't half be cross if she hears you out of bed.' Cuddling the warm body close, Frankie carried his daughter back to her room admonishing her quietly, 'Be a good girl and go back to sleep, sweetheart.' Tucking a thick yellow quilt around her, Frankie bent down and planted a kiss on the smooth forehead. 'Night, night, darling. See you in the morning.'

The little bundle turned on to her side, murmuring drowsily, 'Night, night, Papa. I love you.'

'I love you too, sweetheart,' Frankie whispered. Then he

looked down at the other bed and the small shape fast asleep beneath a matching quilt. He pushed back a lock of dark brown hair from his son's cheek, bent and kissed him, too, before tiptoeing out of the room. On the landing, his expression hardened once more as he thought of Sally's threat to tell Jack Adams about Vicky. Fuelled with rage and anxiety, Frankie took the stairs two at a time and grabbed a heavy coat from the hall-stand. Shrugging his arms into the sleeves, he heard Rose calling out to him to wait. Jamming a hat down over his ears, Frank went out into the night.

Fred and Joe were strolling idly down the Mile End Road, heading for home, when a carriage drew up alongside them. 'Get in. I've got a job for you both.' The terse command brooked no argument, and the two men climbed in.

Frankie was slumped in one corner, his face hidden in the shadows, his mind seething. To think that that *bitch* could turn up after all these years and threaten his family! He'd say one thing in Sally's favour: she had guts. She had always stood up to him, had never been afraid to tell him exactly what she thought, even when her efforts had earned her a smack in the mouth. But she'd gone too far this time. As the carriage rolled over the damp cobblestones through the dark December night, Frankie pondered on how Sally could hurt him if she wanted to.

He had never, in his wildest dreams, imagined he could love Jack Adams's offspring. He had been more than prepared to bring the child up as his own for Rose's sake because, as he had kept reminding himself during those long, anxious months waiting for the birth, the child would be Rose's too, and he had been determined to concentrate on that factor. But the moment the tiny scrap of humanity had been placed in his arms, something had happened inside him. And when the hazy blue eyes had opened and peered at him uncertainly, then closed trustfully again, some tiny corner of him had opened up and reached out to the child. From that moment on Victoria had been his child, his daughter, and he loved her with every fibre in his body. During the first years of his marriage, Frankie had never been happier or more content. He had willingly accepted the platonic relationship that existed between himself and Rose, assuaging his physical needs with a variety of short-term mistresses. But since the first night he and Rose had come together as man and wife, Frankie had never looked at another woman – he no longer needed to.

When Rose had told him she was pregnant, he had experienced a disquiet that had momentarily overshadowed his elation at the news: he had been afraid that he wouldn't be able to love any other child as much as he loved his daughter. Yet when his son was born, he had discovered that love for a child is all encompassing and unconditional, be it for one child or ten. Nor could the intense depth of such love be explained. It was just there.

He had often wondered what sort of father he would make, imagining himself too selfish and caught up in his own affairs to make a good one. Now he knew differently. Frankie shifted restlessly on the carriage seat. He had everything now that he had ever dreamed of, but if Sally opened her big mouth to Jack Adams – and he knew that she wouldn't hesitate if thwarted – then Jack could well cause trouble. He wasn't the kind of man to ignore his own child. Frankie wasn't afraid that he could take Victoria from him – as far as the law was concerned she was his: she had been born inside marriage and she had his name on her birth certificate. But Jack could make life difficult, especially if he insisted that Victoria be told of her parentage. And Adams wasn't a lowly constable any more. He was now an inspector and, as such, a man with considerable clout.

Damn that woman. Damn her to hell for coming back into their lives.

When the driver pulled up outside a seedy tenement block, Frankie was the first to jump out on to the pavement. Issuing a curt command to his men to stay with the carriage, Frankie tore up the rickety stairway, heedless of the damp, decaying walls that brushed against his smart overcoat. There was only one thing on his mind and that was to silence Sally, once and for all. He had come prepared with thirty pounds, a fortune to someone like Sally Higgins, but if that wasn't enough, he wouldn't hesitate to resort to other, more certain, methods.

The stairway and landings were dark, but Frankie found the number he was looking for. Lifting a gloved hand he rapped sharply on the peeling door. There was no answer. His pounding became more insistent as his anger grew, and several other doors opened. Frankie faced the gloomy figures: 'Piss off, and mind your own business.'

When Sally's door remained shut, Frankie kicked it open. 'Sally! Sally, you here, you old slag? Come out and face me.' His strong voice resonated off the walls of the poky room, which appeared to be deserted.

Determined to wait until Sally returned from whatever pub she was spending his money in, Frankie walked further into the room, his nose wrinkling as the rancid smell of body sweat and lice hit him squarely in the face. Then he found himself beside a brass bed. Peering through the gloom he could make out a dim outline on the filthy mattress. With a cry of triumph, he moved forward and grabbed at the arm flung over the side of the bed. But Sally didn't stir. Puzzled, Frank bent closer, ignoring the powerful odours that were emanating from the torn grey sheets.

'Sal! Come on, wake up, you old cow. Sally! Sal?'

Alarm spread through him as the silent figure remained still. Gingerly now, Frankie lifted Sally up, then stepped back quickly as he realised she wasn't breathing.

'Oh, my Gawd!' For a few seconds, he felt a surge of elation. The old cow had drunk herself to death and saved him the trouble. Then his eyes screwed up in bewilderment. Sally might have turned into an old soak but drunks didn't usually die of it at her age. Casting a quick look around the bleak room he saw the outline of a lamp and lit it. The wick was nearly burned out, but the remnant threw out enough light to show the ghastly pallor of Sally's face.

Frankie raised the lamp higher to get a better look, his eyes cold as he looked down at the wretched piece of humanity that had once shared his bed. There wasn't a trace of the young, attractive girl he had once known, yet it was Sally – he would have known her anywhere, despite her drastically altered appearance.

A soft padding of feet sounded outside the door and he whirled round to face the intruder, then relaxed at the sight of Fred's anxious face. 'I thought I'd better come and see what was going on, Guv. You've been a while and – Oh, my Gawd! What's happened to her? She – she ain't dead, is she, Guv?' The fear in the hushed tone was evident.

Frankie hissed, 'Don't just stand there gawping, you stupid bastard. Close the door before all the bleeding neighbours come to see what's going on.'

Fred did as he was told and sidled into the room, his eyes shifting nervously towards the bed.

'And you can take that look off your face,' Frankie barked, 'She was like that when I got here.'

Fred shuffled his feet, his face troubled. 'All right, Guv, I believe you. But we'd better not hang around. The coppers would love to find you here with a dead body. There's still plenty of them as wants the chance to pin something on you. Come on, Guv, let's get outta here, *please.*'

Frankie grunted. Fred was right. If he was found here with Sally it would look bad for him. But something was tugging at his memory, something important. Then it came to him, and as the full import of the situation became clear, Frankie froze in horror. No! Don't be so bleeding stupid, he berated himself. But the persistent voices in his head wouldn't be silenced.

Passing a trembling hand over his chin, Frankie said urgently, 'Hang on a minute, Fred. There's something I wanna look at. Give us a hand, will you? Help me turn her over. Well, come on, man, what you waiting for, a bleeding tip?'

His face creased with worry and distaste, Fred helped Frankie turn over the heavy figure on the rumpled, disgusting sheets. Then Frankie uttered a cry. '*No!* Oh, shit.'

'What's up, Guv? What's the matter?' Fred croaked.

But Frankie, holding the flickering candle, was staring down at the back of Sally's head. He leaned closer, his eyes narrowing at the ugly swelling surrounding a small cut, half buried beneath Sally's matted hair. Dumbstruck, Frankie could only stand and stare at the incriminating evidence. Rose had told him she had lost her temper and gone for Sally, causing her to fall and hit her head against the bureau. But surely the knock hadn't been hard enough to kill her? There was no way of knowing for certain. But once she was found, the coppers would start sniffing around. Knowing Sally, she had probably been shouting her mouth off down the pub about her new-found wealth. Even if she hadn't, the two maids knew of her visits to the house. And the neighbours, too, must have noticed Sally's comings and goings. Once the body was found, the newspapers would carry the story. There would be many people who remembered Sally Higgins from her days at the Red Lion. If that happened, it wouldn't be long before the law came knocking at his door. It would be no good denying that Sally had become a frequent visitor to the house: there were too many witnesses. Maybe the maids would keep their mouths shut, but Frankie couldn't depend on that. Nor could he stop the neighbours from talking. And as Fred had pointed out, there were still some police officers with long memories who would like nothing better than an excuse to even old scores.

But he hadn't done anything, not this time.

No, but Rosie has. Rosie attacked Sally, causing her to fall. It had been an accident, but in the eyes of the law it would be murder.

The enormity of the situation paralysed him. His mind was screaming at him. Sally could have died of anything. The knock on the back of her head might have had nothing to do with her death. But he couldn't take the chance. Not where Rosie was concerned.

Galvanised into action, Frankie began to wrap the body in the grimy sheets. He had to hide it, and the best place to dump it was in the river. With a bit of luck, by the time Sally washed up the fish would have done their work, leaving no evidence of the blow at the back of her head, which could mean the rope for Rose.

Feverishly caught up in his desperate plan, Frankie forgot Fred's presence until the frightened man coughed uneasily. 'What you playing at, Guv? For Gawd's sake, leave her and let's get outta here.' Frankie stopped what he was doing and stared through the gloom at Fred Green. They had been together a long time, had been involved in some unpleasant escapades, many involving violence. But never murder. Frankie surveyed him with affection. 'This ain't got anything to do with you, Fred. This is private business. I never killed her . . . but . . .' Frankie bit down hard on his lip. He couldn't explain any further. To do so would implicate Rose, and as much as he trusted this man, he trusted no one where Rose's life might be at stake. So he nodded and added abruptly, 'Go on, Fred. Sling your hook – and tell Joe to go home an' all. Well, go on, then, you daft bugger. Clear off.'

Fred stood firm. He didn't know what was going on, but Frankie was obviously in trouble, so there was nothing else for it but to help. Filled with quiet resolution, he moved nearer the bed. 'You ain't gonna get very far on your own with a dead body slung over your shoulder, Guv. Here, stand her up, like she was drunk or something. We can carry her between us. No one'll take much notice, not round these parts.'

Hesitating only a second, Frankie nodded grimly. Fred was right. This was one task he couldn't do by himself. Placing one of the corpse's limp arms around Fred's neck, Frankie took hold of the other and swung it around his shoulders. Then, together, they began the arduous journey down the rickety stairway.

Behind them doors opened furtively and Frankie was uncomfortably aware that their movements were being carefully watched, but there was nothing he could do about it. Once out in the street, the two men rested against the rotting entrance, trying to keep Sally's limp body upright. Joe Perkins, who had been lounging against the waiting carriage, a cigarette hanging from his lips, sprang forward in startled surprise. Like Fred, Joe sensed his guv'nor needed help and reacted instinctively. 'Gawd blimey, Guv, what's going on?'

Sweating despite the night chill, Frankie said sharply, 'Keep your noise down.' Drawing in short, ragged breaths, he looked at both his men. He couldn't tell them the entire truth, but they deserved the chance to walk away now. Fred was already implicated by helping to move the body, and Frankie knew he couldn't place either man in any further conspiracy. His breath steamed in the cold air as he urged, 'I

can manage from here. Go on, the pair of you, piss off home
to your families. This ain't got nothing to do with you.'

As one, Fred and Joe stood their ground, their expressions
and bearing resolute. 'Yeah, well, that's up to us, ain't it,
Joe?' Fred said, knowing without doubt what the answer
would be.

'That's right, Guv,' Joe said solemnly. 'You ain't getting
rid of us that easily.'

Touched by their staunch loyalty, Frankie nodded. But
this was no time to stand about talking. 'Thanks, boys, I
appreciate it.' Pushing himself away from the wall, Frankie
grunted, 'Look, the best place to dump it is in the Lea.
What I was thinking of is this . . .' Lowering his voice to
a whisper Frankie outlined his hasty improvised plan, and
the three men began walking back to the waiting carriage,
their voices now raised in laughter for the benefit of the
bundled-up cabbie, their hard stares darting back and forth
on the look-out for prying eyes. The street seemed to be
deserted.

''Ere, what's up with her? You ain't putting no drunken
tart in my cab.' The disgruntled voice of the cabbie floated
in the air. With an oath, Frankie reached into his pocket
and pulled out a five-pound note, while at the same time
bundling Sally's lifeless body into the safety of the cab.
'Quick, Fred, give him this, before he has the street out
with his bleeding shouting.'

The note silenced any further protest from the grizzled
Cockney, and with a sharp flick of the reins and a low,
'Giddy-up', the cab pulled away.

Woken by urgent voices from a drunken sleep, Nobby
Summers opened a bleary eye to see what the fuss was
about. Shuffling from the pile of rags in a corner of the
tenement basement that was his home, the crippled beg-
gar crawled forward tentatively. He stayed hidden in the
shadows, listening attentively to the hurried conversation
above him, then smiled cunningly.

Since Frankie Buchannon's bully boys had broken his
fingers all those years ago, Nobby hadn't been able to
ply his trade. His life had been filled with hunger and

desperation, and a burning desire for revenge. Now he saw a chance to get even with the man who had crippled him and robbed him of his livelihood. Careful not to be seen, Nobby waited until the cab moved away then, with a swiftness that surprised even him, he shambled into the night in search of a copper.

Inspector Jack Adams was in his office working a night shift when the call came through from the front desk. Listening carefully to the desk sergeant's rapid words, Jack's face muscles began to twitch in growing excitement. Before the other man had finished talking, Jack hung up the earpiece, breathing a fervent whisper of triumph. *'Gotcha!'*

Almost at a run, he hurried across his office, dragging his hat and coat from a peg, and within minutes, flanked on all sides by uniformed officers, he ran from Hackney police station and climbed inside a waiting Black Maria.

CHAPTER TWENTY-TWO

The Prince of Wales public house was situated on the south bank of a meandering section of the river Lea. In the summer months, the pub was popular, with families converging in large numbers to sit outside with their drinks while their children fished or sat happily with their feet dangling in the warm water. But at this time of year, with the nights dark and freezing, the pub landlord had to make do with a few regulars from the neighbouring houses, and on this December night, the pub and surrounding area were quiet, almost deserted – which was why Frankie had chosen to come here. It was the perfect spot for what he had in mind. And if someone saw them, well, then, they were just three mates out for a drink with a ladyfriend. Nothing unusual in that.

It was around eleven o'clock when the cab pulled to a stop outside the pub, just in time for last orders. With much guffawing and play-acting, the three men clambered out with Sally's body propped up between them.

''Ere you go, mate. Another ten bob for your trouble.' Frankie grinned up at the now affable cabby and was quickly relieved of four half-crowns.

'Much obliged, Guv'nor. Much obliged!' Tipping back his bowler hat, the heavily wrapped-up man peered down at the unusual trio standing waiting for the tall man in evening dress and high hat. 'Bit of a long way to come for a drink, ain't it, mate? And your ladyfriend looks well gone to me.

I doubt if the landlord will serve her any more drinks. I
. . .' The words seemed to freeze on the man's lips as he felt
menace fill the air around him. Drawing in his chin under
the woollen muffler tied round his neck he decided to keep
any further comments to himself. Clicking his tongue he
urged the horse onwards.

Beckoning his men to follow, Frankie moved quickly
away from the bright lights of the pub to a narrow turning at the side where they could hide until it closed for
the night.

'What now, Guv?' Fred was clutching the body with
obvious reluctance, as was Joe.

Afraid that the two men were losing their nerve, Frankie
said sharply, 'Look, I've already told you both, this is my
problem and I'll sort it out. Besides, the worst part's over.
All I've gotta do now is wait till the pub clears, then take
her over to the bridge at Millfields and chuck her in. So
you might as well clear off home. If – Hang on!' He was
interrupted by a sudden loud discharge of half a dozen
men from the pub. Moving into the shadows, the three
waited with bated breath until the rowdy revellers had
passed on.

Anxious for his boys to leave, Frankie attempted to take
the dead weight of Sally from their grasp, saying gruffly,
'Go on, get off, the pair of you, you're getting on me nerves.'
But both men still stood firm.

'We're staying, Guv.'

Frankie heard the resolution in Fred's voice and nipped
guiltily at his bottom lip. He should never have put either
of them in such a dangerous position. He hadn't intended
to, but when he had spotted them walking ahead of the cab,
he had reacted instinctively. Both Fred and Joe had always
been alongside him in times of trouble, and he had ordered
them into the cab out of habit. Knowing it was useless to
argue, and secretly glad they were staying, he lapsed into
silence.

The narrow turning in which they were hiding was
filled with the sound of their rapid breathing, the air
around them filled with thick grey plumes of the steam
that streamed from their mouths and nostrils as they tried

to ignore the biting winds sweeping in from the dark river.

Another twenty agonising minutes passed before the pub discharged the last of its customers. When Frankie was sure that the landlord had closed for the night and there was no danger of being seen by a last-minute drinker, he beckoned Fred and Joe to follow him. Without the bright lights from the pub, the path leading to the bridge was as black as coal, which was exactly what Frankie had been banking on.

On the short journey he stooped and felt in the dirt road for any large pieces of rock or stone that might be lying around. His fingers closed around a heavy object and he slipped it into his pocket. Then he led the way up the slight incline to the bridge.

Frankie craned his neck to left and right, to make sure they weren't being observed. Then, his voice low and deep, he said, 'Let her go, lads. I'll do the rest.'

The two men stood back panting, glad their nerveracking ordeal was nearly over.

Dropping to his knees, Frankie pulled Sally's skirt around her face and head to avoid any blood splattering on his clothes. Then, raising the heavy rock, he began to pound the covered head and face.

Neither Fred nor Joe would have called themselves squeamish, yet when Frankie began to bludgeon Sally's lifeless form, they turned away. Even though they couldn't see the mutilation being perpetrated, they could hear the dull, sickening sound as the rock thudded down. Assuming that Frank was attempting to obliterate the features of the dead woman, and therefore draw attention away from himself, they waited stoically until he had finished. Then they heard him panting with exertion as he lifted the body over the side of the bridge.

Suddenly the quiet night was rent apart as a dozen wavering torches lit up the night sky and a steady stream of police officers appeared. Immobilised with horror, the three men stood rigid, like rabbits caught in the glare of a poacher's lamp, at the sight of the policemen swarming towards them from the bottom of the bridge, torches and truncheons held out before them.

As the horde of uniformed men advanced, Joe and Fred regained their senses and rushed to Frankie's side, obliterating the sight of the ragged bundle slumped over the bridge. Frankie seized the opportunity with which his men had presented him and, with one last savage push, he toppled the dead weight of Sally Higgins and the rock into the fast-flowing river beneath.

There was a loud splash, followed by a string of oaths from the rapidly approaching policemen.

Knowing it was pointless to run, Frankie turned to meet them, a wide grin creasing his good-looking features. 'Evening, Officers. Nice night for a walk, ain't it? 'Ere, get that torch outta me face, will you? You're blinding me!'

Rough hands grabbed at his arms, but he offered no resistance. He watched in amusement as three policemen scrambled down the grass knoll in a desperate attempt to recover the object that had just been thrown from the bridge.

A man moved forward from the ranks of his colleagues, coat collar turned up around his ears, felt hat pulled down low over his eyes. 'Hello, Frank. Nice to see you again after all these years. How you been keeping?' Jack's voice was pleasant, almost friendly. To the two men holding Frankie captive he added, 'Let him go.'

Freed, Frankie hitched up his shoulders and walked slowly towards the man in plain-clothes, his ever-active brain already formulating an escape route. One of Sally's neighbours must have smelt a rat and fetched the coppers. Funny that. Frankie hadn't thought the kind of people who lived in those rat-infested places would have bothered. But how had they known where to find him? Unless someone had overheard him and the boys talking.

A lesser man would have been terrified at being caught out in such damning circumstances, but Frankie was a past master at pitting his wits against the law. It would be a challenge, and a pleasure, to outwit Jack Adams once again.

Frankie swaggered towards him. 'Wotcher, Jack. I heard you was back in London. What happened? The sticks get too quiet for you?'

All around them, men stood amazed at the almost cheerful conversation that was taking place between the Inspector and Frankie Buchannon. Then the tone changed abruptly. The smile sliding from his face, Jack dropped the guise of friendliness and snapped, 'You ain't gonna wriggle outta this one, Buchannon. You've been caught red-handed. It'll be the rope for you this time. Put your hands out – now!'

Still sounding amused, Frankie said, as he raised his arms towards the threatening figure, 'You gonna read me palm, Adams?'

Jack snapped handcuffs on the exposed wrists then grabbed Frankie by the arm and shoved him down the path back towards the pub, with a loudly cursing Fred and Joe bringing up the rear.

Frantic splashes could be heard from the bank as several officers waded around in the fast-moving river in search of their evidence. A dozen torches bobbed up and down furiously as they tried to illuminate the dark area, hoping to see better.

Frankie's taunting laugh echoed in the night air. 'What you charging me with, Adams? Going out for a late-night walk with me mates an' chucking a few rocks into the river? You'll have to do better than that . . . *Inspector!*'

Jack growled, 'You're under arrest on suspicion of murder, Buchannon. It's gonna take more than a smart lawyer to get you off this time.'

Frankie's eyebrows rose in mock horror. 'Murder, Inspector? And who am I supposed to have murdered? I don't see no body lying around.' Casting his gaze over the taut faces of the officers surrounding him, he said, 'Well, lads, where's the body, then?'

The gloating tone was too much for Jack, and he ground out, through clenched teeth, 'We'll find it, Buchannon, don't you worry about that. If we don't find it tonight, there'll be a police barge out at first light and—'

Frankie swivelled his head round to stare into Jack's face. 'So what if you do find a body? That still don't mean I killed anyone.'

But Jack replied, 'Oh, you killed her all right. We've already got one witness, and there'll be others when the news gets out. Somehow, I don't think you're as popular, or as feared, as you think you are. Then there's all of us . . .' Jack threw out his arm to indicate his fellow officers. 'We all heard the body hit the water, Buchannon, every one of us, and—'

Frankie's eyes glittered like black marbles. Then he spat out, 'So you heard something going in the river. So what? You're gonna need more than that to pin a murder on me, Adams, and you know it.'

The temptation to smash his fist into the sneering face was suddenly overwhelming. Jack bundled Frankie over to his eager officers and snapped, 'Take him to the wagon. Get him outta my sight – and the other two. Go on, take him out of here.'

As Frankie was dragged away, he called mockingly, 'You ain't got anything on me, copper. I'm gonna walk away from this, just like I always do.'

Not trusting himself to reply, Jack turned his back on his tormentor and strode back up the narrow dirt path. His face pensive, he stood on the bank, his hands thrust deep into the pockets of his overcoat, and watched his men flounder about in the dark, murky waters of the Lea.

Despite his confident words, Jack knew he didn't have enough evidence to hold Buchannon for long. All he had was the word of Nobby Summers, who had disappeared as soon as he'd told the desk sergeant what he'd over-heard. According to him, Frankie had taken some tart to the Prince of Wales pub near Millfields, where he planned to chuck her over the bridge into the Lea. And that was all the information, and evidence, Jack had to go on. Damn it! If only they had arrived ten minutes earlier. Because Jack knew, without doubt, that Buchannon had indeed thrown some poor cow's body over the bridge. He'd heard her hit the water. There was no mistaking that sound. If they recovered the body and learned who the unfortunate woman was, then there was a good chance of connecting her to Buchannon. But without a body, or conclusive evidence and witnesses, there was nothing Jack could do. Without knowing who she was, he couldn't even come up with a motive for the murder, which would have been enough to hold Buchannon while he investigated further.

He stared gloomily at the river. He had known of drownings to wash up as far afield as the Thames at Westminster. Many were never found, to remain for ever beneath the dark waters, ensnared in the tangled weed and rushes that littered the river-bed. Pulling his coat collar further up around his neck, Jack turned away sharply and headed back to the pub.

Accompanied by two uniformed officers, Jack stood on the porch of the house in Grantham Avenue, his finger stabbing at the doorbell. To the men with him, the Inspector's expression was filled with resolve. They would have been amazed if they had known how dry his mouth had become, how fast his heart was racing. And not only at the prospect of seeing Rose again after all these lonely years. He was deeply apprehensive at having to give her the news he brought.

Pressing the doorbell with renewed vigour and dogged determination, he nevertheless sprang back in alarm as Mary's familiar voice bellowed, 'Hold your bleeding horses, will you? You'd better have a bloody good reason for getting me outta bed at this godforsaken hour, you . . .' Mary yanked open the door, pulling her thick grey dressing gown over a cream flannel nightdress. Her face fell in dismay at the sight of policemen standing on the doorstep at two o'clock in the morning. Not recognising the plain-clothed man, her eyes were immediately drawn to the dark blue uniforms, her hand clutching in fear at her throat. 'What's up? What's happened?'

Before anyone could speak, another voice, softer but equally worried, came from the passageway behind the stout figure blocking the doorway. 'Who is it, Auntie?'

Jack's heart flipped over as he heard Rose's voice and he warned himself to remember why he was here.

Stepping into the light Jack looked down into the fleshy face and said gently, 'Hello, Mary.'

Mary's large mouth flopped open in stunned amazement, but before she could utter another word, Rose had come to stand beside her aunt, her blue eyes looking up anxiously into the rugged, homely face that had once been so dear to her.

When she spoke it was as if she had spoken to him only the day before. 'What is it, Jack? Has something happened to Frank?'

Jack took off his hat and twisted it between his fingers. 'Can we come in, Rose? I'm . . . I'm afraid I've got bad news for you.'

Swallowing nervously, Rose stood aside to let the three men enter, then, with a regal nod, she indicated that they should follow her. Leading the way to the drawing room, Rose tried valiantly to still her pounding heart. Ever since Frankie had left earlier, she had been afraid. She had tried to stop him going, but he had raced out of the house before she could say anything. Since then she had walked the floor anxiously, before falling into a restless sleep. The moment she had heard the doorbell, she had known instinctively that it meant trouble for him. Exactly what trouble she had yet to learn. Bracing herself for the worst, she led the three men into the plush room and turned on one of the wall lamps. She invited them to be seated, but they declined awkwardly. Wrapping her arms tightly around her upper body in an effort to still their trembling, she looked to Jack for an explanation of the late-night call.

Jack stared at the lovely face, the corner of his mouth beginning to twitch slightly. Rose was clad in a deep green velvet dressing gown, her abundant mass of copper curls falling without restraint around her oval face and shoulders. The years had been kind to her. If anything, she looked even more beautiful than he had remembered.

Jack was about to speak when he found himself thrust to one side by a heavy hand. The next instant he was facing the full impact of Mary Miller's wrath.

'You've got a bleeding nerve, Jack Adams. Coming round to a respectable house in the middle of the night, scaring decent people half to death. Couldn't you have waited till morning before crashing in here with your hob-nailed boots? An' that goes for you two gormless sods, an' all.' She bestowed a look of pure venom on the two uniformed officers, which caused them to fidget uneasily. The furious woman, with her straggly hair bound up in tortuous-looking steel pins was a terrifying sight, but Jack had seen the spectacle too often in the past to be intimidated by it now.

He also knew Mary well enough to understand that beneath the quarrelsome, hostile façade, the elderly woman was badly frightened.

'Auntie!' Rose's voice was unusually sharp, betraying her growing agitation.

Mary, her lips working, fell silent, but her eyes and manner remained malevolent.

In the strained silence, Jack found himself wishing he was back in the peaceful surroundings of Hemerly. But it had been the unending peace and tranquillity that had finally driven him to distraction. He had realised, years ago, that he wasn't cut out for country life, not on his own, anyway.

Perhaps if Rose had been with him it would have made a difference. But deep down inside him, Jack recognised that he was a working copper with all that that entailed. Mixing with the poor and downtrodden, the drunks, the misfits and the downright evil was an integral part of his life as a police officer. Three years ago he had transferred to Scotland Yard and, with hard work, had risen to the rank of inspector. Yet it was only a few months ago that he had asked to be assigned to his old patch. He had asked himself many times why he had wanted to return to a place that held so many bitter, painful memories for him. And while until now he had been able to assure himself that he had had no ulterior reason in wanting to be back in the East End, he knew, as he stared hungrily at the lovely ashen face, that Rose had been behind his desire to be in his old haunts. But he had never imagined they would meet again under such circumstances. Jack had no pity for Buchannon – to his mind, the man deserved all that was coming to him – but Rose loved him, and Jack had heard that they now had two children.

A soft, audible sigh escaped his lips. This wasn't going to be easy. He cleared his throat. 'I'm sorry, Rose, but Frank's been arrested . . . on suspicion of murder.'

A cry burst from Rose's lips, and for a brief, heartstopping moment Jack thought she was about to fall. He moved forward as Rose gripped the edge of a walnut table to steady herself. When she raised her eyes to meet his, he witnessed a sudden change in her. There was a steeliness in the blue eyes he had never seen before. And for a brief, stomach-turning moment, Jack found himself staring into the face of a stranger. When she spoke at last, her voice was clipped and self-assured. 'You say suspicion of murder? And who exactly has my husband been accused of murdering, Inspector?'

Meeting the cool stare, Jack swallowed hard. When he answered his chilly tones matched hers. 'We don't know yet, Mrs Buchannon. Your husband was seen bundling a woman into a cab outside a tenement building in Hackney. Our informant also overheard him planning with two of his men to throw the woman into the river Lea. We arrived too late to stop him committing the act, but we all – that is, my men and I – heard the body hit the water. We . . .'

A surge of hope came into Rose's eyes, and beside her she felt Mary grab her hand. 'Are you telling me, Inspector, that no one actually saw my husband push this woman, whoever she may be, into the river?'

Immediately on the defensive, Jack answered curtly, 'No. That is, we didn't actually see him.'

A smile of triumph swept over both women's faces.

'And this witness you have. Will he or she swear in a court of law to what you have told me?'

Jack thought of Nobby, who had informed on Buchannon and had swiftly taken to his heels. He knew that, for the moment, he was defeated.

Rose saw his confidence collapse and said tersely, 'I'd like you all to leave now, Inspector. I have a call to make, to my husband's lawyer. Good evening, gentlemen.'

There was nothing left for Jack to do except give in gracefully. For now.

Beckoning to the uncomfortable-looking officers standing by the door, Jack left Frankie Buchannon's house, his heart as heavy as it had been on the last occasion he had visited it.

'What now, sir?' one of the constables ventured to ask.

Jack, his expression sombre, answered crisply, 'We go to the address the informant gave the desk sergeant and start knocking on some doors.'

CHAPTER TWENTY-THREE

The body of Sally Higgins was discovered by two young boys, their gruesome find making them local celebrities, at eight o'clock the same morning, wedged between several planks of old timber from the mill further up the river. A jubilant Jack Adams lost no time in formally charging Frank Buchannon with murder – the crime made even more horrific by the brutal mutilation of the victim's face and head, described in the newspapers as 'an unwarranted savage attack on a defenceless woman'. Identifying the body from the river had been relatively easy. All it had taken was a quick visit to the tenement building, where Sally's neighbours had reluctantly co-operated with the police, though none had been able to identify the men involved in her abduction, due to poor lighting in the building concerned.

Jack had also examined the squalid flat where Sally had spent her last evening, and in the lack of any blood found on the premises, it was clear that she had been alive when Buchannon and his men had carried her from the building. The murder must have taken place either near or on the bridge, before Buchannon had callously dumped the body in the river. And that fact had puzzled Jack. Because for all his hatred of Buchannon, he hadn't thought him the kind of man to smash in a woman's face in cold blood, before tipping her into a river. If Sally had been strangled, or even knifed, a killing performed in the heat of the moment, then yes, Jack could have understood that. But this killing didn't follow Buchannon's pattern of behaviour. Also, there seemed to be a complete lack of motive for the murder.

Having known Sally from her days at the Red Lion, Jack was aware that she had had a tumultuous liaison with Frankie. He was also starkly aware that the affair had ended a good ten years ago. If Sally had taken care of herself there might have been a remote chance that Frankie had started up their relationship again but, given Sally's steady deterioration through drink and whoring, Jack knew without a doubt that he wouldn't have given her the time of day. So why had he killed her? And, in doing so, put himself in grave danger of being caught. It didn't make any sense.

To all intents and purposes, Frank Buchannon couldn't have had any reason to want Sally Higgins out of the way, but still, as Jack kept reminding himself, that was up to the court to discover. His job was done.

Meanwhile the press were having a field day. Newspapers that had recently fêted the wealthy self-made businessman had been quick to smell blood, and in a complete turnabout, they began a campaign to expose the man behind the Buchannon empire. There was no real malice on the part of the newspapers, it was all down to business, and how many copies they could sell. People always loved to read about another's misfortune, especially if that person was well-to-do. Throw in a bit of scandal and a juicy murder and you had a recipe for record sales.

Reporters besieged the three-storey house in Grantham Avenue, but the stout door remained firmly shut against the clamouring horde.

Myrtle was sent to order food from a family-owned grocery store where Rose and Mary shopped, the parcels delivered by messenger boys, eager to be part of the excitement.

And for twenty-four hours of every day, a succession of hard-faced, close-lipped men guarded Frankie Buchannon's family in his absence, their rugged appearance keeping the reporters and curious passers-by from annoying the occupants of number 16, Grantham Avenue.

One intrepid reporter decided to chance his luck one day by creeping around to the back of the house and into the landscaped garden. Ten minutes later, he was bundled unceremoniously from the premises and thrown into the road, bruised and bleeding. Despite several entreaties from the police, the thoroughly shaken man had refused to make a statement or press any charges against his assailants.

During this time, Jack had made only two visits to the house. He received a frosty reception from Rose, and a vociferous, hostile barrage of abuse from the volatile Mary Miller, who was still convinced that her Frankie had been 'set up'. Nevertheless, he had completed his task in collecting statements from Rose and the two maids, appertaining to the events of that night. Mary's contribution, too obscene to put down on paper, he had willingly discarded.

The trial date was set for the first week in January, and the police set about collecting further evidence and witnesses to the savage attack on and murder of Sally Higgins, a former mistress of the man accused of killing her. Character witnesses on Frankie's behalf were becoming increasingly hard to find; his respectable new friends suddenly found themselves reluctant to be linked to a one-time racketeer. Equally hard to find were witnesses willing to testify to Frankie's brutal character. Despite the cloak of respectability, many people remembered the Frankie Buchannon of old, and his name could still intimidate. But slowly, as the newspapers continued to rake up his past and proclaim that he was destined for the rope, people began to have second thoughts about testifying. For, if the newspapers were telling the truth, though that would be a first, Frankie Buchannon was never going to come out of prison. If that was indeed the case, then his mob-handled empire would collapse.

All over London, men and women who had a grudge against Frankie and his men considered getting even with him for the injuries and terror inflicted on them in the past. And, as the days and weeks sped by with no sign of Buchannon being released, these same people breathed more easily, becoming confident that they had nothing more to fear from the man who had once terrorised them.

The climax to the whole sordid affair came when a major newspaper offered a substantial reward for information leading to the conviction of Frank Buchannon.

They began to crawl out of the woodwork.

'Is Papa coming home with you today, Mamma?'

Rose was seated at her dressing table, getting ready for her journey to the Old Bailey for the fifth day of the trial, when the heartfelt plea came from the pretty, copper-haired girl who had crept unnoticed into the bedroom with her little brother. Rose laid down her gilt hairbrush and faced her children. What she saw brought fresh waves of anguish to her already heavy heart. Ever since the night when Frankie hadn't come home, the children had been unnaturally quiet. They didn't play any more, or argue or laugh, they simply existed from one day to the next, waiting for their father to return. The only time they spoke was to ask when he was coming home, when she was going to fetch him. Rose held out her arms, and little Ben immediately ran into them, laying his dark head in her lap, but Vicky remained at arm's length. As she stroked Ben's soft curls, Rose said softly, 'We've been over this before, Vicky, darling. I can't bring him home, not until . . . well, not until I'm allowed to. You know that. Now be a good girl and—'

Tears of blind frustration welled up in the child's eyes. 'If you were in prison, he would get you out. He wouldn't let you stay there. My papa's not afraid of anyone. He'd just go into the prison and get you out. He would! He would! He wouldn't let anyone hurt you, or me and Ben, or Auntie Mary. He'd rescue us. Even if there was *hundreds* of policemen keeping us prisoners, he would fight them all and bring us home. Why don't you do something, mamma? *Please*. I want my papa to come home. I want my papa.'

The tearful plea, coupled with the fierce accusation, was too much for Rose. Again, she put out her hand in mute appeal, but the wilful child, her daughter, flounced away.

Rose let her hand fall back helplessly to Ben's head as her daughter ran sobbing from the room. It had always been this way between them, and in the midst of her own fear and grief, Rose pondered on the vicissitudes of life. Vicky was of her own flesh, yet she was Frankie's daughter and always had been. Her first smile had been for Frankie, her first tottering step had been towards Frankie's open arms. Her first word had been Papa. Her child loved the man she knew as her father with a passion that bordered on worship. And while she loved her mother too, it was her father who made the world turn for her, and her days bright. When Frankie walked into a room, Vicky lit up with love, overshadowing her little brother and often stealing his share of their father's attention. Rose had often wondered if Frankie, in his efforts to accept Vicky as his own, had somehow overcompensated in his endeavours. Poor little Ben had frequently been pushed aside by his exuberant, strong-willed sister, although it had to be said that Frankie had never shown any marked favouritism for her.

Cuddling the small body of her weeping son, Rose stared vacantly over his dark head. What was she going to do if Frankie was convicted? She desperately needed to talk about her fears, but there was no one she could turn to. Mary stoutly refused even to consider the possibility that her Frankie would be found guilty of murder, especially of a worthless trollop like Sally Higgins. Rose had had to endure countless hours of Mary's ranting against the unfortunate murdered woman, her aunt laying the blame for all their current misfortunes squarely at Sally's door. And Rose herself had come in for condemnation. Her aunt hadn't actually blamed Rose for Frankie's imprisonment, but Rose knew that Mary thought that if she hadn't given in to Sally's blackmail, he would still be at home with his family.

She blinked back tears. Maybe her aunt was right. Maybe it *was* all her fault. She had tried to stop him from going after Sally, that night, but even if she had succeeded Rose knew he would have gone another time. There was no way he would have let the matter rest, not Frank. Once he made up his mind to do something, nothing and no one could change it.

This was all her fault. If she hadn't become pregnant, if she hadn't asked Rita to find someone to abort her child . . . if . . . if . . . if . . .

Ben stirred in her lap, jerking Rose out of her self-recriminations. Gathering her son into her arms she laid her cheek against his. There was no point in going over and over the whole sorry business. It had happened. Frankie had killed Sally. He had admitted it, but only to his wife. He hadn't intended to, he said, he had only meant to give her a scare but it had all gone horribly wrong. To everyone else concerned, Frankie and his men maintained their innocence. They were sticking to their not-guilty plea. As Frankie said, if the law wanted to pin a murder charge on him they would have to prove it. He wasn't going to make it easy for them.

Rose had been surprised to find she felt no repugnance for what her husband had done. Maybe, she told herself, it was because she had experienced the same murderous urge the night Sally had threatened to tell Jack about Vicky. Oh, yes, she had. How could she condemn Frankie for what he had done in a moment of madness? In different circumstances it might have been her on trial.

'Mamma, when's Papa coming home?'

Rose pulled her son gently around on her lap so that he was facing her, then, gazing down into the dark eyes filled with shimmering tears, she said softly, 'It'll be all right, darling, it'll be all right.'

As more tears threatened to fall, Rose swept the fretful child into her arms and went in search of Mary.

Two hours later Rose and Mary were sitting side by side in the gallery of the Old Bailey, avoiding curious stares by keeping their eyes firmly on the well-dressed man in the dock. The two women were surrounded on all sides by stony-faced men in suits, their one aim to keep reporters and members of the public from harassing the governor's family.

New witnesses were brought in, each with an eager tale to tell in the hope that their testimony would be the vital key to convicting Frankie Buchannon, and that they would earn the newspaper's substantial reward. But even the lure of the hundred pounds on offer wasn't enough to stifle the fear that Frankie Buchannon was still able to instil. One glance at the public gallery was enough to show that the man in the dock had a formidable army to carry out his bidding. Yet still they came, pitiful wretches, spinning out tales of grievance nurtured for years, each one nervously avoiding eye contact with the man who stood accused of murder.

The prosecution made much of these witnesses, encouraging them to make the prisoner's violent character known to the court. It was a cleverly staged manipulation of these uneducated wretches, as the learned gentleman egged them on in his blatant assassination of Frankie's character. Then the defence counsel would take the floor, contemptuously taking these witnesses' testimonies apart with his clever tongue and eloquent wit. Other men in the past had been found guilty and hanged on much less evidence than that against Frankie Buchannon, but none had had Sir Timothy Rhys-Jones as their counsel. A man of whom it was said that he 'could get Judas off'.

Rose let all their words wash over her. She simply didn't listen as the court was regaled with lurid tales of violence, blackmail and extortion by witnesses and the prosecution. It was as if some part of her brain had shut down protectively whenever an accusation was levelled against the man in the dock. Her mind repeated what Frankie had told her of that night. He had meant only to frighten Sally, not to kill her. It had been an accident, that was all. Yet even as his name was dragged deeper and deeper into the mud, the prosecution could still find no new link or motive to tie him to Sally Higgins's murder, without which the case was surely doomed to flounder. For, as the defence argued daily, the accused wasn't on trial for his past misdemeanours. Indeed, the barrister extolled his virtues, pointing out the good he had achieved over the intervening years.

When the court adjourned for lunch Rose was allowed to visit her husband in the holding cell. Leaving her aunt in the protection of his men, she followed a police officer through a maze of gloomy corridors to a row of cells in the basement.

Frankie was standing by a barred window, a desolate look in his dark eyes as he gazed on to the world he was denied. He turned as the door opened, the look vanishing at the sight of his beloved wife. 'Hello, Princess.'

The presence of the guard prevented Rose from throwing herself into his arms, so instead she replied softly, 'Hello, darling,' as she sat down at the small wooden table in the centre of the cramped cell. Then, her composure crumbling, she cried, 'Oh, Frank. Frank!'

Immediately he was sitting opposite her, his strong hands clasping hers tightly. 'Give over, Princess,' he chided her. 'You know what we agreed. No tears and no giving up. It'll be all right, you'll see.' The optimism in his voice brought a wavering smile to Rose's lips and he grinned. 'That's better. Now, then, how's the kids? They bearing up all right? No one's giving you or Mary any grief, are they? 'Cos if they are, you just—'

A strained laugh escaped Rose. 'No. No one's getting at us. They wouldn't dare. The reporters are a pest, but the boys keep them at bay.' As she spoke, Rose realised that *boys* was an odd word to describe the thug-like men who guarded her. Yet it was how Frank had always referred to them, and she felt that if she questioned his term it would diminish him somehow. Patting at her eyes with a lace-edged handkerchief, Rose gave herself a mental shake. It was hard enough for him to be in here without her adding to his worries. Trying to keep her tone even, she told Frankie about Vicky's earlier outburst. She ended, 'Honestly, if she was a bit older, I swear she'd order the boys to come and break you out of here, and she'd be right up the front leading them.'

Frankie's whole face lit up. 'They'd follow her an' all.' He chuckled. 'She's a chip off the old block, ain't she, Rosie?'

Sadness came into Rose's eyes, and when she spoke there was a trace of censure in her voice. 'Ben's missing you too, Frank. I hear him crying at night and he's started to wet the bed again. He's suffering too. He – he loves you so much. They both do, Frank, and it breaks my heart to see their little faces every time I leave them to come here. The minute I get back, they both rush to meet me waiting to hear when you'll be coming home. I – I don't know what to say any more, Frank. I don't know what to tell them . . .'

With a gentleness born of love, Frankie tilted Rose's chin

up until he was staring into her eyes. His gaze intense, he said urgently, 'Just tell them to hang on a while longer. That's all you've gotta say, Princess. Just to hang on a while longer.'

The guard by the cell door cleared his throat reluctantly. 'Sorry, Frankie, time's up.'

'But I've only been here five minutes,' Rose wailed.

'Sorry, Mrs Buchannon. You'll have to go, it's the rules.'

Frankie stood up and pulled Rose to her feet. 'It's all right, Princess,' he said, as cheerful and optimistic as he always was with her. 'Look, don't hang around here all day, Rosie, it ain't worth it. You get off back to the kids and give them a hug from me.' He stroked her cheek lovingly, wishing he could take her into his arms, but it wasn't allowed. And though he himself didn't give a fig for rules and regulations, he didn't want Rose to suffer the indignity of being wrenched away from him.

'I'd rather stay, Frank. I mean, you never know what . . .' Rose's voice trailed off weakly under his understanding gaze.

'Yeah, I know, Princess . . . I know.'

When the guard showed Rose out of the cell, Frankie called after her, 'Give the kids my love, won't you, Princess? And tell Ben I haven't forgotten about our trip to the zoo when Vicky's at school. Just the two of us. Tell him that from me, Princess.'

Rose lowered her head in shame at the love shining in Frankie's eyes as he spoke of his son. How could she have ever doubted it?

Mary was waiting in the visitors' area. 'How is he, Rose? How's my Frankie?' Lumbering to her feet, Mary waited anxiously for Rose to join her, her cheeks wobbling in agitation.

'He's fine, Auntie. You know Frank, nothing gets him down.' Rose tried to smile and failed dismally. It was getting harder and harder to keep up the pretence of normality on which he insisted. The only way she could cope was to take one day at a time and, above all, not to dwell on the outcome of the trial – not to think the unthinkable.

Rose led her aunt out of the grim building and across

the road to the small tea-room they had been frequenting during the trial. As Mary fretfully consumed a large portion of chocolate cake, Rose gazed out of the window at the steady stream of sightseers, all hoping for a seat in the gallery at Frankie Buchannon's trial. Sickened by the public display of morbid curiosity, Rose finished her tea and paid the bill.

Once out in the street, someone recognised the two women and shouted eagerly, 'That's Buchannon's missus. Over there. There she is. Oy, Mrs Buchannon, how's Frankie doing?'

Her head held high, Rose ignored the crowd, her expression almost scornful, while Mary, never one to ignore an insult, immediately gave the heckler a sound tongue-lashing that sent the man scurrying off in embarrassment.

Mary and Rose were flanked on either side by Frankie's men, though as one had remarked to his wife the previous evening, 'I feel sorry for the Guv'nor's wife. But that old battleaxe don't need no looking after. Bleeding hell, she scares the life outta me.'

All the way to the public gallery, Mary rambled on. Rose knew the ceaseless talk reflected her aunt's anxiety, and her mind was elsewhere. Settling back into her seat she sought to allay her own fears. The trial was going well so far. Plenty of people, some of whom were on the jury, didn't care what Frankie had done in the past and were clearly sympathetic to the man in the dock. As the judge re-entered, there was a rustle of movement in the court below. Then Sir Timothy Rhys-Jones was on his feet once more, his cultured voice ringing out clearly. 'The accused is a man of considerable standing in the local community, who had had no contact with the deceased for a good number of years until a few weeks before Christmas. At that time, the court has been told, the former barmaid and friend of the Buchannons had fallen on hard times and asked them for help. As a good Christian, Mrs Buchannon, who incidentally gives a great deal of her time in helping those less fortunate in Stoke Newington, had welcomed the deceased into her home and freely given her a gift of money in a gesture of friendship and compassion – all with her husband's knowledge and blessing. On the night in question, however, Mrs Buchannon had found herself temporarily short of funds and had informed Miss Higgins that her husband would drop by later with a small gift to tide her over the festive season. Mr Buchannon freely admits he visited the deceased on the night in question, and that she was alive and well when he left. This version of events is corroborated by his companions, Joseph Perkins and Frederick Green, both respectable business associates of Mr Buchannon. Furthermore . . .'

Rose glanced absently around the court. She had heard all this before. According to Sir Timothy, there were only a few more prosecution witnesses to take the stand. Well, Rose played with her gloves, if that was true, then surely it couldn't last much longer. The nightmare that had invaded their lives must soon be over. Something Mary had said earlier came to her mind and she had to bite her lip to stop herself laughing.

It had been the day before yesterday when a steady stream of witnesses, including a cabby who swore that he had driven Frankie, two men and a drunken woman to the Prince of Wales public house on the night in question, had eagerly taken the stand. The defence counsel had torn the man's story to shreds, accusing him of concocting it in an effort to obtain the newspaper's reward. Why else, the white-wigged man had asked scornfully of the court, would the cab driver have waited so long to come forward, if indeed he was the honest man he purported to be?

The same had happened to Nobby Summers, the tramp who was supposed to have heard Frank planning to dump Sally's body in the river. The shivering wreck of a man had collapsed under the skilful questioning, and even though, as he left the witness box, he had loudly declared himself to be telling the truth, his credibility had been destroyed.

After Nobby had come a stream of Sally's neighbours, all embellishing their stories of the mystery man who had shouted abuse through the closed door to Sally's room before kicking in the door, who had then, with the aid of another man, carried the unprotesting Sally down the stairs never to be seen again. Then a portly man had taken the stand, declaring himself to be a butcher from Stoke

Newington. Here, Mary, her face suffused with rage, her massive body trembling with indignation, had stood up and roared derisively, 'Bleeding hell! They'll be bringing in Uncle Tom Cobbley an' all at this rate.'

The court had collapsed in uproar, and the judge had ordered it to be cleared for the remainder of the day.

Rose's eyes roamed the packed court-room, and she pursed her lips as she recognised Henry Dixon, her former employer, sitting at the far end of the second row of seats in the gallery. Sensing her scrutiny, Dixon looked up. When he smiled at her Rose sensed that he was on her side and returned the smile gratefully, before retreating back inside the protective shell she had built around herself during the trial.

Lost in a little world of her own, Rose jumped when Mary nudged her sharply in the ribs saying, 'You all right, girl? That feller's just said this is the last witness for today, thank Gawd. Bleeding hell! Where they all coming from, that's what I'd like to know? I'll bet Frankie don't even know half of 'em.'

But Rose had seen something down in the court. In a matter of seconds, her world had begun to crumble.

At that moment, Jack looked up into the public gallery, thinking wryly that, with all Buchannon's henchmen gathered in one place, it looked more like a rogue's gallery than anything else. Then his eyes, as usual, alighted on the elegant figure seated at the front. The unmistakable terror on Rose's lovely face shocked him. What on earth . . . ?

He looked towards the witness stand and the woman who was now taking the oath in a quavering voice. His head swivelled back to Rose as he wondered what it was about this woman that could cause her such terror.

As Rita Watkins had climbed into the witness box and taken the Bible in a trembling hand, Rose had leaned forward in her seat, her eyes wide with fright. She had never told anyone, not even Mary, about Rita's involvement with the botched abortion and she cast a feverish glance at Frankie. As usual, he was watching the proceedings with veiled amusement, probably wondering what grievance Rita Watkins would air about him. As Rose watched in helpless despair, she saw Frank's expression change to one of incredulity as Rita told of her life in exile: she had been afraid to come back to London in case Frank Buchannon did her in for helping his wife try to get rid of her unwanted child.

In an instant Frankie was on his feet demanding that he be allowed to speak, and the court descended once more into uproar as two officers tried to restrain him. Hitting out wildly, Frankie continued to shout to be heard.

Near fainting now, Rose heard him cry out, 'All right, I did it. I killed Sally Higgins. I'm putting me hands up. Now get that stinking, lying bitch off the stand, before I do for her an' all.'

And, in that instant, the veneer Frankie Buchannon had maintained throughout the trial slipped to reveal a savagery that brought startled gasps of fear from several women present, not least Rita Watkins, who screamed for help to all and sundry.

As if in a dream Rose saw Jack coming towards her, growing awareness glinting in his eyes, but Rose no longer cared what happened.

It was over. It was all over.

Frank was going to hang.

Then everything became a blur as she was helped by unknown hands from the court.

CHAPTER TWENTY-FOUR

'Here's the post-mortem report, sir, on Sally Higgins. The doctor says he's sorry it's taken so long to get to you, but he's been swamped with work.' The young constable stood by the Inspector's desk, a slim folder held out in front of him. 'It's always the same before Christmas, he says. Everyone seems to either do themselves or each other in. So much for the Christmas spirit, eh, sir?'

Jack glanced up irritably. Today was the day Frankie Buchannon would be sentenced to death. It was the day he had been waiting for for years. So why did he feel so bloody awful? As if he didn't know.

Rita Watkins's testimony had rocked Jack to the core. It had explained the hasty marriage between Rose and Buchannon. Rose had been pregnant, and in a moment's desperation had tried to abort the child. His child! But the abortion had failed, and Rose had nearly died as a result. He still couldn't quite take it all in. He had a child, a daughter. A child that Buchannon had raised as his own for the past nine years. And, according to all Jack had heard, Buchannon doted on her. The pair had been inseparable. Jack's first reaction had been to confront Rose, but when he had looked into those anguished blue eyes that day in the court, he hadn't had the heart to cause any more pain for the woman he still loved. Nor would he ever bring up the subject. As much as it hurt him to deny himself his daughter, Jack knew that any action he took to lay claim to the child would bring only suffering to all concerned. And Rose had suffered enough. Jack also knew he owed Buchannon a debt of gratitude. Not many men would have brought another's child up as their own, especially if the men in question had been bitter enemies, as he and Buchannon had always been. Not that Jack kidded himself that Buchannon had done it for him. Oh, no! If it had been anyone but Rose, Jack knew Buchannon wouldn't have been so charitable. Still, he conceded, it had been good of Buchannon, and even though Jack would never be able to thank him personally, he was grateful.

Then he remembered the constable's presence. 'Eh? Well, it's a bit late, isn't it? Buchannon's being sentenced this afternoon.'

The constable flushed. 'Yes, sir, sorry, sir. The doctor said to tell you his examination was carried out soon after the body was delivered to him, but then it got so busy down at the morgue that his notes were mislaid, and this is the first time he's had the chance to sort himself out.'

Seeing the nervous expression on the constable's face, Jack relented. It wasn't the boy's fault, after all. If anything the lateness of the report was down to him. As the officer in charge of the case, he should have chased up the post-mortem findings. But there hadn't been any point. It hadn't taken a genius in poor Sally's case to determine the cause of death. Taking the folder he dismissed the constable and laid it on the desk with a wry grimace. It was lucky the Buchannon case hadn't rested on this evidence or he would still be waiting for the trial to start. Jack returned to his paperwork, and for the next hour he was immersed in his task. At eleven thirty he stretched, yawned and leaned back in the comfortable desk chair, his hands clasped behind his head.

Sentencing had been set for three o'clock, so he had plenty of time to get to the Old Bailey. Lowering his arms, Jack stared gloomily across the office. He wasn't looking forward to this one little bit. Not with Rose and Mary sitting in the gallery, hearing someone they loved being sentenced to hang. At the thought a shudder rippled through his broad body. It was going to be grim, very grim, and he couldn't even offer support to the two women, not in the circumstances. Jack picked up the folder containing the post-mortem report on Sally. With nothing better to do for the moment he glanced idly through the doctor's sprawling, uneven handwriting, his eyes screwed up in concentration as he tried to decipher the almost unintelligible squiggles. You'd think, with all the education these doctors had, someone would have taught them to write properly.

Then his attention was caught by one small paragraph. Jack sat bolt upright, his eyes rapidly scanning the page. When he had finished reading, he lay back in the chair, stunned. He reached out for the telephone, and within minutes he was talking to the doctor concerned. What he heard only increased his bewilderment. Gripping the earpiece tighter, he bellowed, 'What d'yer mean, she was already dead when the injuries to her face were administered? How on earth could you possibly know that? What . . . Oh, look, I'm sorry, Doctor . . . No, no, you're quite right, I'm not a pathologist, but . . .' Jack listened intently as the doctor talked about the blood in a person's body settling in one place after death. According to the doctor's findings, Sally had died while lying down and had remained in that position for some time before she went into the river. Also, no blood or bruising consistent with the injuries to Sally's face and temple had been found. At this point Jack interrupted, 'But she'd been in the river! Surely that would account for no blood being found and—' Again, Jack lapsed into silence as the doctor continued, rather waspishly, to explain how he had come to his conclusions. As the doctor continued his narration about blood vessels, skin tissue and lividity, none of which made any sense to Jack, his puzzlement increased. Finally, and with growing alarm, he asked, 'So the cause of death was the wound to the back of the victim's head? How long had she been dead before? Oh, I see, you can't tell the time of death, but it was definitely before she went into the river and before the injuries to the face were inflicted. What? Oh, no. No, it doesn't make any difference to the case. I just wanted to know for my own benefit.' The voice at the other end of the line spoke again, and Jack forced a shaky laugh. 'Yes, it might help me with future cases. Thank you, Doctor. Yes, that's all right. Yes, thank you again, goodbye.'

Jack hung up the earpiece. Something was wrong here, horribly wrong. From the very beginning, Jack had wondered about the method employed to murder Sally Higgins. It just hadn't seemed to tie in with what he knew of Frankie Buchannon. Maybe he had killed Sally earlier, then gone back later with his men to dispose of the body. That would account for the doctor's findings. The mutilation to the face had obviously been carried out to prevent identification. But still . . . Something rankled in Jack's mind and, try as he might, he couldn't shake it off. Cursing beneath his breath, he rose to his feet. What did it matter when Sally had died? Frankie had murdered the woman – he'd put his hands up to it in open court. And he wouldn't put his neck in the hangman's noose for—

Jack came to a standstill. His mouth dropped open in fear as the germ of an idea slowly came to him.

Oh, Christ, no!

Frantically now, he began to pace the floor, his mind in a whirl. Unbeknown to Jack, his tortured thoughts mirrored those of Frankie on the night he had found Sally dead. And, like Frankie, Jack's fevered brain sprang to something Mary Miller had said.

When asked to make a statement about the night in question, Mary Miller had launched into a vituperative attack against Jack. He hadn't taken much notice at the time, his attention caught up in Rose's distress, but now snatches of the angry abuse came flooding back to haunt him. As if hearing Mary's words from a long distance, Jack vaguely remembered her mumbling something about *'If it had been down to me, I'd've given that trollop a lot more than just a push. And if she'd bashed her head when she fell, then it was her own stupid fault, not my Rosie's.'*

Oh, my God!

Jack trod back and forth across the thin carpet before he sank back into his chair, his eyes closing as he tried to block out the images now crowding his mind. If what he thought was true, then it all began to make sense. Why else, if not to protect Rose, would Buchannon have let Rita Watkins's testimony force him into admitting to the murder? Because if Frankie had done it, he would have fought to the bitter end to save his neck.

More to the point, if his suspicions were correct, then he couldn't let Buchannon hang.

Jack's head drooped in despair.

If the doctor in question had been anyone else, Jack would have taken the startling new evidence with a pinch of salt, but James Beecham was highly respected, renowned in the field of pathology. But before Jack did anything rash, he had to make sure. Snatching up his coat, he raced from the building.

Frank was sitting on a narrow bunk in the holding cell. As Jack entered he rose indolently to his feet and came towards him, walking with the easy swagger that Jack had always hated. 'Bleeding hell! I might have known you'd be in at the death, Adams.'

Jack stared into the handsome face, trying to keep his hatred for this man alive, for if he could do that then maybe he could turn round and walk away, forget what he knew. But Jack was a policeman, first and foremost, and his instincts were to see justice done, whatever his own feelings.

'Hello, Frank.'

Frank's dark eyebrows rose in mock astonishment. 'Well, well, on first-name terms now, are we, Adams? Still, I think I'll stick to calling you by your surname. It's a bit late for us to start acting pally, ain't it . . . Inspector?'

Jack blinked rapidly. He had wrestled with his conscience on the journey to the Old Bailey, still undecided whether or not to let the matter drop. But now that he was here, face to face with the man he had always hated, he couldn't do it. He had to give Buchannon the chance to save himself. He had intended to lead up to it. To ask certain questions and see how Buchannon reacted. Instead he said simply, 'You didn't do it, did you, Frank? You didn't murder Sally Higgins. You were covering up for Rose, weren't you? She got into a fight with Sally that night and Sally fell and smashed her head. I know she seemed all right when she

left your place, but that bang on the head is what killed
her, not you.'

Frank's mocking expression changed to one of horror.
And that was all the proof Jack needed.

Frankie glanced quickly to the open cell door, then darted
forward and thrust his face close to Jack's. He hissed
frantically, 'Keep your bleeding voice down, Adams. What
you trying to do. Get Rosie hanged an' all?'

Jack gazed into the contorted face, and felt a great weari-
ness seize him. He walked slowly over to the small, barred
window, his expression bleak.

So it was true. Buchannon hadn't killed Sally. Jack had
been hoping against hope that he would be proved wrong,
but now he knew beyond all doubt. Oh, he had smashed
Sally's face in and thrown the body into the river, but he
hadn't killed her. Rose had. And she wasn't even aware
of it. Of that Jack was certain. There was no way on
earth that Rose would let someone else take the blame for
something she had done. Especially something as serious
as murder. What was he going to do? Dear God, *what was
he going to do*?

Frankie watched the silent policeman, his fingers clenched
into fists, and fought to regain his composure. Then he gave
a harsh, grating laugh. 'What are you playing at, Adams? I
mean, bleeding hell, I'm gonna hang, ain't that enough for
you? Or d'yer want to make me suffer more by making up
this load of old bollocks about Rosie being involved—'

'Save it, Frank. I'm telling you I know. I wish to God
I didn't, but I do. The post-mortem report landed on my
desk an hour ago. There's no mistake. I checked. Sally
was dead long before you got your hands on her . . .
Jesus, Frank!' Jack's face was filled with misery. 'D'yer
think this is easy for me? D'yer think I ain't falling apart
inside, knowing what I know – and knowing what I've got
to do now?'

Frank grabbed him by the throat. 'Listen to me, Adams.
Whatever you think you know, you're wrong. D'yer hear
me? *You're wrong*. And I'll stand up in any court and swear
it was me that killed Sally. I'll send for the newspapers, too,
if I have to. They love that sort of thing. I'll give 'em an

exclusive story. Kind of like an insight into the mind of a murderer. Yeah, they'll lap that up!'

Jack stared into the dark eyes and shook his head in pity. 'You're really willing to hang, ain't you, Frank? You're gonna let them put a noose around your neck to save Rose, ain't you? My God, Frank, what are we gonna do?'

At the helplessness in Jack's voice, Frankie relaxed his grip and breathed a little easier. He stood back a pace and looked squarely into Jack's eyes. 'We ain't gonna do anything, Jack. We're just gonna leave everything as it is and keep our mouths shut. And not just for now either, but for the rest of our lives. Which is easy enough for me, seeing as how I ain't got long to go. But it'll be down to you to keep what you know quiet. It should be easy enough. After all, it ain't as if it's some poor innocent bastard going to the gallows, is it?'

Jack walked slowly to the bunk and let himself drop on to the hard mattress before his legs gave out on him. All Buchannon was saying was true. He couldn't for the life of him understand why he was here. Why should he care if the man swung? If it was a choice between him and Rose, there was no contest, was there? So why did he feel such overwhelming guilt? As Buchannon said himself, it wasn't as if he was as pure as the driven snow, and if he was willing to hang in place of his wife, who was he to stand in the way? Yet Rose wouldn't hang. What had happened had been an accident. But would the law see it that way? Oh, Lord. He didn't know what to do for the best.

Seeing Jack waver, Frankie moved in quickly. Keeping his voice low, he sat on the bunk beside the policeman and whispered urgently, 'Listen, Jack, you know what the law's like. We know what happened was an accident, but that won't stop your lot from arresting Rose if the truth comes out. D'yer really want to put her through all that? Ain't she been through enough? She's already been splashed all over the newspapers on account of that old cow Rita Watkins opening her big mouth about Rosie going to that old butcher . . .' He trailed off, realising that Jack must have guessed about the baby Rose had tried to abort.

Jack's mind was working furiously. Could he do it? Could

he stand by and let an innocent man hang? And the answer, to his shame, came back at him in a blinding flash. Yes, he could. If, by turning a blind eye, he could save Rose, then he would keep what he knew to himself. And it would haunt him to the end of his days.

Feeling old and tired, Jack rose to his feet. Looking straight ahead across the small, gloomy cell, he said quietly, 'Rose was lucky you were there to help her with the baby. It would have been hard for her to manage by herself.' He put his hat back on, and looked down at Frankie. He saw fear in the dark eyes, fear that had nothing to do with the sentence that was about to be pronounced. He rearranged his hat more comfortably, and swallowed hard before he added, 'You've been luckier than me in that department, Frank. You've got two lovely kids. I haven't got any.'

Jack watched the fear fade and felt a measure of comfort. Then the old Buchannon was back in evidence, who said slowly, 'Just to put your mind at rest – about me being topped, I mean – I did kill someone once, and got away with it. That old quack, the one that nearly killed Rosie. Well, I tracked him down an' stuck a knife into the miserable old bastard's guts. You can check if you don't believe me. I left the body in a derelict building off Stamford Hill high street. No one was ever caught for his murder. So, really, you could say I'm hanging for what I did to him. It all amounts to the same thing in the long run, don't it?'

Jack nodded tiredly. There was nothing else to say. He turned to leave, then stopped at the cell door. When he spoke, his voice contained a tremor of emotion. 'I'll see you in court, Frank.'

And Frankie, limp with relief, answered cheerfully, 'Yeah, see you in court . . . Jack.'

The sentencing of Frankie Buchannon was a formality. Everyone knew what the judge was going to say, long before he placed the black cap on his wig. Yet still there was a hushed expectancy in the crowded court-room, as if some last-minute evidence might bring about a reprieve.

Rose had no such illusions. She had begun to prepare herself for this day ever since Jack had first arrived at her door with the news that Frankie had been arrested. Now she sat alone, dressed defiantly in a bright red dress and matching coat and hat, her eyes fixed solidly on the relaxed, smiling man in the dock. Mary had refused to come today, and Rose hadn't tried to persuade her. Indeed, Mary had aged so much over the past months she looked like a woman in her seventies. Gone, too, was the aggressive, strident woman who, to put it in Frankie's words, 'could make a strong man cry and a weak man shit himself'. In its place was a weeping, lethargic woman Rose barely recognised.

Below Rose sat Jack, his strong features set and grim as his conscience waged a war of words inside his head. An innocent man was about to be sentenced to death, and he, Jack Adams, could put a stop to it. But a niggling voice in the far corner of his mind said mockingly, 'Innocent! That's a laugh. All right, so he might not have killed Sally, but he has blood on his hands. He killed that doctor, he admitted it, so don't go wasting any pity on him. He's only getting what he deserves.' But the demons wouldn't go away.

Jack's head jerked back as the judge began his sentencing.

'Frances Albert Buchannon, you have been found guilty of murder. It is the sentence of this court . . .'

Rose's hands clenched in her lap, her face betraying no emotion to the hungry crowd of morbid sightseers.

'. . . be taken from this court to a place of execution . . .'

Jack's mouth moved as if to speak, but he stayed silent, his growing guilt weighing heavier and heavier with each word the judge spoke.

'. . . hanged by the neck until you are dead.'

His eyes darted to the figure in the dock, and the warning shake of Frankie's head, followed by a slow wink, only compounded the heavy blanket of guilt enveloping him.

'And may God have mercy on your soul.'

As Frankie was led away, he glanced up at the gallery where Rose sat and gave a cheerful wave and the lop-sided grin Rose knew so well.

Deathly pale, but composed and steady, Rose left the court-room, her eyes staring straight ahead, which deterred anyone from asking questions or offering false condolences.

Jack watched the slim figure leave, his grey eyes sombre

and ashamed. All around him, his fellow officers were jubilant at seeing their hated adversary finally brought to book, but Jack found he had no stomach for celebration. To the astonishment, and outrage, of his colleagues, he ignored their exultant cries and backslapping, and strode away without a backward glance.

It was the final visit allowed to Frankie before his execution, and as Rose watched the children, almost sick with excitement at seeing their father again, run into his outstretched arms, she wondered dully how much more she could take before she broke down. In the three months since he had been sentenced, she had been in a daze, her shattered mind refusing to accept the horror of what was to come. By her side, a hobbling Mary was assisted by the strong arm of Jack, into the small, rapidly crowding cell.

That was something else she was finding it hard to come to terms with. This new friendship that had sprung up between Frankie and Jack. Not that she was complaining. Lord, no. Anything that would make life a little more bearable was a godsend to Rose. For with Frankie's blessing, Jack had become a frequent visitor to their home these last few agonising months, and Rose didn't know what she would have done without him. Even Mary had buried her animosity towards the hated police force and had accepted Jack's kindness and assistance during this troubled time. Though whether the elderly woman would have been so amenable towards Jack if Frankie hadn't insisted that both she and Rose should lean on him for moral support was another matter. Neither woman had queried his unexpected request. Indeed, it was taking all of their courage and strength just to get through each day. Little Ben had become quite friendly towards Jack, reaching out and clutching at the kindly policeman as a comfort in the absence of his desperately missed father.

Vicky, though, was a different matter altogether. From the moment she had learned who Jack was, she had made it clear she blamed him for her father's predicament, and was openly hostile to him every time he showed his face at the house. It was strange, Rose mused, how she herself hadn't once thought of Jack as Vicky's father. She wondered also why Jack hadn't mentioned it. After all, he knew now that she was his daughter. Rose's eyelids fluttered tiredly. Maybe the truth was that Jack wasn't interested in taking on the role of parenthood at this late date. If so, it was just as well, for Vicky was, and always had been, Frankie's child. In every way that mattered, she was his daughter, and no matter what happened in the future, Rose was adamant that her child would never learn the truth.

Keeping a tight rein on her emotions, Rose took in the poignant scene being played out before her eyes, wondering if she was in the throes of a breakdown. She hadn't cried since that last day in court. In fact, nothing seemed to have registered since then: it was as if part of her brain had shut down to save her from insanity, and to enable her to remain strong for her family's sake.

She felt as she had when she had been taking the pills Dr Maitland had prescribed during her pregnancy with Vicky. This time, though, no drugs were blunting her senses. The anaesthesia was coming from within herself, and she was glad of it, oh, God, how grateful she was.

When the warder announced that the visit was at an end, Rose jolted as if she had awoken from a heavy dream. She could hear Mary's pitiful weeping and the plaintive cries of her children as Frankie, his face strained and tired-looking, relinquished the near-hysterical girl and the wailing boy. Jack, more taut and sad than Rose had ever seen him, was trying to guide Mary and the children from the cell. Then bedlam broke out.

Vicky, her tear-stained face ugly in her childish grief, tore wildly at Jack's hands and face. Kicking and screaming, her shrill voice echoed down the corridor as her terrified young soul tried to comprehend what was happening. *'Don't worry, Papa, I'll save you. I'll get help and come back and rescue you. Don't you worry, Papa, I won't let them hang you. I'll save you, Papa, I'll save you . . .'*

Screwing up her eyes against the raw pain in her daughter's voice, Rose staggered forward then stopped, while all around her pandemonium reigned. Unable to bear any more, Frankie yelled, 'Get them out, Jack. For Christ's sake, get them out of here.'

The urgency in his voice impelled Jack to greater efforts. Picking up the little boy he then tried to take the frantic girl from the hands of the harassed warder, but she turned in fury and spat, 'Get your hands off me, you lousy copper! I hate you. I wish it was you that was going to hang. I hate you! I hate you!'

Then she was scooped up into the arms of the warder and carried from the cell.

Through blurred eyes Rose stared at Frankie's back as he stared out of the tiny barred window. Her lips stiff as if through neglect Rose whispered, 'Goodbye, Frank. You'll never know how much I love you. Goodbye, my darling . . . God bless.'

If Frankie heard her heartfelt words he made no sign, and when he was finally alone, the cell door firmly closed once more, he sank down on the narrow bunk, his face in his hands. But he couldn't shut out the screams of his daughter.

'I'll come back for you, Papa. I'll save you . . . I'll save you, Papa . . .'

His shoulders began to shake then heave as great sobs ripped through his body.

It was a cold, grey morning in early April when Frankie Buchannon, flanked on all sides by a priest, the warder, and several prison officers, made the short journey from the condemned cell to the courtyard. On the way he joked and made light talk with his guards, determined not to show any fear and to die with dignity.

It was as the small group entered the courtyard that another man came into view. When Frankie saw who it was he said, flippantly, 'Come to make sure they do a good job, Jack?'

And Jack, his eyes holding those of the man he had hated and despised for years, but who now had his respect, asked quietly, 'Would you mind if I kept you company, Frank?' His dark eyes growing dim, Frankie replied, 'Yeah, okay. I'd appreciate that. It's always nice to have a friendly face about when you're going somewhere you're not sure of. Thanks, Jack.'

No more was said on the grim walk. But as the priest dolefully intoned his prayers, Jack, his eyes suspiciously bright, stuck out his hand and, in a voice choked with emotion, said, 'Goodbye, Frank.'

Frankie looked down at the hand and shrugged. Clasping the strong fingers firmly he grinned. 'Yeah, 'bye, Jack. Stay lucky.'

When the hood was placed over the dark head, Jack dropped his eyes, and when one of the prison officers murmured mockingly, 'Not so bleeding cocky now, is he?' Jack turned on him with such savagery that the startled man fell back in fright.

It was over in seconds, and as Jack walked back into the prison on that dismal, cold morning, he had never felt so alone in his entire life.

Mary and the children were fast asleep, their heavy slumber induced by a sleeping draught prescribed by the family doctor. He had prescribed for Rose, too, but she had stubbornly refused to take the white powder last night. She had sat all through the dark, lonely hours waiting for the dawn to break, her eyes fixed as if she was in a trance.

At seven o'clock, a red-eyed Myrtle had brought in a breakfast tray, before she ran weeping from the room. The tray remained untouched.

At five minutes to eight o'clock, Rose got unsteadily to her feet and sat down at the dressing table, looking in the mirror at the clock on the mantelpiece behind her. As the seconds ticked by she wondered how grief could be measured, or the pain that seemed to go on and on with no sign of relief. A pain that filled every pore, every inch of you. A pain that throbbed and pulsed with a rawness that was physical in its intensity. When the clock struck eight, Rose's eyes flew open. Slowly, very, very slowly, a chill began to spread through her, spreading its tentacles wider and wider until her throat seized up and her nose, eyes and ears seemed filled to bursting point with sorrow. It was choking her, blinding her. And when the dam finally broke within her, a great torrent of tears burst from her eyes, rained down her cheeks and on to her heaving breasts. Sliding down from the stool, she stretched out on the carpet and gave herself up to the wrenching, tearing agony of grief.

CHAPTER TWENTY-FIVE

The funeral of Frankie Buchannon was talked about for many years to come. Over forty carriages followed the funeral cortège on its journey to Abney Park Cemetery. The route from Dalston Junction along Stoke Newington high street was thronged with spectators, all eager for a last look at the coffin bearing the infamous Frankie Buchannon, the one time self-proclaimed Lord of the Manor of the East End. Rose and Mary sat in the carriage following the hearse, both dry-eyed and pale, determined to maintain a dignified presence for the sake of Frankie's memory.

Rose even managed a tremulous smile as she recalled his words about the funeral. 'For Gawd's sake, Princess, watch what you put on me headstone, will you? Every time I've seen something like "My dearly beloved husband who fell asleep on 4th May", I've thought to meself, Blimey, he must have got a bleeding shock when he woke up, then. So promise, you'll just have me name and . . . well, you know, when I was born and died. That's all I want. Promise me, Princess.'

And Rose had carried out his wishes. He had also asked that she make sure Joe and Fred received the services of Sir Timothy Rhys-Jones as their counsel when they came to trial next month. This request, also, she planned to keep. It would give her something to do in the lonely months ahead. She could have taken over the many businesses Frank had left, but had decided to leave things as they stood. If Frankie had trusted his boys to manage his affairs, then so would she.

As the coffin was laid in the ground, Rose was aware of someone taking photographs. She was filled with fierce rage at the intrusion. But she remained composed. There was nothing the newspapers would like more than a photo of Frankie Buchannon's widow attacking their staff.

As the first lump of dirt fell on the exposed coffin, Rose felt her nose prickle and her throat tighten. She glanced up and saw Jack, his head bent in respect, a few feet away. Then she turned to the frail, weeping woman by her side, and said softly, 'Come along, Auntie. Frankie's gone. It's time to go home to the children.'

With great dignity, the two women left the cemetery, surrounded as always by Frankie's men, many of whom were openly weeping. And, for a brief, shame-filled moment, Rose wished Jack could be by her side to comfort her.

Safely back inside the carriage, Rose pulled down the blinds to shut out the prying eyes of the morbid crowd. Once hidden from view, she threw herself into Mary's large, comforting arms.

Surrounded by suitcases, Rose looked around the hallway as if she was searching for something, then she pulled on her gloves. If she had forgotten anything then they would just have to do without.

It was the end of September. Frankie had been dead for over six months, yet each day when she awoke the pain was still there to greet her, and she wouldn't have had it any other way.

Joe Perkins and Fred Green had been sentenced to ten years each for their part in the murder of Sally Higgins, and many people thought they had got off lightly, considering their crime. It just went to show, it was said, you could get away with murder if you had the money for expensive lawyers. Then they would remember Frankie Buchannon and fall silent.

One of Frankie's last wishes had been for Rose to take the children out of the country for a long holiday. He had thought a change of scenery, and a bit of sun on their faces, might help them get over his death. At the time Rose had protested that it would take more than a bit of sun and sand to put him from his children's minds. But now, looking at the doleful faces at the carriage window, Rose knew he had been right, as always. Nothing would ever wipe out the memory of their father, he had been too deeply loved, but a long holiday, away from the house, which was filled with memories, could surely do the children some good.

At present she had no definite plans on how long they would be away. She would take it, as she was taking her life, one day at a time. Pausing at the door, she said to Myrtle, 'You have the address of the hotel where we'll be staying. Not that I suppose you'll need to get in touch, but you never know.' Adjusting a brown felt hat trimmed with bright green ribbon, Rose added earnestly, 'Now, are you sure you wouldn't like to come with us, Myrtle? Goodness knows, I could do with some help with the children as Mary's still not herself.'

The middle-aged woman looked horrified. 'Oh, Gawd, no, madam. Thanks all the same, but you won't get me going to no foreign place. Southend's good enough for me . . . if you don't mind me saying so, madam.'

Rose sighed and looked out to where the carriage was waiting with her children and Mary inside. When the suitcases had been put on board, she stood in the doorway as if waiting for something or someone. Then she gave a slight shrug and climbed into the carriage.

Arriving at Victoria Station, Rose handed the responsibility for the luggage to the porters and climbed aboard the train. With first-class tickets, the small party had the luxury of a compartment to themselves. As the train sped on its way to Dover, from where they would board a ferry for France, Rose rested her head against the plush seat next to the window and closed her eyes. At any other time, the children would have been raising Cain in their excitement and Mary would have shouted at them to keep quiet. But today, as with all the days since Frankie's death, her family sat subdued in their seats, each one feeding off the others' grief.

Dispiritedly Rose planned ahead. A few weeks in the sun

might be just the tonic the children needed. Also, the change of scenery would do them good. Mary had accused her of running away, and at one point Rose had been afraid her aunt would dig her heels in and stay behind, but thankfully she hadn't. Rose didn't know if she could have managed on her own just now. Lulled by the rocking motion of the train, she wondered what Jack was doing. She had thought he would at least have come to the house to see them off, and his neglect bothered Rose more than she would dared to admit. Mary, too, had querulously remarked on Jack's absence. It was strange how she had come to depend on him being around. Though maybe not so strange. After all, Mary and Jack had known each other a long time, and Rose understood that her aunt had never really hated Jack – just his profession. Not that it made any difference now, she told herself sternly, as the train raced through the countryside. Yet, try as she might, Rose couldn't help the feelings that had been rekindled over the past months. She had loved Frank, truly loved him, but she had loved Jack, too. And, deep down, she knew she still did. The knowledge shamed her: it was as if, even by thinking such a thing, she was somehow desecrating her husband's memory.

The rocking of the train lulled Rose into a fitful sleep, from which she was rudely awakened by voices protesting that they were hungry. Rose stood up and led the children to the dining car, a grumbling Mary close on their heels.

It was as she was finishing her coffee that Rose glanced up. The sight that met her eyes caused her fingers to shake so wildly that the coffee dregs splashed over the white tablecloth.

Seeing the startled look on her niece's face, Mary said, 'What's up with you, girl? You look like you've just seen a ghost.'

But before Rose could reply, Ben, who was sitting beside his mother also looked up, a wide grin almost splitting his small face in two. 'Mr Adams,' he yelled, in boyish glee. Then, digging Rose sharply in the ribs, he shouted excitedly, 'Look, Mamma. It's Mr Adams.' Before either woman could stop him, the little boy had clambered into the rocking aisle, his sturdy legs racing towards the red-faced, awkward-looking man lurching in the corridor.

Stooping down Jack lifted the boy up into his arms, then, hesitantly, as if unsure of his reception, he walked towards the rest of the family. When Vicky saw him she set her face stubbornly against the window and stared out.

Rose gulped as he approached, but she couldn't stop the sudden joy that leaped into her heart. Then he was standing by the table, the little figure clasped in his arms. He had to clear his throat twice before he could get his words out, and when he did all he could say hoarsely was, 'D'yer mind if I sit down, Rose?'

Rose looked at Mary, as if for permission, and Mary, with a trace of her old self, said grudgingly, 'Well, sit down, then, you soppy git, before you go arse over tit.'

Laughing with relief, Jack lowered himself down beside the stout body, his eyes meeting Rose's across the table. Then she smiled and, suddenly, Jack knew it would be all right. Hugging the boy close to his chest, Jack recalled what Frankie had said to him that last night before the hanging.

It had been late, and both men had been tired.

Frankie, with no sign of his usual flamboyance, had said quietly, 'Look after Rosie and me kids, will you, Jack? She'll be worth a few bob when I'm gone, an' I don't want some slimy fortune hunter latching on to her.' When he had noticed Jack's surprise, Frankie had raised his eyebrows nonchalantly, saying, 'Well, you're gonna chance your luck with Rosie as soon as you think it's decent, so I might as well give me approval 'cos there's bugger all I can do about it where I'm going . . . Oh, an' don't worry too much about Mary. The old trout'll come round in the end. Just give it a few months.'

Now, as he held Buchannon's son, Jack found himself trying hard to wipe what felt uncomfortably like a smirk from his face.

Catching hold of a passing waiter he said quickly, 'A whisky, please.' Then, catching sight of his daughter's scowling face, the daughter he would never be able to acknowledge openly, he added hastily, 'Make it a large one.'

He was going to need it.